THE NIGHT HUNTER

MICHAEL G. THOMAS
& ERIC MEYER

ISBN: 979-8656140171

PROLOGUE

May 1969, A Sau Valley, Thua Thien-Hue Province

The formation of helicopters looked like a swarm of insects as they moved into the hotly contested A Sau Valley. There were two separate groups of UH-1 Hueys, or slicks as they were known to the soldiers, plus a trio of the more heavily armed UH-1C variants that bristled with rockets, machine guns, and miniguns. The gunships moved ahead of the slicks, checking for signs of the enemy.

The mist settled deep into the valley, leaving the slopes on each side shrouded in clouds. The effect was made worse by the low light as the Sun rose slowly in the East. It would be hours before it could burn off the worst of the mist, and by then Private Billy Richards would already be on the ground. He watched the fields as they whooshed on by. The formation of helicopters passed the paddy fields and into the long contested A Sau Valley. The border region with Laos was one of impregnable hills and mountains, covered in thick woodland, and a haven to the enemy. Marines, soldiers, and airmen had fought and died in this arca for years now, and not once had they been able to deny it to their implacable enemy, the People's Army of Vietnam, and their Viet Cong allies.

They were a few hundred feet above the surface, and the shadows of the helicopters cast a grim pool of darkness over the damp surface. There were few paths, and yet no matter the weather, there were always farmers out in the fields. He watched one who seemed as interested in them, as they were with him. He appeared to be a farmer, but by now Billy had no idea how to tell friend from foe. The man could be hiding a rifle and waiting for the chance to use it, or maybe he really was just a simple farmer.

"Billy!" The soldier directly opposite him shouted, "Look!"

Private William S. Richards, known as Billy to most of the platoon, didn't hear the words over the thumping sound of the rotors, something they never told you about back in boot. He saw something in the sky, a shadow of a cloud, or something else. That was when Lance Corporal Johnson, the unit's M60 gunner tapped him on the helmet. He spun around as though he was about to be attacked. The man was all smiles, with the belts of ammunition hanging about his body. A pack of cigarettes was strapped to his helmet as he nonchalantly enjoyed their trip cross-country. Billy leaned forward.

"What?" he shouted.

"Look!"

Billy turned back around as a pair of USAF McDonnell Douglas F-4 Phantom IIs came thundering towards them down the valley. They moved quickly, with the shockwave following through the paddy fields beneath them. They were gone overhead well before the sound reached the helicopters, and Billy reached for the side of the Huey as it rocked slightly.

"Hell, yeah, burn 'em!" Johnson yelled as he turned and pointed to the other side. The pair of fighters was pulling up in opposite directions. Small objects tumbled from beneath them, and Billy felt a lump in his throat as they hit the ground. Small explosions grew larger and larger as they engulfed the tree line at the base of the valley. He was sure he could see movement down there as the flames spread far and wide. It was a horrific and sickening sight to see, and something he could not drag his eyes away from.

"Napalm," said one of the others, "Serves them right. Burn in Hell, Charlie!"

Billy shook his head and tried to turn away from the fires. He would do what had to be done while in Vietnam, but he would take no pleasure in killing for the sake of killing. He had known almost nothing of South East Asia until he'd arrived, and the longer he stayed, the less he realised he actually knew. Billy was a New Yorker, and until he landed in Vietnam, he hadn't tasted Vietnamese cuisine, or even met a Vietnamese man or woman. He'd not chosen to be there, and this was his second journey into the countryside. The others seemed to be thrilled at the idea of combat, but for him, just moving one foot in front of the other was often too much. He inhaled slowly to calm his nerves, and then noticed a flicker of light in the canopy below. He might only be three months into his tour, but he knew enough to know this was a problem.

"I see something!"

"You see what?" Johnson grumbled, "There's a lot to see out here."

The experienced machine gunner shook his head and lay back to get some rest. But Billy would have none of it. His eyes widened as he looked down into the cover below. The Valley was a strange place, with a mixture of paddy fields, waterways, jungle, and of course, the tall mountain ranges that flanked it. Every piece of foliage, every hut, and every tree was a potential hiding place for the enemy, and that didn't include those that were hiding in plain sight. A farmer could be carrying a Kalashnikov and might open fire the minute they came into range.

There was something down there. I'm sure there was.

Right away he began to doubt himself. The speed they were travelling at, and the constantly changing terrain, made it almost impossible to identify a thing. And yet, Billy remained convinced he'd seen something.

"There…again."

He pointed off into the distance, but nobody seemed to listen. He looked to the right and found none of the others paying any attention to what he was saying. The fighter jets and large formation of helicopters tearing through the valley without a care in the world fascinated them all.

"I said…"

But it was already too late. The gunfire erupted once more, and this time the effect was devastating. Dozens of small holes appeared in the skin of the Huey, and then the man opposite, Private Guy Gilormini was hit from below by multiple shots. He was physically lifted from his seat by several inches as they punched through his torso and up to the roof of the cabin. Blood splattered the metalwork and the men seated nearby.

"Fuck me!" One man shouted as more fire hit around them. The helicopter started to spin, and it seemed as though the pilots had been hit. But then they levelled off, and the rotors whirred as the pilots struggled to escape.

"Get down!" yelled another, though in the Huey there was simply no place to go, "We've got incoming!"

"No shit!" Billy muttered as he bent down and placed a hand on his helmet to ensure it stayed on, "Why doesn't anybody listen?"

The pilot pushed the nose down and boosted power to try and accelerate away, but more bullets hammered into the helicopter, and they punched through the thin metal skin with ease. These were not the small rounds from rifles and machine guns, but heavy calibre shells designed to bring down aircraft. An alarm sounded, and Billy held on for all his life. He'd seen the burnt-out wrecks of choppers on the ground, but he'd never seen one fall before. And that was when he spotted a second Huey going down, with a long column of smoke following right behind it.

"Bastard Gooks!" Johnson shouted, "When we get down there, we're burning you up. All of you!"

He almost screamed the last few words, but Billy's gaze was locked onto the burning Huey. It was going down fast, and soon vanished in the mist where the open fields rose up into the gentle gradients of the valley.

They're going down. Nobody gets out of a crashed slick.

The aircraft appeared once more, and then dipped below

the tree line and out of sight. Billy tensed up as he waited for the blast, but there was no flash or explosion. A few more seconds passed and still nothing. He exhaled, and he could only hope it had landed safely.

"Kill them!" said one of the newer enlisted men as he leaned out to open fire. He lifted his rifle and then tipped forwards as the helicopter changed course again. The pilots were obviously doing all they could to shake off the fire and make it as hard as possible for the enemy to hit them. Even so, the occasional bullet still hit the metal work, with some punching inside the craft. As the man was about to vanish into the air, the muscle-bound Sergeant Jones grabbed him, a mountain of a man that no one would dare argue with. His skin was as black as tar, and he wore a short-trimmed moustache that angled down to the corners of his mouth.

"Get back inside!" His voice was so loud he could just about be heard over the sound of the rotors. He looked to the canopy below as more shots hit the helicopter, and then shouted one word at a time.

"They're got a fifty mike fifty in the tree canopy!"

Just hearing that sent shivers through Billy's body. That was a fifty-calibre machine gun, a weapon that hurled 12.7mm slugs into the sky. Those bullets could tear off limbs and smash through any part of the helicopter with ease. A hit to one of a hundred different components would see the chopper fall from the sky, killing everybody onboard. The Sergeant leaned forward and shouted to the pilots.

"Call the fighters back!"

The co-pilot looked back, though he said nothing. Even as he looked away, the nose dropped and alarms sounded. He looked back and struggled with the controls. The helicopter was a strange machine, a lump of metal trying to rip itself through the forces of gravity and its two rotors. Even at the best of times, it seemed as though it would take little to bring it down, yet the pilots somehow managed to keep the craft moving, even when damaged. Sergeant Jones tried to speak with them again, as a burst of fire punched up through the shattered glass in the lower left nosecone and up through the top of the Huey. It tore off toggle switches and left a hole above their heads. Miraculously, it avoided the clutch and rotors, but it still managed to disable several systems.

Sergeant Jones moved back into the blood-splattered crew compartment. The door gunners were already in action. One shouted directions from the left, while the second put down a hail of fire into the mist-covered tree line. As Billy watched, he could make out the spinning blades of the landed Huey and shook his head in amazement. Either by luck or judgement, the crew had put it down just yards from the tree line. There were men around it, as they jumped out, they were engaging something in the trees.

I can't believe it! They made it!

"Help them!" screamed one of the men.

Billy had been so transfixed on whether the men would land safely, he'd completely forgotten about the enemy hidden on the surface. He lifted his M16 to his shoulder and aimed off roughly at the tree line. The sights on the rifle were relatively simple, and he'd been well above average during basic training. But this was nothing like what he'd practiced for. There was no discernible target, and the buffeting and shaking helicopter made aimed fire all but impossible. A hand hit him on his helmet, and he looked back at Johnson.

"Open fire, Newbie! Just shoot!"

Billy pulled the trigger, firing one shot at a time. Had he been able to aim carefully this might have been enough. But the others were firing with wild abandon. The door gunner unleashed a long burst as he swung from left to right. There was no real target, though the muzzle flashes at least gave them a rough idea of where they needed to aim. Lance Corporal Johnson appeared to be having the time of his life as he fired from the hip, spraying bullets down into the trees.

"Yeah! Who wants some?"

A dozen tiny flashes in the canopy seemed to answer him, as scores of assault rifle bullets hammered into the Huey. This time they succeeded where the larger calibre weapon had failed and struck something in the rotor assembly. A plume of smoke blossomed from aircraft as the crew struggled to stay airborne. But Billy knew better than that. He grabbed the straps and called to the others.

"Hold on! We're going down!"

Most were already doing the same, with just Johnson remaining next to the door gunner and still firing. His mind seemed focussed on one thing, blasting the unseen enemy. But when another burst of flame from the engines spread above him, he ducked back inside.

"Oh…shit!" Johnson yelled, "We're going down, baby!"

He pulled on the straps as the helicopter dropped down lower into the low-lying mist that seemed to carpet the ground everywhere. Billy had heard stories of what happened when helicopters crashed, and try as he might, he couldn't shake his mind from the prospect of being torn apart by whirling blades and still running engines. The mist looked like an ocean, and as he looked off to the side, he was sure he could make out a pair of red glowing lights. They looked almost like eyes watching them come lower. Then the mist separated and there were trees.

"Oh, no!"

The ground came towards them much faster than he'd ever thought possible. The whine from the engines and the thump of the rotors transformed as they struck branches. For a second it didn't seem quite so bad, but then they slammed into the ground just as Billy lifted his arms in front of his face.

This is it.

* * *

Billy could see nothing, but he could hear shouting and gunfire. Everything was slower and lower pitched than normal. He felt sleepy and just wanted to rest. He opened his eyes, but it was a tortuous effort, and they soon closed again, and the sounds began to fade. In place of the helicopter was the new reality that they were on the ground, and nowhere near where they had intended to land.

"On your feet, soldier!"

Billy looked to his left, but all he could see were the blurred shapes of people moving. Some carried weapons. Others dragged the dead or the wounded with them. There was no sign of the helicopter, or even the smoke that might be expected from the burning wreckage. Something pinched his shoulder, and then he was being dragged along the damp ground. Based on the state of his clothing, and the complete change in scenery, they must have been moving for some time.

"Wake up!"

He shook his head, and finally his eyes began to open. There was greenery all around him but not the jungle of his imagination. This was the brutal and dense interior of the lower slopes of the A Sau Valley. The long elephant grass cut skin, and the foliage was tall and tough, making progress slow and difficult as they moved into the tree line. Billy blinked again, and this time he was sure he could see glowing red eyes in the distance.

"I'm okay. Let me go!"

Private O'Malley, the young soldier from Boston dropped him to the ground, and then turned away. He carried his M16 on his shoulder and pulled it down to ready it for combat.

"You took your time. You've been out for fifteen minutes."

Billy was about to reply but was drowned out by the unmistakable rattle of an AK47 clattering away in the distance. O'Malley staggered backwards and hit the floor next to Billy. More shots followed after him, but as the adrenalin pumped through Billy's body, he all but forgot about the enemy and focussed on his friend.

"O'Malley!" he screamed as he scrambled to the man.

There were a few yards between them, and as Billy slid down alongside him, he knew the man was in trouble. O'Malley was gasping for breath as blood pumped from wounds in his chest and neck. As Billy grabbed him the blood spurted out, and the poor man gasped one incoherent word before falling limp. Billy tugged away at his jacket. The fabric was already damaged, and as he tore it away, he found the wounds from at least three penetrations to his torso. Blood had poured from them, and he had to turn away to stop from vomiting.

"Private…keep moving!" said a stern voice.

He looked up at Sergeant Jones who looked as angry and confident as he always did.

"Sarge? We can't leave…"

Billy pulled at his friend, but O'Malley wasn't moving. Blood trickled from his mouth and joined the blood that had poured from the rest of his body into the damp earth. He was dead, but Billy didn't want to leave him behind. It wasn't just for O'Malley, but for himself. If one could be left behind, so could he.

"We've got Charlie in through the mist behind us, and the rest of the platoon is moving forward and scattered. Get into the trees, or get a bullet in your back. We're being hunted."

Billy's eyes opened wide in surprise. He'd seen his friend cut down, but it hadn't occurred to them that theirs was the unit being attacked, let alone hunted. It was a sobering thought.

"Now move!"

Billy struggled up to his feet, and something made him look back. It was a tingle in his body, as though he knew somebody was watching him. He looked into the mist that now seemed to be everywhere. There was no sign of the helicopter, only the stink of burning fuel and smoke. And there were the two distant red lights again. White and yellow flashes around it were followed by the crackle of gunfire.

"Move it, you ape!"

Billy turned and chased after the Sergeant into the undergrowth surrounding the trees. The mist was with them but seemed to disperse a little the further inside they went. He could hear his own panicked breathing as he ran, all while shots crashed around him. He felt terrible leaving O'Malley behind, but as he kept on moving, that thought quickly faded.

"Hold them back!" shouted a voice off in the distance.

Billy slowed, and then turned back to open fire. Another American ran past him to the right carrying an M79 grenade launcher, shortly followed by a radioman. Billy took aim and waited until he saw movement. He fired at the targets coming from behind the thicker trees, but the shapes kept on coming. Sergeant Jones was some way ahead, and it did not take long for him to be on his own, and that set his heart pumping. He took aim at the shadows and fired three bursts, but then the reply was shockingly brutal. Scores of flashes showed dozens, maybe even hundreds of enemy soldiers were right behind him. The bullets hit all around him, and yet thankfully managed to not strike him.

Run, you idiot.

Throwing caution to the wind, he turned and broke into a run. He passed another body and stopped to check. He could see the blood around the neck, and dozens of smaller wounds at the face and chest. He had no idea who it was, but the sound of shouting in Vietnamese pushed him along. Finally, he reached a series of shattered trees lying horizontally where they'd fallen. Five or six soldiers were hunkered behind one of them, with Johnson in the middle and positioning his M60. Another stood up and fired his M79 grenade launcher before ducking back down. A moment later the 40mm explosive shell detonated with a loud thump.

"Get out of the way!"

Billy leapt over the fallen tree and ended up catching his jacket on the many smashed branches jutting out. One split a pocket wide open, spilling its contents onto the jungle floor. He looked back as several personal items vanished from sight.

"What the Hell?"

He grunted and then slid down next to the others. They looked as confused and tired as he was, all while preparing for a major firefight.

"What the hell is going on down there?" asked one.

"They're in the mist. They got O'Malley, hit him in the back."

Sergeant Jones was next as he appeared from the West, and with a soldier holding onto his arm. He vaulted the tree with no effort and dropped the soldier down next to him.

"We've got a company strength unit coming after us. They must have planned this. You all ready?"

"Yes, Sarge," said Billy. The others joined in with a mixture of grunts and acknowledgements.

"Good. Hold your fire, and wait until you can smell 'em. Then we shred them."

CHAPTER TWO

The column of soldiers marched through the jungle, accompanied by the sounds of the distant battle. For Private Linh Hoa it was a day like any other, one made up of marching, fighting, and then more marching. She couldn't remember a time when every bone in her body didn't ache, and yet she would not want to be anywhere else. To those around her, they were merely soldiers of the Vietnamese Army, or more officially known as the PAVN. But to the Americans and their puppets, they were the North Vietnamese Army. Linh Hoa kept on moving as she listened to the unmistakable sounds of a battle raging in the distance. Just minutes earlier she'd heard the staccato rattle of anti-aircraft weapons firing out from inside the jungle canopy. They would be well screened from the sky, and based on the smoke and explosions, they must have shot down at least one helicopter, maybe even more.

Linh Hoa did not smile knowing this, because she knew where they were going. The gunfire was increasing in volume, and in her experience that meant one thing. They were moving closer to the battle, not leaving it. After years of death and destruction, the leadership had finally realised that the only way to neutralise the strengths of the Americans was to get close. It had been known simply as the *'grab them by the belt buckle'* tactic, but it did work. The closer they moved to the enemy, the less artillery and aircraft would be used against them. Linh Hoa was a quick runner, perhaps the fastest in the entire platoon. She leapt over the stumps and foliage and made so little noise that she had been nicknamed the Ghost in the battalion.

"Airplanes!" said one of the soldiers.

Many of them lifted their weapons as they usually did. It was standard practice to fire on anything low flying. At the very least it made their ground attack more dangerous, and sometimes, though rarc, they might even damage or destroy one. And each of them knew that taking pilots prisoner was considered a top priority in gaining leverage in forcing out the Americans.

"Do not fire," said the Captain far off towards the front of the unit.

Some lowered their rifles, but the rest continued looking up to the sky. A Sergeant moved among them barking orders.

"Lower your weapons!"

The aircraft were close now, and the mood in the unit changed in a matter of seconds. It was one thing to face an enemy with rifles, but to be destroyed from the air was like being smote by a supernatural force, and one they could not fight back against.

Another jet aircraft screamed overhead, and Linh Hoa flinched at the sound. She'd seen the results of enemy bombing attacks many times before. The Americans excelled at fighting from a distance, using technology and cruel weapons to maim and kill while exposing few of their own soldiers to danger. High explosive bombs would blast apart trees and soldiers with ease, leaving anyone nearby crippled and traumatised. They sprayed chemicals over the jungle, destroying vegetation, and poisoning numerous animals and people. But the weapon Linh Hoa feared more than any others was the dreaded napalm.

Please do not attack us. Not today.

Any moment she expected a metal canister to fall around her and detonate, killing her in an instant. Even worse would be to be left maimed or severely burnt, making her useless to the war effort, and a lifetime cripple. She could not see the Sergeant from where she was, but every man and woman in the unit obeyed his commands. There were standing orders to always attack aircraft once their position was known, but so far, they had moved unobserved.

"Do not move."

Blasting away at the aircraft would guarantee a response within minutes from fighters and artillery. Linh Hoa was one of a few dozen women in the company, but she had proven her worth over the last year in combat with ARVN soldiers three times, and a single pitched battle with the Americans. Each time she'd lost friends, and with each passing battle, she found it harder and harder to retain friendships. She did her best to keep people at arm's length, to protect her for when the next casualties would occur. Because she knew, perhaps more than most that it was not a case of if they would be taken, but simply when.

Do not move.

Linh Hoa had to fight against her muscles to ensure she remained utterly still. A year ago she might have broken and run, but not now. She was nineteen and had been married a month when her husband Chí was sent South. Linh Hoa received some letters, and then nothing. Now it was three years later, and that nineteen-year-old had aged in both years and experiences. She'd been involved in more battles than she could remember, survived the bombings, and killed the enemy so close she had seen them die before her. Officially, she did this for her country, and for the ideals of the Communist Party. But in reality, she was out there looking for Chí. Every day she prayed she would have the strength to keep going, and that they would be reunited.

Sergeant Thanh hissed and then lifted his hands. The entire unit took cover as a pair of American aircraft flew overhead. They were not the terror inducing jets, but the thumping sounds of rotors. Linh Hoa inhaled slowly, gladdened that they were not about to face the flames of jellified petroleum as it melted trees and flesh with equal ease. That sound could only mean helicopters, and where they were, the American soldiers were soon to follow.

"Listen," said the man immediately in front.

Linh Hoa turned her head to the side so she could hear more clearly. Her right ear was noticeably worse than her left, and almost certainly due to the bombing in the North that she'd endured for so many months. The local doctor had only been able to irrigate her ear, but it had done little to help. As far as she was concerned it was a war injury, and she would simply have to manage with it.

"You hear it?"

The gunfire increased in volume, and right away she knew it was an engagement perhaps a few hundred yards away.

"I hear it," she whispered, "They're close."

The weapons used by both sides had a particular sound to them that a veteran would understand immediately. A grenade exploded far off in the distance, and that meant both sides were awfully close now. One man whistled, and the unit started to move once more. They covered ground quickly, and Linh Hoa thought they might make good their escape when something exploded twenty or thirty yards away. It was so close she tried to turn away and inadvertently tripped over a tree stump. As she hit the ground hard, she could see the feet running past her. Two of the soldiers stopped and reached down to help her.

"Quickly," said Quang Cong, one of her three-man cell, "Get up!"

He sounded stern, but in the Army, they were all pushed together into groups of three. They watched out for each other, helping where needed, but also ensuring loyalty to the cause. If one were hurt, the other two would always help. She grabbed his arm, and he helped her back to her feet. The man was almost skeletal in build, yet he remained strong and capable. Months of being in combat had seen deprivations of a kind Linh Hoa never imagined. Lack of food, replacement clothing, and unending marching left the entire battalion hungry, tired, and in a ragged state. Yet for all this their morale was high. They were in the South, taking the fight to the American invaders, and they knew they were going to win.

"Are you hurt?"

She shook her head. "No."

"Good. Keep moving!"

They pushed on, and it took a few steps for the pain in her feet to subside from the fall. It was nothing major, but it did mean that her cell had fallen behind towards the rear of the unit as they worked their way through the jungle. She kept looking up as though a long arm would reach down and scoop her away. She was scared, just as she had been in the other battles she had been involved with. After all this time, it was not the Americans on the ground or their rifles that scared her. It was the screaming jets overhead that put terror into her heart. She had seen the random death that came from the skies, her comrades blown apart and burned alive in the brutal conflagrations.

Where are they?

It was difficult to see those in front of her as they darted in and out of the trees. They were only a detachment from their battalion, and part of the massive force based around the 29th Regiment sent in to secure this part of the valley. Then they slowed, stopped, and melted into the trees. Corporal Quang gave a signal, and she remained completely still so that that she would be unseen, even by a soldier passing by a few yards away.

Quang was one of the best-educated young men in the entire regiment, and he found himself constantly in trouble with the officers. A student from Hanoi, his round glasses with crooked wire frames made him look like a young professor. That meant little to any of them as they were all equals in the new regime, and united against the common enemy. And right now, Linh Hoa didn't care about any of it. She was sure she could feel her chest pounding. She sniffed the air and right away knew they were in for a storm. In Vietnam one became accustomed to the weather, and its whims and whiles. A native to the land could feel the changes through the trees and the air, while the invaders always seemed surprised.

Rain. The land offers us protection again.

She smiled, imagining the pilots being forced to turn back due to the clouds and weather patterns that would make flying dangerous for them. A deluge would make life even less tolerable than normal, but Linh Hoa would happily accept that as the price for avoiding being blown apart by American aircraft.

What's that?

Something moved in the trees off to her right. She didn't see what or who it was, but she did see the wake it left in the foliage. The greenery shook behind it as it raced away, and then it was gone as quickly as it had arrived. Linh Hoa shook her head and tried to shake it from her mind, but then a soldier five yards away lifted from the ground and flew through the air. Another turned, lifted his Kalashnikov, and was in turn cut in half. Something seemed to lash out at him, but it was too fast to see. The bloody remains of his body scattered to the ground, while some of his blood flicked towards her. A splatter of the fluid hit her forehead and nose, and she instantly recoiled. Without even thinking, she opened her mouth to scream, but Quang grabbed her and placed his hand over her mouth. The scream came from her lips, but he kept up the pressure, and may have saved all of their lives in the process. He moved in closer so she could feel his breath on her cheeks.

"Do not move," he whispered, "They're close."

Linh Hoa wanted nothing more than to run, but he held her tightly. Her chest felt like it was going to explode, and his hand interfered with her breathing. She started to struggle when she spotted the shape pushing past but was hidden by the greenery. It was big, much bigger than a water buffalo. Perhaps even the size of a fully-grown adult elephant. Yet it moved quickly and effortlessly through the jungle. She could smell it now, and it made her recoil in horror. It was like a decaying corpse, the stink of flesh left too long in the Sun. Her entire body shuddered, and she almost lost her grip on her rifle.

"Kill it!" A soldier broke ranks and opened fire. The AK47 fired wildly into the shadows, with the bullets shredding bark and greenery as it thundered off into the distance.

"Idiot!" Linh Hoa muttered.

One of his comrades grabbed him, but it was too late. The shape in the shadows stopped and changed direction as it came for the man that had spoken. Each time it moved closer to the light, it veered away, always travelling in the shadows as though the light itself would burn the thing. Then something lashed out, and the soldier dropped to his knees, while his head vanished into the jungle. Linh Hoa placed her hand over her mouth to stop herself from screaming.

Do not move! Move, and you die as well.

The shape moved again, and this time something like a metal whip lashed through the undergrowth. Branches and entire trees were torn apart as it injured another, and then wrapped itself around a third man. He screamed, as he was pulled away and dragged off into the jungle.

"Do not move!" snarled the Sergeant, but already the fear and panic tore through the group.

Another man vanished, and that was the moment when discipline finally collapsed, and the massacre truly began. One by one they opened fire, some at the moving shape, and others at shadows and demons they conjured up in their own minds. AK47s hammered away as they blasted the thing, and it responded with howls of a kind Linh Hoa had only ever heard in nightmares. The dreadful cacophony of sounds was worsened as light machine guns joined in, filling the jungle with the din of battle. Linh Hoa turned away and then spotted the thing moving quickly to the next densely wooded part of the area.

There it is.

She pushed Quang's hand away and lifted her weapon before firing. The rifle thumped into her shoulder as she fired four or five shots at a time. She was no expert with a rifle, but at this range accuracy was hardly important. Men and women were being cut apart or dragged away all around her, and still she fought on. Corporal Quang Cong did the same, with the pair putting down a hail of fire that allowed one trio of soldiers to fall back from the rampaging shadow. Captain Nguyen, a veteran of six years in the field stepped out into the open, with two of his men at his side. As always, Sergeant Thanh was right next to him and brandishing his rifle. The Captain held a MAT-49 submachine gun, a weapon that dated back to the French War. It had been modified, like most of them to fire the to the Soviet 7.62 mm Tokarev pistol cartridge, available in large quantities from the Soviet Union and the People's Republic of China. It was a weapon he carried with much pride.

"No running. Fight!"

He held the small metal wire stock to his shoulder and opened fire. The modified weapon unleashed a torrent of fire into the greenery, and many others joined him as they opened fire from their assault rifles. The shape came towards them, but as Linh Hoa was about to make out its position, it would duck down or move behind the other soldiers. All she could tell was it was big, fast, and violent. Bullets crashed around it, with some making a meaty thud as they struck flesh. It was then among them, but Linh Hoa was already running. Others in the group broke and ran, and in seconds the column had been shattered. Scores of veteran soldiers were killed, captured, or their will broken by something they had never seen.

Linh Hoa stumbled past bodies, and one in particular was terrifying to see. A man had been split open from head to groin, with his innards splayed about in the foliage. She staggered past, retched, and then vomited onto the grass. More screams filled her ears, and she looked to the right as her friends and comrades ran for their lives. As she waited, she could see three other soldiers, as well as Captain Nguyen who had somehow survived the initial brutal assault. They all hid in whatever they could find as more soldiers ran past them. The Captain held a hand to his left shoulder, and it was covered in blood. He waited behind a tree, panting in terror.

Linh Hoa removed the long, curved magazine from her AK47 and pushed in another as quietly as she could. Pulling back the bolt on the side seemed excruciatingly loud, but at least she could now defend herself. One soldier started to breathe louder and louder, even though his comrade struggled to silence him. Then the stench of death returned, and Linh Hoa knew what was coming. Deep, guttural breathing followed it, and then a spike appeared that pushed out from the man's chest. He tried to shout, but blood spurted out instead. He reached out to Linh Hoa as he tumbled forward. And there behind him was the thing of nightmares. It seemed to have no discernible shape in the foliage, but it was the eyes that drew her in. Dull red bowls of light that sucked her in.

"Ky Lan!" she hissed, "You're real!"

Captain Nguyen stepped to her side and pushed her aside. He screamed something before opening fire. The bright flashes from the muzzle partially lit up the features of the thing, but it was so close it was impossible to make out its complete shape. It lashed out at him, but he sidestepped and opened fire with his submachine gun again. One soldier tried to throw a grenade at it, but it lashed the man's legs, and he went down hard. A second later the grenade exploded below his body, physically lifting him up but sheltering both him and the creature from the worst effects. A half-rotted tree splintered and collapsed down on him, and for a few seconds the pair was engulfed in flame and smoke.

Linh Hoa watched all of this with a look of astonishment and terror on her face. She'd heard stories of all kinds of creatures and beasts of the ancient past. But not once, not even as a child had she heard of a thing that was so strong and so brutal. It had torn through their unit in a way a company of American soldiers could never have imagined. A second blast followed the first, as another grenade was detonated. This time the creature was either hit or surprised, based on the noise it made. Entire trees were torn down as it flailed about, but it was enough for them to break and run. She knew she should stay and fight, but what use was she to Chí if she was torn apart trying to stop this animal? Nobody would bring back her body for her parents to take care of. Death was an important business to her people, in some ways more important than life. No, it was better to run and fight another day. And so Linh Hoa ran for all she was worth.

Run…or you join the others under the ground.

Nothing, not the howls of the beast, or the screams as it tore her friends and fellow soldiers apart; all that mattered was staying alive, and she had no desire to be ripped apart by this terror that has risen from the shadows. She ran and ran, leaping through the long grass, the greenery, and the mass of trees as the sound of the terrible thing began to fade. She kept on going until her body would take her no further. She sank to the ground and panted. Her clothing was ripped and torn, and there was blood scattered over her as though she'd been bathing in blood. She still carried her rifle on its sling over her shoulder, but her supplies were gone, along with the rest of her ammunition.

A Ky Lan, can it be true?

CHAPTER THREE

1km West of Landing Zone Bravo

Billy had never encountered anything quite so stressful and terrifying as the wait in the jungle. Most of his squad had made it out safely from the wrecked helicopter, but there were injuries, and he could see that two men were missing. He wanted to ask after them, but as they waited, he knew it was not the time. The other helicopters had apparently landed long enough to deploy the rest of the platoon, but so far, he'd seen no sign of them and wondered if they'd been scared off by the growing battle on the ground.

This must be the calm before the storm, and they all knew that a sizable number of enemy soldiers had been in this area. The tension while they waited worsened as the seconds turned into minutes. Billy had rested his M16 on the tree trunk, but there was nothing to aim at. Just tree stumps, elephant grass, and the tall tree trunks rising high above.

"Maybe they've gone?" Billy suggested as quietly as he could.

"Are you kidding me, Fresh Meat," said Lance Corporal Johnson, "They just hit us, and they hit us hard. They ain't leaving till we're in body bags. Trust me, I've been here before."

He spat on the floor, gazing into the mist as though only he could see through the clouds. He then sniffed the air, and Billy nearly laughed at the absurdity of it. But the other men in the squad seemed to be acting very differently. They looked to Johnson, and then followed his gaze.

"Yeah," he said quietly, "They're coming this way, all right. Of that, you get my personal guarantee."

Sergeant Jones nodded and gave a hand signal. Billy almost choked as he realised the Sergeant had spotted the enemy. He looked in the expected direction and was sure he could see leaves moving. He wanted to fire, and his finger even moved to the trigger, but the others remained still. Then something happened that no one would have expected. A shrill scream of the kind only heard by somebody that had lost any sense of control. It came again, and then a crackle of gunfire that rose into a crescendo.

"Shit," said Johnson, "That's a lot of Gooks. What are they shooting at?"

Even the hulking figure of Lance Corporal Johnson seemed unsettled.

"Quiet." Sergeant Jones nodded towards the mist, "Check your weapons and be ready. We've got friends out there, too. So be careful."

Billy looked to his M16 and noticed the mud running along the side of the barrel. He reached forward to wipe it off when he saw the shapes. They were little more than shadows, but there was a dozen, perhaps more, and they were moving fast. Sergeant Jones gave them a hand signal, and each took aim at the approaching shapes. Billy licked his dry lips and rested his finger on the trigger. He'd never knowingly killed a man before, though he'd expended hundreds of rounds of ammunition. There was shouting, and it was definitely Vietnamese. The enemy was usually much more careful than this, and whoever had decided to speak had just sentenced his soldiers to death.

"Fire!"

Billy pulled the trigger and opened fire. The M16 kicked into his shoulder as he moved from left to right. The shapes were coming fast, and a few dropped to the ground. But more came towards them, and though he could hear gunfire, nothing seemed to have come close.

"Johnson, slow them down!" Sergeant Jones said.

The M60 roared as Johnson unleashed burst after burst. He was through the belt in a short time and pulled back behind the felled tree to reload. The man must have practiced it a hundred times as it took seconds before he was back in action. Billy had already loosed off two magazines' worth of ammunition and was reloading himself.

"What's wrong with them?" Johnson fired again, "They ain't shooting!"

That was when they broke out of the mist and the tree line and into view. They looked little different to any of the other civilians with their ao ba ba farming garments and hats. Most carried the venerable AK47s in their hands, but they seemed more interested in running right at the Americans, rather than fighting.

"Put 'em down!"

They were so close that Billy could see their faces, and they looked a mixture of grim determination and terror. One spotted the soldiers waiting for them and opened fire. The burst of rifle fire thudded into the tree, blowing pieces of bark into the air with small puffs. Billy dropped back to avoid the fire, but Johnson simply swung his M60 to the left and fired again.

"Yeah…yeah!"

Three more bursts, and then he was back and changing the belt.

"You hit?" He'd spotted Billy sheltering behind the tree. Billy shook his head, "Then get back on the line!"

Billy nodded and moved back while adjusting his helmet. The enemy soldiers had scattered, with some moving off to the sides, but a number continued to come right at them. He aimed in their direction and fired. For the first time since his arrival in Vietnam he was certain he'd shot somebody. It was a horrific thing to have happened, but he also felt a moment of relief that he'd done it. More shapes were coming for them, and they fired as they ran. Bullets hit around him, but this time he hunkered down as low as he could go and returned fire. Another magazine was gone, and he fumbled looking for another.

"Looking for a clip?" Private Jayden Hohner asked. Like Billy, he'd recently been shipped over to the unit, and was one of a dozen young men sent to reinforce the unit. While Billy continued to get into trouble, often for situations beyond his control, Jayden seemed to stumble into every problem. Billy had never found a more accident-prone individual in his life, and though he'd refused to join in, he had heard many of the others saying he'd never complete his tour. If somebody were going to step on a landmine or get hit by a stray, it would be Private Jayden Hohner. Billy looked at him and shook his head, as he grabbed another of the short 20-round metal magazines and pushed it into the rifle. He then pulled back the charging handle and took aim.

"It's not a clip, Jayden…it's a magazine."

Lance Corporal Johnson laughed as he fired another burst.

"The Private is learning…finally!"

A few more came at them, but the last group were completely different. They kept turning back and firing into the mist before then running at Billy and his comrades. They emptied what ammunition they had left in their weapons, cutting down every single one of them. Two more came running out, but then the sharp crack of carefully aimed M16 rifle fire hit them in the back. The shooting stopped, all apart from Johnson who continued to fire short bursts into the mist.

"Hold your damned fire, Johnson," said Sergeant Jones, "Cease fire."

This time Johnson stopped, and the gun hissed away from the repeated firing of short bursts. They watched carefully as four men crept through the foliage and into view. They wore the same uniforms as the rest of the soldiers, and Billy breathed a sigh of relief.

"Thanks for not cutting us down as well," said a thick Texan accent. A Hispanic soldier emerged and walked up to Sergeant Jones. He reached out and shook his hand. They were clearly old buddies, possibly from back home.

"You joining us, Rodriguez. Because I tell you now, we

could use you up here."

The man shook his head.

"That's a negative, old buddy. Only got half a squad with me, the rest are scattered further down the hillside. We're going back to collect them all before they get lost."

Sergeant Jones didn't seem impressed.

"You need a hand down there? That's a lot of ground to cover."

The Sergeant shook his head.

"Between us we scattered 'em pretty good. We've got a full company inbound to mop up. We've got our orders, Jones. And trust me, if we had a choice, we'd be following you up that hill."

He smiled as they grasped hands.

"You know how it is, I can't leave 'em wandering this place. The Gooks are waiting for that. We've got your back, now get up the damned hill before Charlie does."

Billy looked back and watched the shadows. He was sure he could see movement, but then the man vanished back into the foliage as quickly as he had arrived. The soldiers waited and listened, half expecting to hear their comrades come under fire. But there was nothing. Sergeant Jones looked around at his depleted unit and then whistled. Radioman Thomas Jeffries slid down alongside him.

"Where's Lieutenant Weston?"

The radioman pointed off into the distance.

"He's ahead with the scouts. They've spotted NVA regulars heading back up the hillside."

The Sergeant spoke into the unit several times as he authenticated with the radio operator back at their forward base.

He didn't waste words and finally handed the receiver back to Jeffries.

"Our people have secured the crash site and are medevacking the wounded."

The man wiped his brow before continuing.

"We've got fresh boots coming in behind us, and we're gonna need them. New orders. We're pushing up this hill. Apparently, there's an SF base camp three klicks from here, and they've gone dark."

Billy had no idea what was going on and looked to the others.

"Special Forces, Newbie," said Lance Corporal Johnson, "And if they've gone dark, there's only two outcomes."

"Yeah," said Private Freeman, a man who always seemed to be at Lance Corporal Johnson's side. The machine gunner seemed to attract the rougher elements of the squad to him, as though he was their unelected leader. And in doing so, each of them felt able to say and do things they might never do alone, "Special Forces think they're kick-ass, but usually they just get themselves into trouble. If they're dark, they're about to be overrun."

"Or they've already been overrun," said Johnson in a grim tone, "Either way, it's not good."

The ground shook, and shortly afterwards came a great rush of air from the shockwave. Billy instinctively ducked down, while Lance Corporal Johnson simply remained upright and began laughing. The thump from a dozen bombs crashed through the trees as they exploded in the distance. With the green canopy overhead and the slowly thinning mist, it was impossible to see what was happening. But as Billy looked back, he saw flashes, a sure sign that the bombs were closer than he might think.

"Close air support," said Lance Corporal Johnson, "You're not the one that needs to keep your head down."

The bombing went on for a few more seconds, followed by the screaming roar of jet engines as fighter-bombers left the scene.

Sergeant Jones nodded to himself, and then looked back at his men.

"ARVN are already on the ground. We're going to support their advance and chase these bastards down."

"Whoopi!" Corporal Johnson said, "ARVN Marvin is back."

Sergeant Jones simply looked to him, silencing the man with his gaze.

"Grab your gear, we need to ruck. We've got a fair way to go, and not a lot of time to get there."

Billy looked at his clothing and his rifle. Everything was as it should be, but then he noticed the bodies littering the ground behind them. He could see their weapons on the ground, and some appeared to be unarmed. He'd heard stories of Viet Cong soldiers that were effectively slave soldiers, but until now he'd thought they were nothing but propaganda from the South Vietnam government. After all, he'd never been given a chance and had been sent overseas to fight in a war he still didn't fully understand.

"Isn't anybody wondering why they came running at us, screaming?"

Some of the other soldiers muttered explanations, but Sergeant Jones answered him.

"Two companies were coming in right behind us, Private. Trust me, the one place Charlie doesn't want to be is out in the open. If I had to guess, I'd say they were running from the napalm. Nothing gets them moving like a dose of burning gasoline."

"Hell, yeah," said Johnson.

"Trust me, anybody still in the valley will have our air support turning them all into fried chicken out here. Now…move out."

One by one the squad moved away from their hastily defended position, but as they walked away, Billy just had to step back to look at one of the bodies. It was a young woman, maybe nineteen or twenty. She'd been hit once in the chest, but was unmoving, and surrounded by blood that had sprayed over the lower branches and foliage. He reached down to touch her arm when Sergeant Jones grabbed it.

"Private. Do not touch the dead…ever! This country is littered with people and devices designed to maim and kill you."

Billy's hand lingered over the body, and then he stepped back, even though his hand seemed to hover over the dead soldier. He turned his head and looked to the Sergeant. The man's black skin glistened with sweat, and as always, he was all business.

"I've lost too many rookies to booby traps. Trust me, leave them where they are. Unless you want to find your legs blown off at the knee, or your junk hanging from a tree." He then grimaced, "We need to keep moving. The mop up crew will clear this area behind us. We've got our own job to do. We're off to do some hunting."

"Yes, Sergeant."

Billy moved to join the rest of the squad and began the slow and tortuous journey through the thick woodland. From the air the place had always seemed so open and easy to move through, but the reality on the ground was quite another. Some parts were more open than others, but sections of the jungle out there were almost impossible. It didn't take long for him to reach the rest of the platoon, and out at the front was Lieutenant Weston and the small unit that had moved ahead to check the area. The Sun was much higher now, and it sent scattered beams of light down through the jungle canopy and around the soldiers.

"Any news, Sir?"

The officer looked back at Sergeant Jones and shook his head. He was quite different to many of the platoon commanders Billy had met so far. This one was hardened by the war, and rumour had it that he'd volunteered to return to at least two more tours. At first glance he had a boyish, soft-looking face that one might expect to see back home with some National Guard unit. Those boyish looks had changed over the months and years, and were barely visible through the lines and gentle stubble at his face. His gear was stripped down to the bare minimum, and hanging from a sling at his side was a XM177E2 carbine. It was something of a rarity, and Billy had heard he'd been given it by one of his wounded comrades in the MACV-SOG. Being shorter and smaller than the M16, it was ideally suited to the platoon commander and looked more like a toy hanging at his side than a combat rifle.

"The camp is up over the next ridge and on top of the little hill," he said while pointing ahead. Billy followed his hand and noted that the small hill was currently in the shadow of the much larger peak that rose up to the East.

"Sarge!" said one of the men, "We've got movement."

A hand signal was all it took, and the entire platoon went to ground. Billy could feel his heart pounding as shapes emerged from the shadows. A voice called out in thickly accented English, and he knew right away it was Vietnamese.

"It's the Striped Tigers," said Private Thompson.

"Who?"

Johnson slapped the side of Freeman's head.

"Striped Tigers, asshole. ARVN Rangers."

Billy had never seen them before, but as they emerged from the trees, he could tell they were nothing like the ARVN soldiers he'd met on base camp. They wore tiger-striped camouflage and were heavily armed and equipped. But it wasn't the clothing or gear that set them apart, it was the way they moved. They were quiet and quick, much more so that his own platoon. One moved to Lieutenant Weston, and they spoke quietly for some time. Sergeant Jones was with them, nodded, and then moved back to his own squad.

"What's happening?" Private Thompson asked.

The Sergeant looked to him and then back at the others.

"Command screwed up. We came in too far East, and right into elements of an NVA division being monitored by the SF unit in these hills."

"Well, that's just great." Corporal Johnson shook his head, "So, they dropped us into a shitstorm…again."

"Enough," said Sergeant Jones.

"What's the plan?" Billy asked.

Sergeant Jones wiped his face and then nodded to the half strength Ranger platoon that was with them. There were less than twenty of them, and some showed recent injuries.

"We've surprised them and interrupted whatever they were up to. The mission has changed. We're here to hunt and destroy any Regular Army units we can find. We've already dealt with their rear-guard, and the rest scattered into the jungle. Anybody not in the jungle is getting bombed by the hour, every hour."

He pointed ahead to the dark shapes that were barely visible due to the trees and mist.

"That means we are to push into the hills, secure the SF base, and then pursue the NVA into the hillside. ARVN forces are going to be airlifted in tomorrow to block their movement to the West and South.

"So they'll do what they always do," grumbled Johnson, "They'll escape to the North."

"No." Sergeant Jones moved right up in front of the soldier. He was so close that his breath almost warmed Johnson's cheeks.

"We've got a division on the run. Either they stand their ground, and we surround them and kill them man-to-man, or we drive them out into the open ground, and they'll be dealt with by bombs and artillery."

He paused for a few seconds and then stepped away.

"Get your game faces on. We're going up country."

Billy gulped as he checked his gear, and then stepped after the others, and up through the winding animal paths in the jungle, all while keeping a careful look for the one of a hundred different things that could kill him.

"I hate the 'Nam," grumbled Private Thompson, drawing a smile from Billy.

You're not the only one.

Then came a scream. A hideous, terrifying sound that chilled him to his soul. And it was then followed by gunfire.

"Move it!" Jones shouted, and the platoon threw any semblance of discretion out of the window as they raced through the undergrowth and towards the screams and gunfire.

CHAPTER FOUR

They'd been working their way up the hill for the best part of the day, and a quick glance at his watch confirmed it was nearly four o'clock. Billy wiped the sweat from his eyes for maybe the hundredth time that day and instinctively reached for his canteen.

"Save it," said a voice from just behind him. He didn't need to look to know it was Sergeant Jones. The man seemed to be everywhere at once, and never appeared tired.

"We're stopping soon."

The slog through the jungle seemed to make time slow down to something truly unimaginable. Billy found that combined with his unending terror of what lurked in the shadows he could barely stay upright. He'd seen old Westerns and war movies at home with his family, but never had he expected this. Each step was agonising, and his chest felt like it was being compressed inside his body. Those films showed great deeds being the definition of heroism, but for him being a hero was putting one foot in front of the other. That took every ounce of courage and drive he could muster. Up ahead he could see the long column of ARVN Rangers moving out in front of them. There were large gaps between each of them, and they made half the sound of the Americans, even though Billy and the others struggled to maintain their pace through the jungle.

"Man…these Rangers are fast. Makes you wonder why they need us here."

Jayden was right behind him and nodded as he stepped carefully over a splintered tree partially blocking their path.

"Yeah. I've been wondering that for some time."

Something flashed around them, followed by a crackle far off into the distance. For a second Billy thought it was gunfire, and instinctively dropped to a crouch. Johnson laughed as he watched him taking cover. But then it became so much worse as the sky darkened above the green canopy.

"Oh, great," Private Thompson muttered, "Now we've got rain?"

Lance Corporal Johnson laughed.

"It's 'Nam, either you burn, or you drown. Today ain't no different. Just be thankful we've got friends behind us and gunships watching topside."

The rain started with a gentle shower and then increased in intensity. At first it was the heavy patter in the leaves above them, but soon the water was running down to the undergrowth and soaking the men as they trudged ahead.

"What about our bodies back at the landing zone?" Jayden

asked, "We don't leave people behind."

Johnson heard them speaking and called back in an irritated tone.

"Foxtrot Company is already there. All we have to do is keeping moving forward."

Then came a whistle. It was subtle, almost birdlike, and the Rangers vanished into the woodland. Billy strained his eyes but could only make out two of them. The rain was coming down hard, and it reduced visibility further, even though it was the afternoon. Sergeant Jones crept forward and waited just behind the Rangers. He then gave a signal, and the soldiers moved forward. The rain thankfully covered the sound of their footsteps, but it also made it all but impossible to make out what was in front of them. Billy could see the shadows again, but as he passed a set of trees, he was stunned to see the clearing. It had come out of nowhere, and yet now he could see the large area that had been cut away on this level section of the hillside.

"Wow."

"Jayden, cut it," said Billy, "You're ghosting me."

Jayden lowered his body down in subtle acknowledgement, and one by one they stepped out into the clearing. The rain was still coming down, but enough sunlight beat through to give them a fairly good look at the place. Sergeant Jones gave the signal to spread out, and they quickly responded, moving apart in small groups. Billy, Jayden, and Private Thompson moved closely behind Lance Corporal Johnson as they picked their way to the left. The lightning crackled again and acted like a flare being sent up over the base. Billy had expected to find a few sandbags and tents, but this was more like a small firebase. Just ahead of them off to the left and right were trenches. They approached at a corner and could see the trenches worked back to create a triangular moat around the base.

"Inside," said Johnson quietly.

They moved to the edge of the trench, where the only barrier was a single layer of sandbags to mark the top. There were no steps, and each dropped down inside. Billy lifted the muzzle of his M16 as though he expected a North Vietnamese soldier to charge out of the shadows. But nothing happened, so they continued forwards. The trench was deep enough to stand in and still see out over the top, but only just. They continued forward, and then Thompson stopped and bent down. He reached for the surface and lifted up a handful of bullet cases.

"5.56mm." He pulled them closer to his nose, "And fired really recently."

He dropped them, and Johnson grunted before moving away. He held the machine gun at the waist and moved left and right, checking for signs of the enemy. He could see a mark on the side wall where panels from wooden crates had been used to shore up the sides of the trench. He followed it for a few feet and then stopped. It headed into a small dugout facing away from the base. It was like a pillbox, but a lot smaller, with perhaps enough space for two or three men only.

"Corporal," said Billy, "I've got a blood trail."

"Nice. Follow it. And be careful. Watch for traps."

Billy slung his rifle as he bent down to examine the blood. He reached forward and was stunned to see it was still wet.

"Fresh, this happened recently."

The lightning crashed again. It surprised Billy enough that he stumbled forward and fell partially into the dugout. He waited there, still and shaking. Right there in front of him was a soldier, much like him, but brutally disfigured. Deep lacerations to the flesh had cut through his uniform, clothing, and webbing with ease.

"I've got a body in here."

"Yeah," said Johnson, "There's another one here, and it ain't pretty."

Billy looked to the body and noticed the small metal table with a cup of fluid still sitting on it. A cigarette was burning, and that could only mean it had happened a matter of minutes ago. He lifted himself up and stumbled back out.

"Sarge wants us at the main building. Let's go."

They moved in through the trench and then veered off to the right. There were a number of dead Vietnamese soldiers, most wearing the uniforms of the North Vietnamese Army. There were also several irregulars, though they'd all been shot, or worse.

"Keep moving," said Johnson.

The side walls of the trench seemed shorter, and then they were completely gone. To the left was a watchtower, made from timber and relatively short and squat. Sergeant Jones and two other men were with him at the top of the tower. And to the right, half buried in the ground was a single-storey structure, like a barrack room. There were sandbags all around the outside to protect it from debris. Waiting at the doorway was Lieutenant Weston. He was next to a pile of broken bodies. Most had been shot, but several showed signs of having been mutilated and one had a curved object embedded in his torso. There were also three more dead enemy soldiers, with one still brandishing what seemed to be a fire hardened stake in one hand.

"So much blood," said Johnson, "It's like a slaughterhouse here."

Sergeant Jones came down the wooden ladder and leapt the last few steps, hitting the sodden ground. He moved next to the other and shook his head.

"Same in the tower. They came in and hit this place hard."

As he spoke, his gaze was drawn to one of the bodies. At first glance it was just one of many, but as he gently pulled back the torn jacket, it revealed something unexpected.

"What in the name of Moses is this?"

He gently touched the object embedded into the body of the dead soldier.

"I've never seen anything like this before. It looks like a claw."

"No." Billy moved alongside them, "That's not a claw. It's a talon."

Sergeant Jones laughed.

"Are you kidding me? You think there's a bear out here?"

Billy shook his head.

"No, Sergeant, that's much too big to be a bear."

"Then what is it, professor?"

Billy licked his lips as he scanned the tree line all around the small clearing. Something made a terrible howl far off into the distance. A cross between a wolf and something so much bigger.

"I don't know."

"Look!" Private Thompson said, "In the tree line."

Billy looked to the tree line and cried out. There were red lights, like pairs of eyes once more. But this time there were five pairs of them. As he watched, more and more of them appeared.

The howl came again, and then more noise in the trees.

"Uh...Sarge, what's going on?"

Lieutenant Weston pulled back the charging handle on his XM177 and held it low but at the ready.

"I think we're going to find out soon. Jones, on the tower, everybody else to the trenches. If they hit us you will pop flares. Understood?"

"Yes, Sir," replied Sergeant Jones.

"And Jeffries, get over here. We're gonna need help up here. Things just went from bad...to really bad."

The men grabbed their gear as they prepared for a fight.

"I want a strong perimeter defence. But be ready, if they get through, we'll fall back to the stockade right here." He stamped on the ground between the sandbagged covered structure and the watchtower, "This is where we stand our ground if this all turns to shit. Understood?"

"Yes, Sir!" they replied in unison.

"Good, now get to work!"

The men scattered, leaving just the radioman alone.

"Let me guess. The radio's not working?"

Jeffries shook his head.

"Radio is fine, Sir. But nobody is responding."

Lieutenant Weston sighed.

"It just gets better and better, doesn't it?"

CHAPTER FIVE

The light was fading as the Sun began to drop down behind the hills of the valley. In theory, it should remain light for at least another few hours, but the weather and thick clouds made it seem much darker than it should be. Occasionally, a gap would appear, and warm yellow light burned through to the surface. He could make out the entire compound as the men prepared for battle, and it was not a pretty sight. At first glance the base was intact, but closer examination showed signs of damage and destruction. Much worse was the blood. Billy found the sight of fresh blood to be vomit inducing and made so much worse by the gore around him.

"Get on the line!" Sergeant Jones ordered, "Now!"

Billy moved to a small dugout positioned along the outside of the base. The soldiers were well equipped for a firefight. But as he slipped into position, he felt a nagging doubt in his body that he had enough ammunition for the coming battle. He'd already expended several magazines, and he carried no sidearm should his rifle fail him. He looked to the weapon, and then spotted something in the distance.

"Look," he whispered to Private Hohner as he lifted his hand. The two men looked to the tree line, and the ever-shifting tree trunks and foliage. The rain was lighter, but it still obscured the greenery, making it difficult to see.

"What?"

Then the rifles opened fire. The AK47 made a particularly distinctive sound when fired, and the bullets hit close to their position. The wooden posts and sides of wooden crates could do little to protect them, but the sandbags and mounds of dirt and mud were perfect at absorbing energy. Even so, the gunfire was enough to force Billy to want to drop to the floor and stay there. But he knew he needed to fight. Hiding from the attack would simply allow them to get closer, and then it would not just be him in danger, but all of the men in the platoon.

"Hit 'em," he said as confidently as he could.

Private Hohner took aim and fired a long burst. Billy joined in, but he used single shots, demonstrating the excellent control he'd shown back at boot camp. Billy might not be the bravest soldier in the Army, but he had what it took to be a rifleman, perhaps even a sharpshooter. Private Hohner was already reloading when Billy had only expended six rounds. He watched the trees for signs of danger, and as before, the gently glowing red lights reappeared. It was soft now and difficult to see. But as he looked to the lights, another crackle of fire hit around them.

Something hissed, and then a bright flash above them bathed the entire base in red light. Right away the tree line was lit up, and Jayden gasped in horror. There were so many soldiers he could scarcely believe himself. Dozens and dozens, each standing upright, and right at the edge of the trees. They seemed to be stunned, almost dazed, yet unmoving. Then their eyes blinked that terrifying red, and they started to move forward. Many had no weapons, but enough carried rifles to be a problem. They opened fire, putting wild bursts of fire into the compound.

"Holy crap. It's like Night of the Living Dead out there!"

"What?"

"You, know, Jayden. The movie."

Billy fired more rapidly and quickly expended the last few bullets in the 20-round magazine. He released the magazine, pushed in another, and readied the weapon to continue. The crackle of gunfire was all around the compound as the platoon and the ARVN Rangers fought back against the advancing shapes.

"They just keep coming!" Private Hohner pushed in yet another magazine. Billy opened fire, and then the first of the enemy soldiers was at the dugout. The soldier reached forward to grab at the loose logs and tugged at them. Another pushed forward with a rifle fitted with a long bayonet. Billy fired, but after three shots, his rifle jammed.

"No!" He stumbled backwards as he tried to find the problem. More shots hit around them, and then a bayonet stabbed forward, catching Private Hohner in the shoulder. He cried out and fell to the floor.

"Out of the way!"

Lance Corporal Johnson pushed past them and dropped his M60 onto the log at the base of the firing position. He was firing before the weapon was even stable and cut them down like wheat. Billy propped his rifle against the inside wall and bent down to check on Private Hohner. There was blood all along his upper arm. He reached inside his jacket and withdrew a US Army Carlisle first aid field dressing. In seconds, he had torn open the pack. Private Hohner groaned as he wrapped the dressing tight around the wound and slightly above it.

"Apply pressure here, and keep your arm raised."

The two exchanged looks, and Billy could tell it wasn't just the injury. Private Hohner was terrified, and yet somehow Billy was finding his second wind. Maybe he was just in too much shock, but whatever it was, he was able to function, and that was good enough right now.

"Private, over here now!" Johnson said.

Satisfied that Private Hohner was safe for now, Billy took his comrade's functioning rifle, checked it was loaded, and positioned himself alongside Johnson.

"They're everywhere. Cover me while I reload."

Billy nodded and began firing short bursts. Twenty rounds didn't go far, and he was on another magazine before the M60 was ready. More enemy soldiers were at the entry point, and Johnson moved back, nearly tripping over the empty boxes inside.

"No way, man. Get back!"

Billy grabbed his friend, dropped his arm over his shoulder, and started to drag him back out of the dugout and into the trench. Johnson opened fire again as the Vietnamese soldiers ignored the dangers and climbed into the dugout. He cut down one after another, and still they came. Billy could see them close up and lit by the flares falling slowly over the encampment. They staggered as they moved, an unnatural way of walking, and they seemed focused not on the base, but only those defending it. Some carried rifles, others sticks, stakes, and knives. And all of them staggered forwards while hissing and groaning. But as Billy opened fire on them, he noticed something else. Their eyes.

"Fall back to the stockade, move it!"

The men broke from the dugouts and trenches, racing back over the mud and dirt. The enemy were already through parts of the perimeter, and the flares revealed hundreds of them coming into the Special Forces camp.

"Hurry!"

Billy used every muscle in his body to drag his comrade along, and finally one of the other Privates raced across to help him. Together they pulled him to the open door of the small structure and threw him inside. There were several soldiers already there, plus four of the Rangers, and they were knocking holes into the walls to use as loopholes.

"Corporal, take two men and get on that tower."

Johnson looked around him and whistled to Billy and Thompson.

"With me!"

They climbed the short ladder to the top of the tower and moved into position. It was a sturdy tower, with more than enough thick wood to protect them against debris and perhaps even a stray round.

"Be ready," said Johnson.

A flare flashed bright red, and they could see the

Vietnamese soldiers coming for them. Lines and lines of them as they ignored any kind of cover or secrecy. It was like a human wave attack like the Communists had used on Korea.

"Kill them all!"

Billy had so many targets to choose from he only needed to pull down the trigger. As usual, he concentrated on aimed fire, conserving his ammunition and making maximum use of every single round. One enemy after another fell to his fire, but more took their places. Several were carrying flaming torches, and though most were shot down, some were able to toss them onto the wooden structures, while others ran inside only to be shot down. Soon the main building was on fire, as well as one dugout. Two soldiers came running from one, shouting as they went. Seconds later, the dugout exploded, spreading its flames to other wooden structures. From these flames emerged more enemy soldiers, with some burning alive as they came on to attack.

"Thompson, grenades! These bastards won't quit!"

The soldier nodded and proceeded to use their small array of high explosive grenades. Every few seconds another would explode, throwing the enemy aside, and blowing some of them apart. Billy saw one Ranger out in the open with a submachine gun blasting away. He shot several enemies, but more threw themselves onto him. They stabbed at him, and he was sure one was even biting him. Knowing the Ranger would die without help, he opened fire, hitting two of the enemy. They fell, but more took their place. Billy reached for another magazine, and then spotted a rough-looking M79 grenade launcher stacked to the side, along with a vest with several grenades still fitted and unused. He rolled along the floor and grabbed both.

"Private, get back on the line!" Johnson screamed while still firing.

"I am."

Billy moved to the South side and aimed roughly at the enemy. The M79 thudded as it tossed the grenade slowly towards the ground. It hit and exploded in a bright fireball. He loaded another and another, and soon multiple fires were burning near the central building, and atop one of the fallen dugouts. Billy fired once more, and then a long burst from Johnson thinned out the few still left.

"Beautiful," he said happily, "Nice shooting, Private."

Billy smiled for the first time in days. Lieutenant Weston stepped out into the open, flanked by two soldiers.

"Check the perimeters, stock up on ammo, and get ready for another attack. The rest of you, get what you can out of the buildings before this place is burnt to the ground."

Billy dropped down the ladder and moved to join the others as they dragged the wounded, and as much as they could carry while the flames continued to spread. It didn't take long before the blaze had spread through half of the base, leaving just one dugout, the tower, and part of the trenches intact. They waited with their weapons at the ready, but no more enemy came forward.

"I think we've scared them off." The Lieutenant moved out into the middle of the remaining base camp.

"Corporal, your squad is on first watch. This is gonna be a long night."

Billy moved back to the ladder and slowly climbed to the top. Johnson was still there, watching the trees for dangers. Billy took the M79 and loaded in another grenade, and then rested against the side of the tower. He looked to the trees for signs of the eyes, but there was nothing, just the groan of the wounded and the dying. The Rangers moved out to check on the injured, and he shuddered as they finished off the mortally wounded enemy. This went on for some time, and finally they were in the night, and still he remained where he was. Johnson tapped his arm.

"Get some shuteye while you can."

Billy didn't argue and sunk down into the corner, pulling his helmet down over his eyes. The night felt like an eternity, and though he was able to sleep, even the subtlest of sounds woke him from his slumber. Finally, the Sun began to rise, and Billy could feel a warmth in his body. One of the lookouts whistled, and it was back on as before. He took aim and waited.

"Nobody do nothing until I say so," said Johnson as he swung his M60 into position. The soldiers on the ground rushed to the trenches to join those already inside the dugouts.

"Listen," said Billy.

They all remained silent, but they could make out the crunching of branches and the footsteps of people coming up the hill. Lieutenant Weston nodded and gave a simple hand signal. One by one the men resumed their stations.

"What do we do, Sir?" asked one of the men.

"We do what we're trained to do, soldier. We fight."

The men looked to Sergeant Jones as he scanned the tree line. Small fires still burned, and the acrid stink from the ammunition expended, mixed with the sweat of the men from both sides gave the place a foul atmosphere.

"We're coming out," said a voice in the trees, and then a smile spread across the Sergeant's lips as soldiers emerged from the tree line. They looked exhausted. At the front was Platoon Sergeant Rodriguez. They were bloodied and filthy and had clearly been engaged in combat.

"About time. Thought you'd all left hours ago."

"Not likely, Jones."

Lieutenant Weston appeared, and the man saluted. The newly arrived Sergeant shook his head as he looked at what remained of the Special Forces camp. The buildings were all burnt to the ground, and smoke still rose from the smouldering ruins.

"Report. Where are the rest?"

He looked to the tree line, and at the small, battered group of men.

"Sir, this is it."

The Lieutenant looked stunned.

"Sir, the wounded were airlifted out. We waited until more troops had been landed as ordered, and we were coming back here with thirty guys."

"Where are they?"

The man wiped his face with the back of his hand.

"Only seven of us made it here."

"Seven?"

"Yes, Sir. We ran into these crazed NVA. We stopped 'em. But they kept on coming out of the mist. Some of our guys went back down to the LZ, but we heard them screaming a minute later. The rest of us slogged it back here. We followed the sound of the firefight. We've been on the move for hours."

Sergeant Jones shook his head.

"There's something not right here. You ain't gonna believe what we've seen so far."

Billy could see something in the Sergeant's eyes. It wasn't fear. He suspected the man had never known fear in his life. No, it was something else. A mixture of surprise and revulsion. At that moment, he knew they were in real trouble.

"Sir," said Sergeant Rodriguez, "There was something else out there. It waited until the dead of night before it hit us."

Sergeant Jones looked to his friend, and his eyes opened wide in surprise. Sergeant Rodriguez looked like he'd seen a ghost.

"I sent one squad East, and something swallowed them up whole."

He shook his head.

"What?" Jones asked, "Like smoke?"

"No, not smoke. It tore them apart in the darkness. We heard the screams and the sound of breaking bones. We chased in after them, and it took down three more of my men."

He whistled, and one of his soldiers approached. The Sergeant gave him a nod, and the man lifted his jacket away to reveal the torn olive drab underclothing. Running from the shoulder to his upper ribs was a deep cut that was fused by heat as though a soldier had used a heated iron to seal it up.

"You used fire to seal up the wound?"

"No. Something in the shadows gutted my men. Kowalski was dragging one of them away when he was attacked. The blades scorched his flesh like red-hot iron.

"It's got to be the Gooks," said Lance Corporal Johnson, "Has to be."

Sergeant Rodriguez shrugged.

"I dunno. Whatever it was, it butchered my men. We called for help, but the radio's down."

"Same here," said Lieutenant Weston, "We can't pick up a damned thing. We'll have to get higher. Or wait here."

"We did track it following the trails heading up into the hills."

He pointed towards the vast canopy of trees that went on for scores of miles in every direction.

"Okay. We've secured this site, and we'll need to dig in and wait for…"

"Lieutenant, they took two of my men. Maybe it's NVA, maybe something else, but I'm not leaving them behind. They left a trail behind them…I know they're still alive."

Lieutenant Weston looked to the bloodied Sergeant and then back to his men. The compound was shattered, and with the smoke rising up high, it was a signal to any and all NVA and VC in the area that an enemy was there.

"We've got no reinforcements, no supplies, and no communication. We should head back down to the…"

"Sir, comms are back," said Radioman Jeffries. The relief was evident in his voice.

"Finally." Jones beckoned him to come closer. He was surprisingly quiet on the radio and kept looking back at the hillside rising high above them.

"Aerial recon confirms sighting of NVA forces to the North."

"Bastards are bugging out," said Sergeant Jones, "Told you. They always slink away."

He looked to Sergeant Rodriguez.

"Probably got your boys, too."

"Negative," said Lieutenant Weston, "The opposite, they're heading right there."

He nodded towards the distant peak.

"You're kidding?" Lance Corporal Johnson asked, "They're heading to the peaks?"

"Correct, and our mission stands. We came here for one reason only, to find and destroy the NVA. We've got two platoons coming in within the hour."

He stopped as the distant, barely audible crack of small arms fire caught his attention. He looked in the direction of the sound. The look from his Sergeant told him everything he needed to know.

"No more running," said Sergeant Jones, "As soon as they get here, it's time to go hunting."

CHAPTER SIX

The rain returned at first light, and by the time the reinforcements finally arrived he was soaked through. His quick drying clothing seemed irrelevant in this weather, and it did little to improve his mood. He looked down on the burnt-out Special Forces camp as more troops were brought in. The first helicopter had already left the base, and more were coming in low and fast. The Hueys ferried squad after squad to the base, with each touching down for only as long as was required. Others brought in fresh supplies, including much needed food, water, and ammunition. Billy was much more interested in the pair of armed escorts, though. The AH-1 Cobras known as Snakes to many of the men on the ground. They sounded little different to the normal Hueys, but they looked nothing alike. Whereas the UH-1 was a simple utility helicopters, the Snake featured a slender airframe and was designed around a two-seat tandem cockpit. A ball-turret in the nose carried the main guns and stub wings for mounting rockets, missiles, and other weapons.

"They're sweet rides, ain't they?" Private Hohner was wiping the rain from his face. There was still mud, and a few drops of blood had spread out along his skin. Billy looked at the marks, and then did his best to shake thoughts of the battle from his mind. He nodded while turning his attention to the helicopters circling about. From atop the watchtower they had the perfect view of the base, as well as the ground around it. With the daylight, more soldiers and air support, Billy didn't feel quite so alone anymore. As he watched, the gunships pulled back further into the valley, but not too far away.

"What are they doing, though? They're holding back."

A voice from directly behind him made him jump. Billy turned around to find Lance Corporal Johnson chewing down on a cookie he must have packed with his gear. Billy immediately felt his stomach growl as he watched the man chewing slowly.

"That is a ploy for hunting Gooks." He nodded at the gunships.

"How?" Private Hohner asked.

Johnson spat out one part of the cookie and wrinkled up his nose.

"The Gooks don't like the gunships. Why? Because they shoot back. So, what happens is…"

He stopped as a much smaller helicopter screamed overhead, and little more than tree height. It was moving fast, as if some great flying beast was hunting it.

"There you go," said Johnson, "Just on time. The little

one, the Loach, it goes on first to flush out Charlie. It's low and slow, and they always fall for it. Once they've pinpointed the ground fire, the Snakes come in and mop up."

Private Hohner shook his head.

"How can we lose this fight? You've heard the stories back home. They want us out. But we're winning."

Johnson nearly choked on the last part of his cookie.

"How are we winning, Private?"

"We win every battle. We kill more of them than they kill of us."

Another Huey came in over the base and hovered just off the ground. Men leapt from the side, and one lost his foot and stumbled. He must have hurt his leg or broken his ankle because he was pulled back inside and left once the rest were on the ground.

"Idiot," said Johnson, "And that's the difference. We're just visitors in 'Nam. We win battles, but did anybody tell Charlie that? All he knows is he fights and he kills, and he's been doing this since the Frenchies were here."

"What?" Private Hohner asked, "French?"

Johnson shook his head and walked away, leaving the two soldiers atop the tower while he pulled out a cigarette.

"What's the French got to do with this?"

Johnson continued to laugh to himself.

"They were here long before us. Back in the 1890s, and right up until they were kicked out fifteen years ago."

"Wow. I've never heard of this."

"Well, the Vietnamese people have fought the French, then the Japanese occupation, then the French again. We're here because the French couldn't win."

Private Hohner laughed.

"When did they last win?"

"When did we, dumbass?" Johnson asked, "Korea…a draw, against the Brits, a draw. We only came out on top in the big ones because everybody else was involved. If you ask me, we should have marched on Saigon with the Commie Gooks the day we arrived."

Even Billy couldn't argue with that.

"He's not wrong. If the ARVN fought like they do, this war would be over by now."

Johnson pointed at Billy and nodded.

"Exactly."

Lieutenant Weston appeared in the middle of the base as he spoke with a captain or colonel, it was hard to tell from the tower. The conversation didn't last long before he turned away and headed toward the tower. Johnson tossed what was left of the cookie to Billy, and then headed for the ladder.

"It's time."

Billy wolfed down the tough cookie and nearly choked as the dry, mealy food almost stuck in his throat. He then dropped down the ladder to the ground as the rest of the unit assembled. Fresh troops continued to arrive as the US and ARVN troops reinforced the base and began stacking boxes of ammunition and supplies. Others went to work with hand tools and chainsaws, cutting down more of the foliage around the base to create a larger landing ground. Lieutenant Weston looked to his weakened platoon. The rain did little to improve their mood, but they were relatively unhurt, and finally fully equipped with rations, supplies, and ammunition.

"This is now Forward Base Alaska. From here we're

launching our attack up into the mountains. By the time we're done, we will have crushed an entire NVA division."

Platoon Sergeant Rodriguez and Sergeant Jones were standing next to him, as well as Lieutenant Van Quyen, the leader of what remained of the ARVN Rangers. He looked tiny next to the Americans, with his gaunt frame and diminutive build. His uniform was loose fitting, and the tiger strikes looked worn and faded. None would doubt his resolve in combat, with the lines and the immaculately fitted beret perched atop his head. He was a proud man, and more than likely had ten times the experience of almost any American on this hill.

"Charlie Company, 1st Battalion is already heading up the hill. They're fresh and full strength and going up ahead of us."

"It's our hill, Sir," complained Johnson.

"Right now, it's nobody's hill," said the Lieutenant in something close to irritation, "The enemy has withdrawn, and you know as well as I do, that if we are not fast they will vanish, like they always do. So, we're going after them, like I promised."

"Good. Time to give the Gooks a reminder why we're here."

"Johnson!" Sergeant Jones said.

"Sorry, Sarge."

"Charlie Company will tackle them head on, and trust me, if the enemy are dug in that's a fight we want to avoid."

He nodded to himself as he glanced at the battle-hardened Rangers.

"Lieutenant Van Quyen has seen us in action and has asked for us to work with them as we move up their flank. We might be half strength, but we've got an interest in this damn hill. Now…are you ready?"

He looked to the men of the two remaining squads. Each nodded in agreement, but there was a mixed response in eagerness. Some like Johnson seemed ever eager to get to grips with the enemy, but others were less eager to see combat. Normally, there would be four squads in their platoon giving them a fighting strength of up to fifty soldiers, but with the fighting, and not all of them being landed in the same place, they were down to just eighteen men including NCOs and Lieutenant Weston. Less than half of their normal strength. The ARVN Rangers padded out their number to around thirty, but it was still a sombre reminder of what the brutal conditions of Vietnam could do to a military unit.

"Okay, then, it's time to move out. We've got plenty of light, and Command wants us in position before nightfall."

"We're attacking at night, Sir?" asked a Private from Sergeant Rodriguez's platoon.

"If all goes to plan, we'll just be mopping up. Command has put air cover on standby for us. Once we find 'em, it will be time to let them know the true feeling of fear."

"Arclight?" asked one hopefully.

"Let's hope so. Any other questions?"

The unit remained silent, but there was one thought on Billy's mind that he couldn't shake. The images of the red glowing eyes in the night seemed so far away now, yet when he looked off to the trees, he was sure he could still see them.

"Sir, what about the things in the trees?"

A few of the others looked to him, and one chuckled nervously.

"Son, we don't know what we saw. We have flares going off, tracer, mortars. The works. Trust me, we don't know half of what was being fired at us."

Some nodded along in agreement, but Billy could sense the unease in the unit. Weston looked to them, and then back to his NCOs. Sergeant Jones shrugged.

"No idea, Sir. I guess we'll find out on the trail."

"And the talon?" Billy asked, "That doesn't worry you?"

"It's a talon, son. You'll find them two a penny back home. Those NVA soldiers probably found an old bone and used it as a weapon. There's not a lot we can do about it now, is there?"

Billy gulped as he realised what was about to happen. They would be leaving the safety of the base, with its burnt down trenches and dugouts, and the tower that provide both height and a perfect view down onto a possible enemy. Worse than all of that, he would be heading back into the jungle, and to face the unknown.

"Now, grab your gear. We've got marching to do."

In ten minutes, they were marching away from the base and back into the jungle. Although this time there were wider gaps through the trees, making movement so much easier and faster. The ARVN Rangers went out ahead as before, using their speed and expertise to check for traps and other dangers. Billy looked back at the base one last time as the foliage obscured it, but all he could see were the bloodied bodies, and the great talon embedded in the man's body. He turned back to speak to the nearest soldier, but it was Johnson. And the man looked like he was in no mood for chitchat. They exchanged looks, but then Johnson did something he would never have expected.

"If you see those red eyes again, you let me know. Right?"

"Uh…of course."

"Good. There's things in this jungle no man should see."

They continued onwards, and with each passing hour Billy began to calm down. Until today he'd been terrified of moving through the jungle. There were the Viet Cong, the North Vietnamese Army, the animals that could bite or sting him, and the fauna that his body would react to. All manner of illnesses and diseases, yet all of this paled to insignificance next to the true horrors he'd experienced first-hand. They'd come up against a strange and determined enemy, as well as the thing that no one wanted to discuss, and they were all still there.

The trees seemed to change colour, depending on where they were on the hillside, and occasionally, they would reach a point where they could see back into the valley. At one such area, they paused and stopped for a short break. That was the perfect opportunity to rest his legs, take on water, and get through some of the rations he'd brought with him. Like most soldiers, he'd broken up his rations before leaving, reducing the weight and material he needed to haul around with him. Most of the platoon sat around, with just two keeping watch, as well as a handful of the Rangers. They never seemed to rest or relax, their eyes always on the trees all around them.

"What are they looking for?" Thompson asked.

Johnson tossed a can of jerky at the man's head, and it glanced off his helmet before dropping to the floor.

"What do you think? Charlie is out there, and he's not our friend. These Rangers know their shit."

Until the battle at the Special Forces camp the Corporal had been nothing but dismissive of them, but having seen them in combat on their side, his mood seemed to have shifted. That, or his attitude to the enemy had simply hardened further. They sat and chatted like they were old friends before finally stowing their gear and moving back to the trail. Minutes stretched into hours, but they were all thankful for no more shouting and gunfire. Billy lifted one leg in front of another, and slowly but surely his confidence grew. They passed all kinds of peculiar foliage, but there were also some surprises in store for them. Entire sections were almost like cultivated fields back home, though as they moved into them, they could see it was more a place devoid of trees than pastoral land. The grasses were tall and could cut if slid along at the wrong angle.

A Ranger up at the front stopped, gave a hand signal, and then moved ahead.

"Oh…crap," Thompson muttered, "Not good."

The Ranger returned, and the column continued forward. They were now away from the trees and in an area of scrubland, where much of the larger vegetation was missing. Sitting out in the open, and half buried in the ground was an aircraft.

"C119," said Sergeant Jones as he moved around it.

Billy was close behind, and he found the wreckage fascinating. It was not recent, and greenery was already growing inside the structure. Much of the aircraft was missing, presumably scattered about. But the markings on the side intrigued him.

"French?" Thompson asked.

"Yeah. We loaned them these plans in the 50s."

"Well, looks like somebody hit them hard back then." Johnson walked around to the rear of the aircraft; "Yeah…they've got cannon damage to the main structure. Guns brought her down as she moved through the valley. Probably heading out from Da Nang."

The box structure was mostly intact, though the twin booms were broken and half hidden under greenery. A Ranger appeared from the rear of the boxy main fuselage holding webbing and a rifle. The kit was quite different to that used by the soldiers, and the rifle especially odd. More wood than metal, and like a rifle from World War II.

"What is that?" Johnson asked.

"MAS-36 rifle," said Sergeant Jones, taking it from the Ranger. He looked at the weapon with interest and then worked the bolt. It moved effortlessly.

"Standard French bolt-action rifle. Carbine length, and ugly as sin."

"You seen our rifles, Sarge?" Private Thompson said, "They look like a kid designed 'em."

Sergeant Jones ignored him and continued to turn the weapon around.

"They're reliable, like the Kalashnikov. Kick it, stamp on it, bury it in the mud, and it still works."

Billy looked to his own rifle. It looked like something from a comic book, with its curved and plastic fittings. But he was also familiar with the fact that it would prove useless if not cleaned and maintained all the time. There were times when he'd have given his right arm for something simpler and more reliable.

"This must have been hauling French paratroopers. Maybe even the poor bastards heading out to Dien Bien Phu."

He checked the webbing and removed a number of stripper clips fitted with bullets, as well as some personal effects. He squirreled all of it away, and then slung the carbine over his shoulder.

"You're gonna use that thing?" Johnson asked.

"We'll see."

He looked to the rest of the squad, but before he could speak, the Ranger dragged out the remains of a man. Billy turned away and retched, but Sergeant Jones seemed unaffected by the grizzly remains.

"Half eaten. They've definitely been here for some time."

The Ranger spoke with him, and Sergeant Jones responded in short, guttural words in Vietnamese. It sounded like they were arguing, but Billy could hardly tell. The language was so different to his own. Jones turned away, shaking his head.

"What is it, Sarge?"

He looked to Billy and shrugged.

"Our ARVN friends say he was killed by a puncture wound from an animal. Right through his chest."

Something clicked off to the left and far off into the distance. It wasn't particularly loud but was then followed by several others.

"Listen," said Sergeant Jones.

The unit remained utterly still, each looking left and right for signs of danger. Back home they'd trained for combat against an enemy they could see, but the reality of combat in Vietnam was very different. Aimed fire was almost irrelevant, and instead it came down to combat at close ranges, often never seeing each other. Just muzzles flashes, the sound of gunfire, and the screams of the wounded from both sides.

"I can't hear a…" said Private Thompson, but then the sounds increased in number, followed by the telltale thump of a mortar. Lieutenant Weston was just visible ahead, and he also gave the signal to move forward.

"We've found 'em," said Jones, "That's got to be Charlie Company going into the fight."

He looked to the men of his squad.

"Our guys are in the fight. You ladies up for a scrap?"

Lance Corporal Johnson pulled the M60 down from his shoulder and held it out from his hip. The rain started again almost on cue, soaking the soldiers and reducing their visibility.

"Are you kidding?" he said with a grunt, "It's game time."

CHAPTER SEVEN

The battle had seemed so distant as they worked their way up the hill, and every single step was a struggle. Billy found it almost impossible to stay upright and take aim with his rifle. It was difficult going at the best of times, but the unending rain was making their lives almost intolerable. As they moved forward, a soldier towards the front lost his footing and slid back down towards Billy and his comrades. The man's struggles seemed to hasten his fall back down the hillside until Johnson reached out and grabbed his pack with one arm.

"Hold onto something!" he said angrily, "We ain't surfing to the bottom of this hill. We're going up it."

He pushed the man's forearm, and though exhausted, he started the slow, brutal ascent to his unit. In the distance was the unmistakable sound of rifle fire, mixed with the thunder of

AK47s assault rifles firing in fully automatic. It was a sound all of them were by now familiar with, but that didn't make it any less unnerving. Occasionally, a stray bullet whistled past them, and one even hit the tree just in front of Billy as he was climbing over a mound of moss-covered rocks.

"Not much further," said Sergeant Jones, "One more push."

But as soon as they reached the next small clearing, they ran directly into the path of a group of enemy scouts. The ARVN Rangers pushed forward to attack them with rifles blaring as they went. Seconds later a flurry of rounds was all around the American soldiers coming up behind them. It didn't take much to scatter the soldiers.

"Take cover!"

Billy had no idea who was speaking, and quite frankly, he didn't give a damn. He hit the ground, and a moment later a burst of fire hit overhead. The high-pitched crackle of bullets flying over him was a sobering thought at the best of times, and Billy knew that all it would take was one to end his life, or worse it might leave his body with injuries that would ruin the rest of his remaining life. Billy looked off into the distance while struggling to hold onto his helmet. The ARVN Rangers were falling back. One was shot, and another was blown through the air as a grenade exploded.

"Suppressing fire!"

Johnson was already ready and began firing from the hip. There was no enemy to be seen in the jungle, so he tracked from left to right, blasting away. Even if he hit somebody, there would be no way of knowing he'd been successful. Thompson was at his side and ducking down while readying a belt of ammunition.

"Yeah!" Johnson shouted as the M60 thundered away. The heavy weapon left Billy's M16 looking like a plastic toy, "Eat this!"

Billy lifted his own weapon and fired four bursts into the trees. He felt powerful as the weapon shook, but still there was no sign of the enemy being hit. He hit the magazine release and loaded in the next one. Something then went boom, and he threw himself down to avoid being blown apart. There was never a way of knowing where incoming gunfire was coming from. And by the time you heard it, the thing was exploding in your face. He saw two flashes off to the left, and then another just behind them.

"Mortar!" shouted a voice from up ahead, near to where Sergeant Rodriguez's men were, "We need to get closer to these bastards!"

Billy wiped the dirt from his face and reached for his rifle. Thankfully, he'd managed to push the next magazine into place before dropping the weapon. He looked to his right, and there was Sergeant Jones ducking behind cover. He was reloading his carbine, and as he slid in the magazine, he looked back to the others. Lieutenant Weston was there, as well as the radio operator.

"We're moving as fast as we can, dammit!" grumbled the Lieutenant as he handed back the radio handset. The PRC-6 Radio Transmitter & Receiver unit had taken a near miss, and part of the outer bodywork was cracked and damaged. Lieutenant Weston snarled and then looked to Sergeant Jones.

"Charlie Company has 'em pinned down on the next ridge. There's a bunker and tunnel complex, but they can't break through."

"Let me guess, they want us up there?"

Weston nodded.

"Yeah, something like that."

He reached for his map case and held it out, all while the battle continued to rage.

"If we keep pushing up through the next two hundred yards, we'll hit this ridgeline."

The Sergeant looked at it and nodded.

"Once there, we can hit them with enfilade fire and take some of the pressure off Charlie Company."

"Understood. We're going to have to break through."

Lieutenant Weston put away the map case and then lifted his rifle.

"Exactly. On my command we push, and we don't stop till we take that ridge."

The hill was a relatively gentle gradient, but the rain and muddy animal paths made it slow and difficult work.

"Get past the range of their mortars. Push!"

One by one they rose from the mud and began to walk, crawl, and drag themselves up the steeper parts of the trail. Off to their flank, and in the distance a massed battle was taking place. But they were hardly out on a picnic where they were. Billy spotted something ahead and took aim ready to shoot. But an M79 took care of the enemy. The grenade hit a little to the side of their position, and a cheer rang out as two enemy soldiers were thrown through the air.

"Push!"

Billy was third from the top. As he reached the top of the ridge, there was sparse foliage, as well as a raised ridge of solid rock, like the spine of some long dead beast resting on the ground. He stayed low behind it as he looked for signs of danger. He could already make out at least four enemy bodies, as well as a shattered radio and a pack with used up ammunition. A soldier from the other platoon bent down to check, and Billy swiped away his hand.

"Never…ever touch the dead. Unless you want to join them."

The man pulled back his hands as though they were about to catch fire. He looked to Billy, and his face was white. There was a terror to his face that Billy knew only too well.

"You okay?"

The man nodded and clambered over the rock. For a few seconds he was completely exposed and raised up way too high.

"Get down, you…!" Billy called out, but it was too late. Something slammed hard into the man's chest, and he was thrown down hard. Billy ducked down to help him as the roar of a heavy weapon opened fire. This wasn't the sound you'd expect from something like the M60, but the roar of something designed to knock out aircraft. The body on the ground had been hit just once, but the hole was the size of a dinner plate, and there were no signs of life.

"Jesus, this is one of their anti-aircraft batteries!" Lance Corporal Johnson yelled as he settled down next to Billy. He looked across to him, and any sense of past antagonism was long gone. Now they were just a pair of soldiers in the jungles of Vietnam.

"You up for a sprint to the next tree line? Because if we stay here, we're not leaving."

Billy looked up from where he was sheltering. The next ridge was much brighter and looked as though it led to a clearing, presumably where the guns were located. The weapon fired again, powerful thudding sounds four more times, and then fell silent.

"That's a 37mm gun. It will cut you in half if they get a bead on you."

Billy could feel his poor legs turning to jelly. There was absolutely nothing he could do against such firepower. A tree would do nothing, and nor would flak jackets. Even most tanks would struggle at close range against such a beast.

"Haha! The stupid bastards can't get the depression, and that's a 5-round clip."

"You're sure?" Billy asked.

"Pretty sure."

There was a short pause, but the gun then fired again. Billy stayed low, even as more soldiers reached their position. Some opened fire, but most hunkered down in the mud and prayed they wouldn't be hit.

"See," said Johnson, "If you keep down, you're fine."

"And that's another five," said Billy as he counted the shots.

"Yeah. Be ready."

Billy's chest pounded as he waited. Both sides fired back and forth, but it wasn't the rifle fire he was listening to, it was the deadly hammering of the gun. Johnson looked to the soldiers around them.

"Put down suppressing fire when we attack. Once we get there, climb up and haul ass. Ready?"

The small group nodded as the gun fired again. Lieutenant Weston and eight other soldiers threw themselves to the mud further down the slope as the heavy shells ripped apart trees with ease. It was having a devastating effect on the morale of the men, and they were now all but pinned into place as the rounds threatened to cut them down. Billy looked to Johnson and nodded.

"Go!"

The two broke from cover, and right behind them came Private Hohner. The three ran, stumbling and sliding as they worked their way up. Two rifles fired down at them, but they were then hit by massed fire from the American soldiers. Billy felt like they had been running for several minutes when Johnson dropped down. Billy did the same, but Hohner kept on going.

"Get down!" Billy screamed.

Then the guns opened fire again. The shells ripped down the hill, and one narrowly missed the Private before he dropped down. Five shells were soon expended, and they were back to their feet. This time Private Hohner remained face down in the mud, and Billy knew that the worst must have happened. But Johnson was already pushing ahead, and he had to do the same. With one last glance at his friend, he rose up and chased after Johnson. They slipped about, but somehow reached the next ridge, and into a clearing. There before them was a pair of four-wheeled platforms, each fitted with a massive anti-aircraft gun. One remained pointing up to the sky, but the second pointed downhill, and a number of crew were around it as they were about to fire.

"Bastards!" Johnson opened fire. The M60 was brutal at this range, and Billy stepped to the side as he did the same. Shots hammered into the crew, with many glancing off the metalwork of the gun itself. They killed or wounded the entire crew, and two of the men slunk off into the jungle. Billy moved back and called down to the soldiers on the slope.

"Clear!"

There were shouts from Lieutenant Weston and his NCOs as he ordered the rest of the unit to move up to join them. Then Billy moved to Johnson, and they inched their way past the two anti-aircraft units. The place was relatively open and provided a good view of the sky around the hillside. It was also possible to make out the entire side of the hill heading off to the North. He made out undulating ridges, trees, and some of the sparser locations.

"There," said Johnson, "Charlie Company."

Lieutenant Weston arrived, along with six others who quickly spread out to check the area. Weston moved closer and stopped alongside Billy.

"Good work, you two."

"Sir," said Johnson, "Looks like Charlie Company is taking a beating getting up that hill."

Lieutenant Weston lifted his binoculars and checked on their progress.

"There's a line of bunkers. I can make out four of them, all reinforced and sunk into the ground. And look there, to the rear. They've started work on trenches."

"We got here early?"

"Maybe. In any case we've got their flank."

He turned and signalled towards Sergeant Jones as he appeared from the slope with the rest of the squad.

"Lt?"

"Get your men ready. We're gonna put some hurt on the NVA flank. That should soften em up enough for Charlie

Company."

"Yes, Sir."

Jones looked to Billy and Johnson. "You two, with me."

"Yes, Sarge." They both replied and moved to join him after receiving a nod from the Lieutenant. As they joined the others, Billy gasped in surprise. There, being carried by two of the privates was Private Hohner, and he was partially conscious.

"What happened?"

The two men dropped him next to one of the guns and then tapped his helmet.

"Lucky bastard took shrapnel to the head. Knocked him out cold."

Billy placed a hand on his friend's shoulder and bent down to speak.

"Private," said Johnson, "Later. We've got work to do."

Billy tapped his friend, and then moved off to line up with the others. They'd taken position on the edge of the anti-aircraft position, and behind the stacks of now empty metal and wooden boxes and crates. They created an improvised wall over three feet tall. Johnson placed his M60 atop the boxes and deployed the bipod. Billy moved alongside him and rested his rifle.

"Watch your fire," said Sergeant Jones as he used his binoculars to study the open ground along the hillside, "Charlie Company is off to the left, and they're taking a lot of fire."

Billy watched carefully and soon spotted the dull green shapes of US and ARVN regulars exchanging fire with the entrenched enemy all along the hillside. The bunkers were impossible to hit from where they were, but he could see movement near to them, as well as others rushing boxes of supplies via the half-completed trenches, they could now see into.

"Ready…" Sergeant Jones said, "Fire!"

CHAPTER EIGHT

The ARVN Rangers appeared to be having the time of their lives as they tore up the hillside. Half of them were mixed in with the Americans, the rest slightly further up the hill to protect their flank. All of them were firing with every weapon they had, and a number shouted in English as they gunned down their hated foe. Billy looked at one man nearby who seemed to reload and fire without a moment's pause. He might be on his side, but he had to admit, if he'd run into the man in the jungle, he would have fired right away. Apart from the tiger stripes, he looked just the same as the NVA.

"Die, man!"

The accent was thick, and Billy was convinced they were trying to prove something to him. But as the man looked back at him, he could tell it was nothing like that. There was a fire in his eyes, a fire that dripped in hate and violence. Billy shuddered as the man returned to his workmanlike approach to the fight.

This is insanity.

All thoughts of the red eyes and the thing in the jungle were gone now. This was a gun battle like no other, and as they watched down on their opponents, Billy could feel his rage beginning to rise. He had never felt quite so confident and powerful as he did right now. From their position in the clearing high up on the enemy's flank, they had the perfect enfilade position. The entire platoon brought down a hail of fire. The M60s rattled away, while intermittent explosions from the M79s hit around the bunkers. The rest fired bursts into the enemy positions as they rushed to find cover.

"Nice shooting." Sergeant Jones took aim with his rifle, "Keep putting the hurt on 'em."

He was so calm it was a little unnerving to watch. Unlike the rest of the platoon, Sergeant Jones operated like a machine. Bullets came close to him, but never enough to really do more than cause the odd flesh wound. Other men were just as brave, yet it was Jones that was never hit. As the bullets thudded into the trees and even the metal work of the guns, he simply waited, took aim, and fired. Burst after burst at the enemy, with almost no discernible recoil. As he reloaded, Private Thompson looked back at their current position.

"What asshole builds an air defence position with so few defences," he said with a laugh, "They should have positioned this site further up the hillside."

"Maybe they would have if we'd given them more time," said Sergeant Jones, "Now keep your eye on the enemy. This ain't over yet."

He unleashed two long bursts that chased a trio of men

into a bunker. One stumbled and took the brunt of the fire, while the others vanished from view. They found no safety inside though, as grenades hurled by the advancing men of Charlie Company fell inside. Part of the roof collapsed under the brutal flashes of fire and light.

"Yeah!" Thompson shouted.

"If I have to say it again, you'll go down and join them."

That seemed to silence Thompson, who went back to firing down on the helpless enemy. The Sergeant, on the other hand, continued his own methodical slaughter until his rifle ran dry. After expending it, he swung it back around his body to hang from its sling, and in its place, he brought up the French weapon. It looked gleaming compared to when they'd found it, and Billy could only assume that in their down time the Sergeant had performed some basic cleaning on its components.

"Sure that's wise, Sergeant?" Lieutenant Weston asked as he placed the shoulder stock of his XM177E2 up to his shoulder. He then fired short, rapid bursts, though it was impossible to tell what effect it had on the enemy. He certainly looked competent, though he'd spent much longer before firing than the Sergeant had.

"It's solid, Sir."

Sergeant Jones lifted the MAS-36 bolt-action military rifle to his shoulder and took aim down the iron sights. It looked strangely familiar in his hands, as though it was a weapon he'd used many times before. The bolt moved smoothly as he loaded in a single bullet into the chamber. He tracked a target far below, moving slowly to the right. The rifle kicked hard into his shoulder, along with a brutal crack from the muzzle. Billy saw him fire and half expected the weapon to tear itself apart. Instead one of the men quickly whistled.

"You winged the officer, Sarge! That was a hell of a shot."

Sergeant Jones worked the bolt quickly and smoothly, while keeping the weapon to the shoulder and fired again. The 7.5 x 54mm rimless bottlenecked rifle cartridges were ballistically comparable to the rounds fired by the platoon's M60. Sergeant Jones outshot the others as he hit two more NVA soldiers, with only two misses.

"Nice shooting," said another, but he merely grunted and slid in another stripper clip of five bullets. It was quite different to the system the other soldiers were used to. The strip slid in, and he pushed in the five bullets before throwing the clip aside. It was the same system used by most rifles of the World Wars, and had proven sturdy and reliable.

"Like I said, it ain't pretty." Sergeant Jones took aim again. This time he put down all five bullets into a group struggling to drag a machine gun into position. One was killed instantly, another wounded. The rest scattered, leaving the weapon in place, "The French can make some good firearms."

"Yeah," said Thompson, "Except when they're busy surrendering."

Some of the others laughed at that.

"Frenchies. What is it the Limeys call them, Frogs?"

There was more laughter, but as always, they were shut down by a brutal stare from their Sergeant.

"This isn't a stroll in the jungle for your personal edification, Private. Get your eye on your rifle and keep shooting. Charlie Company is depending on us."

"Yes, Sarge."

A pair of ARVN soldiers moved out from the jungle, and

Lieutenant Van Quyen moved a short distance behind them. There was blood on his jacket, but he seemed uninjured. He spoke rapidly with Lieutenant Weston, who in turn replied in rough Vietnamese. He was no expert, but he was more than capable of communicating with them. Van Quyen finally gave the messiest salute Billy had ever seen, and then moved back up the hill. Lieutenant Weston shouted after him in English so everybody else could also understand.

"Advance half a klick and dig in."

Lieutenant Weston saw Billy watching and whistled, while pointing back down the hill. He turned away, but kept one eye on the ARVN Rangers as they once more vanished into the jungle. He should have felt safe knowing they were advancing ahead to protect their right flank, but something deep inside left him distrustful. Maybe it was little more than pure racism, but he doubted that. He trusted nobody out here other than the men in his unit. American, Vietnamese, or even Korean. They were all here for different reasons. He just couldn't wait to get back home and to put all this behind him. Even this battle on the hillside of some place in the middle of the jungle seemed to mean little in the grander scheme of things.

"Hell, yeah!" A corporal pointed to the muddy hillside as Charlie Company pushed on forward, "Keep moving, guys! We've got ya!"

The riflemen fired again, a mixture of aimed shots and bursts of automatic fire that hammered away at the NVA defenders. A ripple of explosions crashed along the frontline as the Americans coming up the muddy hill tossed grenades at the defences. In the movies the grenades had always seemed so powerful, but out here in the open they seemed very different.

Short flashes and a loud crack, but then just a cloud of dust and smoke. Not that Billy wanted to get close to one. He'd seen the consequence of a grenade blast on more than one occasion already. The thud of mortar shells then marked a savage change in the battle. They dropped down and hit the mud around the soldiers as they struggled in the mud. They were having a hard time fighting against the enemy with the light rain and the conditions of the hill. And now the mortars made that battle so much deadlier. One man tried to run backwards and was hit by a mortar shell. When the dust cleared, there was no sign of him.

"Damn!" Billy said in surprise, "Nasty."

He tried to spot the mortars, but they were not visible, and presumably sited further back on the hill somewhere. So he fired off a burst into the tree line behind the enemy defensive positions. It was a pointless gesture, but it pained him to know the enemy were fighting with impunity from the haven provided by the woodland.

"Private. Help me out here," said Johnson.

Billy lowered his muzzle and moved to the machine gunner. It was then he noticed Private Thompson, the machine gunner's assistant having a bandage applied to his right arm.

"You hurt?"

"No, just thought I'd put a bandage on for kicks!"

Billy was about to say more when another flurry of bullets hit nearby. He moved over to where Johnson was waiting with his machine gun.

"What do you need?"

"Barrel change."

He tossed a slightly damaged glove over to him as a burst of fire hit nearby. The bullets hammered into the foliage, but right now he was completely focussed on the job that needed to be done.

"You got a jam?"

"Not yet, but it's coming. You can do this, right?"

Billy nodded slowly.

"Yeah, but it's…"

"Yeah is good enough for me."

Johnson raised the barrel locking lever, ducking as a bullet snapped past.

"Come on, Private. Move it."

Billy twisted and pulled on the barrel, and the entire unit pulled away from the main body of the weapon. The bipod remained attached, and as he placed it to one side, it hissed when the metalwork touched the wet greenery. The spare barrel waited on top of a pack and looked pristine and new compared to the worn one he'd been using so far. Billy positioned it carefully and pushed it into place. Johnson lowered the barrel locking lever and checked it was all fitted securely.

"Good, now give me another belt."

Thompson heard that and grunted as he removed one of the two belts strapped around his torso.

"Here!"

Billy took one and moved to the left-hand side of Johnson. Though he was not technically a machine gun assistant, he'd gone through the training, and they'd had a refresher back at base, as insisted on by Sergeant Jones. As he'd said, when it came to combat, he wanted everybody capable of taking over when the 'shit went down.' It had seemed a little pessimistic at the time, but as he moved into position, it all came back to him. Johnson tapped the plate to ensure it was down and physically checked the bolt was forward. Billy then placed the first bullet on the ammunition belt over the belt holding pole. Johnson pulled back the cocking handle lever to the rear, fully loading the gun.

"Good," said Johnson.

He swung the weapon to the left and took aim at the enemy. Billy grabbed his M16 and rested on the crates as he took aim once more. He spotted a pair of enemy soldiers moving through a secondary trench. It was half completed, and the gaps gave him a perfect view into their position. One of the soldiers carried a weapon on his shoulder.

RPG. Now that's a problem.

He took careful aim, even as the shots from the others continued to cascade down into the enemy. Several more fell, but the man with the rocket-propelled grenade launcher seemed impervious to fire. Even the M60 did little more than warn him as the fire raced up to him. The enemy soldier ducked down behind mud and splintered wood for several seconds.

"Damned Gook!" Lance Corporal Johnson muttered.

He adjusted his aim and opened fire again. Flashes along the ground kicked up a storm of dirt that provided more cover for the soldier to hide in. As the cloud subsided, the man was already gone.

"I see him," said Billy as he squeezed the trigger.

The rifle kicked into his shoulder, and though well aimed, the man seemed to have a sixth sense. He dropped to the side and then looked up at them.

"Crap!" Billy ducked down. A flash from down below them marked the launch of the rocket, "Incoming!"

Most of the soldiers took cover, but a few either ignored

him or continued to fire down at the enemy. The rocket screamed towards them but dropped off a little too low. It hit the ground a few yards short and detonated. The blast was enough to throw some of the Americans to the floor. One lost his footing, but no one seemed too worse for wear.

"Put him down!" Sergeant Jones snarled.

Billy moved back to his feet, but when he aimed into the distance, the man was gone. And in his place the front rank of Charlie Company surged over the front lines. Two of the bunkers were already under their control, and the flash of grenades marked another that was about to join them.

"Bastard!" Billy said, "He's gone."

Lieutenant Weston was speaking on the radio and looked agitated. Finally, he looked back at his unit that were spread out all along the ridge looking down on the hillside.

"Charlie Company needs us to sweep in and clear the upper trenches. They're too dug in to be hit from here."

Billy licked his lips nervously. It was one thing shooting at the enemy from a distance, but scrambling down the scrub and mud to the hillside was not his idea of fun. The enemy was spread out and well defended, and he knew once they were down there, it would be impossible to get back to safety.

"3rd Squad will stay back at this position. You'll provide supporting fire."

He pointed to the machine gunner who looked like a shorter, Hispanic version of Lance Corporal Johnson. His jacket was torn, and he was missing his helmet.

"And watch your damned fire. It's one thing being hit by Charlie, another from our own gunners. Understood."

"Yes, Sir," replied the men of 3rd Squad.

As Billy looked at them, he could feel doubt building in his body. 3rd Squad would be staying behind, while the ARVN continued to push up the hill to protect them. But it would fall on the rest of the platoon to do the really hard, nasty work. Sergeant Jones moved to the centre of the group as they readied themselves. Lance Corporal Johnson swung his M60 from where he'd rested the thing on the crates, and brought it up to his hip. Sergeant Jones had returned the French rifle for the time being, and as usual held his M16 at the ready. He then reached to his side and stunned Billy and most of the others by withdrawing his issued M7 bayonet from its scabbard and clipping into place just below the muzzle of his rifle.

"If you've got bayonets. Fix 'em!"

Though they were available, most of the unit had not bothered to request a bayonet, and Billy was one of them. Half a dozen began fitting them to the M16s, and it was obvious that they had never done this before. The M7 bayonet was a useful tool for sure, but only for every job other than actual combat. One soldier yelped as he managed to cut his hand fitting it.

"You're kidding, right?" Sergeant Jones shook his head.

"All right, then," said the Lieutenant, "Let's move out."

CHAPTER NINE

Billy's heart pounded as he moved from the safety of the battery they'd captured, working their way through the broken tree stumps and scrub, and advancing down the steep bank towards the side of the last few trenchworks. They managed to get halfway down before the enemy opened fire on them. Luckily, 3rd Squad did as intended and put down a massed volley of fire that quickly silenced the defenders. It took some time, but eventually Billy reached the wasteland that was now the side of the hill. Half completed defensive works spread out for hundreds of yards, and when he looked to his left, he could see the green shapes of Charlie Company pushing on upwards.

"Okay, people, sweep through and head towards the tree line at the top," said Lieutenant Weston.

Billy looked where he was pointing and could just make out the trail leading back into the jungle. There was a partial trench there, plus the beginnings of a bunker, though most of it had now been blown apart.

"And watch yourselves," said Sergeant Jones, "Don't advance too far. Charlie is moving up to meet us as we go."

A handful of enemy soldiers rose up to fire at the Americans moving up the hill, and never even bothered to check their flank. Billy could see them plain as day in front of him, but being so close he felt a pang of guilt at firing. But then one spotted him and shouted out at him as he swung his AK47 around to face him.

"Caca Dau! Caca Dau!"

Billy pulled the trigger without even thinking, expending the entire magazine of twenty bullets in a single burst. Several of the rounds hammered into the NVA soldier, sending him crashing to the ground. Another rose up to fire, only to be hit in the chest and face.

"Nice!" Lance Corporal Johnson moved past him. He held the M60 up to his shoulder, something only the strongest in the platoon could even consider trying.

"Now keep moving…Killer!"

Billy knew it wasn't an insult, or at least it wasn't intended as such. And he felt bizarrely pleased that he'd been recognised. But then as he moved forward to stay at the man's flank, he could see the result of his handiwork, and the guilt quickly returned.

"Don't stop." Sergeant Jones moved off to the right and above the trenchworks. He was slightly crouched and with his rifle at his shoulder ready to fire. The other soldiers were advancing in a wide crescent so that the largest number of them could fire without being entangled with the others. A whistle blew off to the left, and a line of green rose up and started to break out into a jog. Hidden North Vietnamese soldiers broke from cover and tried to move back, only to run into Billy and his friends.

"You know what to do!" Sergeant Jones shouted.

It was a massacre as they gunned down a total of seven enemy soldiers, each of whom tried desperately to escape. In the end all that remained was a single bunker half collapsed, and still occupied by at least one man. Charlie Company move closer, and many of their soldiers swept around to the left. But then a second machine gun from the bunker opened fire to the side. Billy took aim and fired into the log structure, but the bullets seemed to have little effect. A shape appeared at the back, and Billy hit the deck as a machine gun opened fire towards them.

"Get down!" he shouted as he hit the mud.

Something whooshed past and exploded, followed by a second. And when Billy looked up, he could see the bunker had been ripped open and was now burning away. He reached for a fresh magazine when he was sure he spotted movement in the jungle directly above them.

"Okay, sweep and clear," said Lieutenant Weston, "Let's make sure there are no surprises left here."

Billy shook his head, and the shapes vanished as quickly as they'd arrived.

Game face, idiot. This is 'Nam.

They passed the wrecked bunker, and all that remained of the enemy were small pockets of resistance. Charlie Company was now close enough that they could advance as a single spread out unit, and Billy felt immediately safer seeing so many Americans. Some of the North Vietnamese soldiers returned fire, but then he saw something that he'd never come across before. Two of the men lifted up their hands to surrender.

"This way!" said a corporal from the extreme left. The surrendering soldiers dropped their weapons and moved closer, but then they broke into a run.

"Drop em!" shouted another, but it was too little, too late. Bullets cut down the first soldier, but the second ran at the Americans, and then exploded as he detonated a bomb of some sort. Two Americans were killed instantly, and many more were left screaming in agony. One rose to his feet, his entire left arm missing and blood pouring from the wound.

"Medic!" came the familiar cry.

Billy looked to his own unit, but as he looked at Sergeant Jones, he was sure he could see movement again. Normally, he might have discounted it, but in the last few days he'd already seen things he would never have believed possible. As the others continued to fire away, he turned around and looked more carefully. The magazine was in the rifle, and he began to lift it as he spotted what appeared to be branches coming right towards him.

"Behind us!"

Sergeant Jones responded instantly and fired his last two shots with his rifle before his magazine ran dry.

"Watch out!"

And then the trees burst to life as the shapes came rushing down the hillside towards them. They came out of the trees like howling banshees, coming at the scattered Americans with a ferocity Billy had never seen before. Lieutenant Weston turned around and lifted his carbine. He barely had time to bring it to his shoulder when the true danger revealed itself. He held down the trigger and emptied the entire magazine in one go.

"Shit!"

These were not the soldiers they had been battling for the last hour, but they looked like Main Force Viet Cong. Some wore the familiar black clothing, disparagingly nicknamed black pyjamas. Others wore civilian clothing or even regular army gear. They came out of nowhere, and their dark clothing made them difficult to spot as they charged onto the battle-damaged field. It was now littered with collapsed trenchworks, crippled bunkers, and hundreds of boxes and crates, many of which were split open. All were armed with AK47s, save for one who held a machine gun down at the hip, hanging from an improvised leather sling. It was a Degtyaryov DP-27 fitted with its distinctive pancake magazine that looked like a cymbal attached to the top. The soldier fired as he ran, spraying the unit with bullets.

Billy swung his M16 into position even as he lay there in the dirt, firing one short burst after another. He missed the enemy machine gunner, but managed to hit the man coming right behind him. He swung his rifle further to the right so that he could line up on the gunner, and instead found a female soldier twisting the base of a stick grenade handle. He closed his eyes as he fired, and when he reopened them, she was gone. A second late a thump and a flash of light marked the denotation of her grenade, right where she'd been standing.

"Keep firing, dammit!" Sergeant Jones said.

He reached down, grabbed Billy's elbow, and pulled him up to one knee.

"You'll see a lot better from the. Now, if..."

He stopped as a bullet hit his jacket and must have

skimmed his ribs. It was an incredible miss, but still caused him to be in great pain. He then took aim and fired a single shot at his assailant, putting the man down and onto his back. He then tracked to the right as more of them came rushing out to attack.

"It's a damned trap!" Sergeant Jones said, "Everybody back to the trenches, now!"

Billy need no further encouragement and moved back, not before grabbing the arm of a Private who seemed intent on keeping his head down for the entire fight.

"No way, man! I ain't moving."

Billy was not in the mood and struck the side of the man's helmet with the muzzle of his rifle.

"Move now!"

The man hesitated, but something about Billy's behaviour forced him to rise up. He then ran off down the hill, muttering to himself. Charlie Company was coming right up, and they all took whatever cover they could as Lieutenant Weston's platoon gave up ground to join them. Billy dropped into one of the incomplete trenches and turned around. It was not a second too soon, as the wave of fighters came at him. They were enraged and screaming as they came, all while firing wildly.

"Kill them all," said a surprisingly calm Lieutenant Weston.

The platoon was spread all over the hill, though Charlie Company was close enough that their troops mingled with the others, creating a scattered group of defenders. Billy saw several cut down by the enemy charge, but much worse was that they kept on coming, and physically threw themselves into the trenches. Two came at him, and Billy tried to move back, only to be stopped by the trench wall itself. He lifted his rifle and fired into the smoke. At first, he thought this was another attempt to detonate a grenade amongst them, but as one fell onto him, he could see they simply want to get close. The dying soldier slumped to the floor, while the second staggered into view, his AK47 pointing right at Billy's chest. He pulled his trigger, but the M16 simply clicked.

You idiot!

The enemy soldier seemed to be laughing at him as he pushed forward to stab with the bayonet fitted to his weapon. Billy lifted his rifle to try and beat it aside when the roar of a machine gun almost deafened him. Lance Corporal Johnson was right next to him and blasted the soldier with a dozen rounds.

"Reload, and fast. This is falling apart!"

Billy looked down to check for ammunition. He was getting through it at a prodigious rate and had only brought fifteen magazines with him. He'd used four in the firefight so far and now pushed the fifth into the rifle. Once expended he would have used up a full third of all that he had. And as every soldier in Vietnam knew, once you were out of ammunition, you were a dead man.

"Back, back! And keep shooting!"

An RPG whistled past, narrowly missing Billy, and then hitting one of the distant trees. It exploded with a great roar that did little to calm Billy's nerves.

"Come on," said Sergeant Jones, "Get back!"

The Americans were forced to abandon the last of the trenches and moved back down the hill, as yet more enemy soldiers streamed towards them. Most moved slowly and carefully, but a handful broke from cover and simply ran. Billy spotted two take fire as they ran away and dropped down into the mud. Maybe they'd been hit, or they could just as easily have been throwing themselves to the ground.

"What's going on now?" Thompson fired blindly into the smoke, "We just took this position."

Lance Corporal Johnson somehow managed to keep firing, even as he walked back down the hill. He crashed into Thompson, sending him sprawling and hitting the ground face first.

"Get up and fight, damn you!" he spat as Thompson struggled to get back up.

Billy knew what he had to do, and even though his legs were shaking, he still reloaded and put down more fire. As he stepped back, it was clear that any semblance of a defensive line had collapsed. The men were scattered in small groups, with perhaps seven or eight now running about alone. Johnson continued firing, while shouting orders to those around him.

"Into the trench, hurry!"

Billy nodded and moved back while firing. Johnson was right next to him, and somehow, he was able to begin moving into the trench, while putting a long, raking burst into the advancing enemy soldiers. His balance and confidence put Billy to shame, especially with the weight and recoil of the firearm. Billy kept on moving back and fell twice as he struggled to stay upright. He stopped alongside his comrades and ejected the magazine from his rifle. He had no idea how many more he'd used, and he really didn't care. There were bodies all along the ground, and he could see at least three enemy rifles just waiting to be picked up. He reached for one, and his arm was instantly grabbed.

"No," said Sergeant Jones, "Do you want to be mistaken

for Charlie? Trust me. It's tough enough not dying out here. Save the AKs for when the shit really gets bad."

The man then proceeded to fire some of the most careful bursts of fire Billy had ever seen. A perfect three-round per burst until the gun was dry. He then reloaded and did the same again. Billy moved away from the dead enemy and towards the half-collapsed trench wall. He did his best to avoid the blood that seemed to be everywhere.

"Okay, this is the last line," said Lieutenant Weston, "We hold here, no matter what they throw at us!"

A shell exploded just in front, and almost all of the men ducked down. Billy lifted a hand to hold onto his helmet, and more mortar shells dropped down around their position. Somebody screamed, but Billy dared not turn to see what had happened. More shells landed around them, and then came the next charge. Some of the enemy came running down the hill, but others jumped into trenches or ducked behind the debris, broken cases, and bodies littering the torn-up ground. The Sun was finally beginning to drop below the trees, and with it the long shadows returned as before. With reduced light and the patter of rain, visibility in all directions dropped by the minute.

Stay together." Sergeant Jones checked on his men. The conditions were changing so rapidly it was almost impossible to make out the men from Charlie Company now deployed to their flanks, and even worse trying to see the enemy in the tree line. The only sign the enemy was even there was the constantly crackle of lights like some decorative display. It was almost beautiful to watch, save for the constant stream of bullets coming for them.

"Fire!" Sergeant Jones ordered.

A crackle of rifle fire erupted along the trench. M16s fired in bursts, while two or three M60s opened up with a roar. Every few seconds the gunfire would be punctuated by the sound of grenades detonating. Nothing could surely survive in that maelstrom of violence, but as Billy aimed into the smoke, something shook the ground. He knew it well enough for his nerves to almost break.

Artillery.

One thump after another shook the hillside as shells came down all around them. Some hit the Americans, and some the attacking Vietnamese soldiers. Billy had never been so confused in his life, especially when a wave of soldiers raced out of the smoke, some of them actually on fire. They screamed in both anger and pain while still fighting. Billy could make out the shape of Lieutenant Weston and the radio operator as he shouted desperately for help. At least one base was operating close enough to provide gunfire, and there were always aircraft on standby, even in this weather.

"Here they come!" Sergeant Jones shouted as he turned away from the officer and opened fire, "Kill the bastards!"

Shadows shifted in the smoke as the burning enemy came out and charged across the mud. Some slipped and fell, but others surged past them. Thompson was directly in their path, and instead of fleeing, he stood his ground and opened fire on fully automatic. It was a brave but futile gesture, and though he cut down two of them, others kept on coming. One thrust a bayonet into his chest, and the two dropped to the ground in a brutal melee. Billy fired, but the smoke now fully enveloped him, and he could see nothing further than a foot in front of his face.

"Help me!" screamed one soldier.

Billy spun around, but a heavy object hit his leg. He lost his footing and dropped to one knee. A man came running at him with only a pistol in his hand. Billy stabbed forward, forgetting he had no bayonet. Incredibly, the man's pistol failed to fire, and Billy pulled the trigger, cutting him down. Something exploded next to him, and he was thrown hard against the side of one of the partially collapsed bunkers. The impact should have knocked him out cold, but somehow his vision remained, though everything around him was blurred and confusing.

"Private!"

He shook his head and spotted two soldiers running from left to right. One was firing a machine gun from the hip, and another spraying wildly with an M16. Something whooshed past them, and they ducked down. His vision was then blocked out as something moved in front of him. The enemy were on top of them in massed numbers.

"It's a trap!" screamed one of the men as the Vietnamese regulars swarmed the trenchworks. Billy reloaded, and for a second he thought he was out of ammunition. It was every soldier's fear that they would run out in combat. It was well known that a soldier with no ammo was a dead soldier. It was why they carried so much of it with them. When Billy had first arrived, he'd chosen extra rations if he had the space, now it was always ammunition at the expense of food. He could afford to go hungry for a few days. But running out of bullets? There was no chance he would let that happen.

"Billy, help me!"

He turned, but he had no idea who was speaking. An entire platoon of the enemy was now at the trench and physically threw themselves into the fight. They fired wildly as they came, with others going in with the bayonet. Billy swung his rifle around like a club and managed to miss the first soldier. He slipped past him and ended up right in front of another pair. He brought up the butt of the rifle and connected with the metalwork of the nearest man's AK47. It lifted the firearm high as he fired. With no idea what to do next, Billy pushed forward, physically pinning the pair against the trench wall. There was no technique, and he was forced into doing little more than using his larger size and weight to try and keep them away. One tried to pull a knife, but there was little Billy could do.

"Incoming!"

The voice was familiar, and Billy strained his eyes trying to see who it was, but the sound was drowned out and followed by a series of massive flashes of light that temporarily blinded him. The enemy soldiers in front were just as confused, and one turned to look around. Billy staggered back and managed to reload. By the time they turned to him he was ready, and this time he didn't hesitate. The rifle spat two bursts, killing both men. The stink of burning wood and foliage was mixed with gasoline as the napalm strikes turned everything out in front into a wall of fire and smoke.

"Stay down!" Sergeant Jones shouted.

Billy did as was ordered as yet more bombs began to fall. Each impact expanded into a cascade of colours that were almost beautiful to watch. But as he began to enjoy seeing his hated enemy being pounded and burned into submission, one detonated much too close. An American soldier appeared to melt before his eyes as the jellified fuel burnt the poor man to death. A second man tore off his jacket as it caught fire, and he leapt into the trench. Other soldiers rolled him about in the wet dirt to try and douse the flames. A wall of heat then crashed into them, and Billy could feel the stubble on his face being singed off from the soaring temperatures.

"What's going on?" muttered a partially delirious Billy, "We were winning this thing."

He hunkered down in the mud and looked around him.

"How did it get to this?"

There were two men from Charlie Company, and both looked as stunned as he was. One held his hand onto his helmet, and the other kept repeating something in Italian, while clutching a small cross about his neck. The bombs kept on falling and were punctuated by the screaming sound of jet engines. That meant low flying ground support aircraft were smashing the hillside. It was a small thing, but at least it meant that it was not B52s this time. He had heard enough horror stories of the massive bombers wiping out entire units with their indiscriminate carpet-bombing.

"Yeah," said a voice, "Have some more!"

A final aircraft screamed past, and moments later a ripple of explosions tore along the hillside. These were not napalm canisters, but conventional bombs that exploded in blinding flashes of light. Even worse, when they detonated, they sent massive shockwaves along the hillside. Dirt, rocks, pieces of broken wood, and even the dead and dying were hurled away from the blasts. Billy lifted his left hand to his face to shield his eyes as all manner of flotsam crashed into their trench. Clouds of smoke followed, turning the entire area into a grey swamp. Billy blinked, and then right before him all he could see was teeth, and a single red glowing eye. It was right in front of him as it roared.

"Oh…shit, not again!"

Billy took aim with his rifle and fired. The shape moved again, and Billy tracked it to the right while continuing to fire. But then something struck him and caught onto his leg. He looked down and found a reptilian hand wrapped around his leg. A single claw or talon bit into his flesh, causing blood to well up around the wound.

"Let me go!"

The limb yanked hard, and Billy went down onto his back. He still held his rifle as he was dragged away as though being pulled behind like a cart. He lifted his rifle, fired a burst, and then was struck in the face. The impact was hard and crushed his nose, causing blood to spray over his face. The surprise of the impact caused him to lose grip of his rifle, and he was dragged off into the dust and mist, all while the battle raged on all around him.

CHAPTER TEN

Linh Hoa was no native of this region, and though she'd been on the move for years now, the mountainous terrain of the A Sau Valley was taking its toll on her body. The entire Thua Thien-Hue Province was a strange place, even for her. On one side a long coastline with views out to the ocean, but on the other the vast forests of the Laotian border. There were lagoons and mountains to cap it off, all administered from the ancient Imperial capital of Hue. It was a region steeped in history, but none of that interested her in the slightest. She was utterly exhausted, yet she continued forward like an undead corpse being willed along by some dark magic. The light was already beginning to fade, and as the shadows grew longer, so did the memories and fears of the brutal attack.

One forest trail merged into another, and soon she had no

idea where she was anymore. This was just another mountain in a region filled with them. She reached for her canteen and took a sip. The foursome had not spoken for hours, and they kept on moving away from the scene of the brutal battle. At one point they had heard the sounds of a mighty battle taking place, but with just four of them there was little to do. That had been hours and hours ago. Instead, they followed the tracks and continued up the slope towards one of the many strongholds their regiment was supposed to be establishing in the valley. There was no sign of battle there, no gunfire, and no roar of engines from the dreaded helicopters.

The leader of the column was the unstoppable Sergeant Thanh. No matter how tired or hungry he was, he kept on moving. Linh was right behind him, with Captain Nguyen next, and Quang Cong some distance behind to watch the rear of the group. It was a shadow of the large unit they'd brought into the Valley, but something each of them had experienced before. Three of Linh Hoa's units had been wiped out by enemies she'd never seen, only the scream of jet engines and the smell of burning petroleum. Like all Vietnamese, North and South, they were well used to suffering.

Sergeant Thanh was so far ahead that occasionally he would vanish. But he always checked back to make sure the others were following close enough to not lose them. Linh Hoa watched as he moved ahead once more, but this time he did not return. She didn't panic, but as she moved closer and closer, she began to wonder what had happened to him. The trees ahead were becoming lighter, and she could tell they were coming to a clearing, or at least an area less densely filled with trees. As she passed a particularly thick clump of trees, she found him. He'd stopped as though he'd hit a rock wall and remained completely still. Linh Hoa barely noticed for a few more steps, and then she realised that he was stationary. She did the same, but also lifted a hand to warn the others. In seconds they were all as still as the foliage around them, blending in beautifully as they had done a thousand times before.

"What is it?" Captain Nguyen asked in hushed tones. Linh Hoa looked back at him and shook her head.

"Sergeant Thanh has stopped."

The Captain was a brave man to be sure, but he was also completely indoctrinated and dedicated to the cause. If he was asked to attack a position, he would do it until every soldier was expended, and do it with a smile at his face. It might be terrifying for an enemy to face, but it also meant that soldiers like Linh were expendable, and he would cast her to the fire without hesitation. And right now, that offered her little solace. Even so, he waited until there was no obvious sign of the enemy. He crept forward and moved past Linh Hoa, his submachine gun at the ready. He looked into Linh's eyes as he passed her by, and she could see a blackness inside them. He was gaunt, tired, but there was more than that. His very soul seemed broken, perhaps even crushed by the most recent battle. But then he stopped next to the Sergeant.

Linh Hoa watched them both, but neither moved, and after standing there for almost a minute, she could take it no longer. She inched forward, with her AK47 lowered and ready just in case. She moved alongside them and looked out into the opening. At first it seemed quite natural, but then she saw the damage to the trees. Dozens were shattered and broken, but many more were simply not there anymore. The clearing was large enough to land several helicopters, though it was not entirely flattened, and would require further clearance before it could be properly used. About a third of the space was still covered in greenery, as well as partially exposed rock in the centre.

"Landing ground," she whispered, "It must be."

The Captain looked back at her and nodded. He looked shattered, and just saying those few words seemed to be a significant effort.

"The Americans."

He then gestured and whispered much more quietly.

"Move more slowly."

Linh Hoa nodded and moved off to the right. She ran her hands gently along the splintered trees and tried to imagine quite what could have caused the destruction. This was not the attacks of a wild beast or an explosion, but instead the area had been carefully cleared with sharp blades. The more she looked, the more she was convinced the enemy must have carried this out.

Maybe the beast found them?

She'd kept all thoughts of the thing that had attacked them to the back of her mind, but try as she might, there was no way to hide the fact that the thing existed, and had wiped out almost her entire unit. Flashes of its claws and the destruction it had wrought came back to her, sending a tingle down her spine. And yet the further they moved from the scene of the massacre, the less real it became. Now she wondered if she'd imagined half of what had happened, and it had merely been a combination of a ground battle and aerial bombing that had shaken her senses.

Quang Cong caught up with them and stepped forward into the open. Linh Hoa looked to him as he moved. He was slow and just as exhausted as the others, but this place seemed to intrigue him. It was unnaturally barren, though they were all familiar by now of the destruction wrought by the Americans and their allies. Where they went, bombs and destruction always followed. But as they waited there, it was clear there was something quite different about this place. Linh Hoa moved towards one of the large clumps of rocks and bent down to examine them. She was careful in case of traps or other hidden dangers, but even at this distance, she could see it was not as it appeared. The other three spread out, with Sergeant Thanh moving to the opposite side of the clearing. But as he moved away, something glinted inside the greenery.

What is this?

Linh Hoa instantly raised her rifle. The others hadn't noticed, and as she watched water dripping slowly from a moss-covered rock, she sighed with relief. It had been a trick of the light, nothing more. She swung the rifle back to her side, but as the light shifted, it revealed more of the rock's shape, and there was something very odd about it. She stopped in front of the clump of foliage and reached forward. She was careful and used the muzzle of her AK47 to push aside the foliage. It took a second before she realised what she was looking at.

"Beautiful."

With one hand she gently moved back the moss to reveal the carefully carved scales of a fish or other animal. More of it slipped away, but the rest of the animal was gone, broken and lost to time, or possibly intentionally smashed and taken away by a collector. It left her saddened to know that another piece of her culture was now in ruins.

"Captain!" Sergeant Thanh said, "There are broken walls

and steps here. I think this is the remains of a temple. There's not much left of it."

Captain Nguyen lifted his map case and examined it for some time.

"This isn't right. There is nothing in this area. This is tribal territory. These people hunt and farm. They build nothing."

"Maybe it was lost centuries ago," said Quang, "I believe these date back to the Trinh–Nguyen War. Four hundred years ago."

The Captain looked at him with suspicion. Discussion of Vietnam's past was a topic usually avoided at all levels. More attention was placed on family, local society, and social responsibility. Captain Nguyen was no great intellectual and knew little more of his country's history than the average Vietnamese man.

"What do you know of Trinh–Nguyen?"

"I was a student in Hanoi. The Trinh–Nguyen War was what gave us a split Vietnam long ago. It is…"

"Enough. There is no split in our country. We are one people, and we will be united and strong."

Quang Cong placed a hand on the dragon.

"The House of Nguyen controlled this area. This must be where one of their nobles was buried."

"That makes no sense," said Captain Nguyen, "Revered figures were never buried on the sides of mountains far from villages, towns, and roads. You are mistaken. They would have been taken to the Imperial capital, or to one of the great shrines."

Linh Hoa could tell that a major argument was brewing. There was little time for Imperial history in a military unit, especially by the devout Communist Captain Nguyen. Such knowledge was more than likely to result in execution than praise. She stepped away and circled around the broken statue of the animal. The clearing behind it was relatively large, though partially overgrown. As she stepped forward, she nearly tripped over the broken stone and rocks. She steadied herself and then gasped. The others looked directly at her, knowing right away she'd found something important. Quang Cong moved away from the area he'd been examining and to her side. He made it to within two yards and then stopped. He bent down and reached out with one hand.

"They're dead."

Captain Nguyen remained where he was, while Sergeant Thanh inched closer to the bodies. He moved lower and lower, and then checked carefully for traps. It took some time, but they were not in a hurry. Inch by inch he checked, and then finally signalled to Quang Cong. The two grasped the shoulders of the body and pulled him up and settled him back against the nearest rocks. The man wore clothing and beads that instantly marked him out as being different to them. He was not a town or city dweller, yet there was something about his face that was not significantly different.

"He is Ta-oi," said Captain Nguyen, "The mountain people of Thua Thien-Hue Province and Quang Tri Province."

Linh Hoa knew of them and had met them in battle twice already. The Americans called them the Montagnards, and they were the indigenous peoples of the Central Highlands of her country. The centralised state of North Vietnam and communism's hostility toward religion had driven them away as allies, and now they were often found fighting alongside the

Americans as scouts and guides. She knew too well their skill in the jungle, and their ferociousness in battle.

"There's another one here," said Quang Cong.

Linh Hoa circled around them to look for more, but instead found a circle of stones, each beautifully cut to fit together into a low wall. On the other side was a pit like the entrance to a well, but much wider. Foliage partially covered it, but when she pulled it back, she could see down inside, as well as steps running down the inside wall and circling into the shadows. Quang Cong kept pointing out more bodies, with each of them positioned in a perfect circle around the pit.

"They were praying to an animal god. Look."

He opened the hand of one of the dead and revealed a small wooden carving. He threw it across to Captain Nguyen who examined it carefully. It was crude and could not have taken more than a few hours to make. He sighed and then tossed it aside.

"Tribal mysticism. It has no place here. These people must be re-educated, or they will all fall to such a fate. It is our duty to help them."

He looked to the others, but there was no great fanfare or excitement over his statement. The area was one completely unexpected, and of far more interest than discussing Communist ideals right now. Linh Hoa moved around the outside until she'd completed a full circuit of the mouth of the pit, and pulled back moss, plants, and other greenery to reveal the full scale of the pit. There were shapes carved into the stonework. But the bodies all positioned uniformly around the entrance were the most interesting, and also the most disturbing. As Linh Hoa checked, she found the small carvings in their hands.

"The markings, they look very old." She took a step inside the pit. There were more shapes cut into the rock showing more animals, "There are all kinds of strange animals here."

Corporal Quang picked up one of the carvings. "The Ta-oi have unorthodox views of animals' spirits and deities. There are stories of them bringing monsters to life to defend their lands. Great beasts that can swallow rivers and…"

"We were taught about the primitive beliefs of these cultures," said the Captain. He reached for one of the dead, and then made a strange sigh as he removed another object from its hands. He held it up to see in the light.

"A knife."

Linh Hoa looked at it, but there was something odd about the shape. It looked more like a horn but twisted into a point. The last half was dark and stained with red, presumably blood.

"These beliefs are dangerous," said Captain Nguyen.

"What is this pit for?" Sergeant Thanh asked, "A place to sacrifice animals?"

"Or people," suggested Linh Hoa, "The markings show people bowing next to a temple, and they stand in front of a great monster."

"Savages," muttered the Captain while tossing the knife into the pit, "There are no monsters here, only these primitives. The best thing we can do is…"

He stopped as the trees made a rustling sound. As one, the four soldiers lifted their weapons and took aim. But then the rustling increased until it sounded like an elephant was coming for them.

"Run!" Sergeant Thanh shouted.

Linh Hoa and Corporal Quang wasted no time in dropping down behind the mounds of broken rock. The Sergeant was a little further back, but for some reason the Captain refused to move. He just waited there out in the open, with his MAT-49 submachine gun lifted and ready to fire. Linh Hoa wanted to call out to him, but then the terrible stench of death returned, and she knew that the great terror had come back. Her hands turned weak and soft, and she knew there was little she could do against it. So she kept her body down low, so that Captain Nguyen's head was the only part of him visible, with the rest obscured by rocks and foliage. He shouted a party slogan as he pulled back the bolt, and then he fired. It was a short burst, followed by a guttural roar. It was hard to see this low to the ground, and nothing short of being dragged from her hiding place would reveal Linh Hoa to the beast. The ground seemed to shake, and then came a sickening cracking sound, like that of a tree branch snapping against a rock. Something hit the ground nearby, and she began to panic. The white face of the Captain looked right at her, but even now he said nothing. The man was frozen in terror, and Linh Hoa lifted a hand to her face to force herself from screaming out. The terror rose through her body, made worse by the sound of the thing coming closer.

Do not let it take you.

She reached for her weapon, but then his body was pulled away, and the thing moved away with it. It was at that moment that the Captain cried out. Throwing all caution to the wind, Linh Hoa rose to chase after him. It was only for an instant, but she caught the rear legs of the monstrous beast as it leapt into the pit. A long, narrow tail swung behind it like a whip, and lashed to that whip were two people. There was no time to help as they vanished into the darkness, and when she raced to the edge, she could see nothing far below her. Corporal Quang and Sergeant Thanh were at her side in an instant, with both pointing their weapons into the darkness.

"Did you see it?" Linh Hoa asked.

Corporal Quang nodded quickly.

"It is a monster. The Ta-oi were sacrificing something to it."

"No." The Sergeant sat with his back to the low wall that ran around the pit, "They were not sacrificing something to the pit. They were the sacrifice."

Linh Hoa gulped nervously.

"You have heard of this before?"

Corporal Quang looked about nervously, but with the Captain gone his lips seemed freer than normal.

"What do you know, Corporal?" Thanh asked.

"I've read stories of the mountain tribes summoning monsters to punish invaders."

"You think they raised a monster to fight the Americans?"

"No. I believe the Ta-oi sacrificed themselves to bring it to stop anybody coming to their mountain."

"Nonsense. It is an animal, a big, dangerous animal. It must be hunted, and the Captain rescued."

The ground shook a little, followed by snarls and snaps.

"It's coming," said Corporal Quang.

They each hid behind whatever cover they could find as the creature returned to the surface. It climbed up from the darkness, and for the first time Linh Hoa could see it in its entirety. It stopped at the surface and looked about, sniffing the air for its prey. The head was as big as a buffalo and looked like a great reptile, like the sculptures of dragons she'd seen at the Imperial Capital of Hue. Its tongue flicked out, and then she could see the long teeth, each like daggers. Its eyes blinked red, and then it was gone as quickly as it had arrived.

The Ky Lan!

CHAPTER ELEVEN

The world was nothing but blackness, and as Billy lay there, he found some comfort in the calm and serenity. He had been unconscious for a long time, and a bizarre amalgam of images and thoughts drifted through his mind. His arrival in Vietnam, his first ever mission, as well as the recent battle. They merged together and somehow transferred back home to the United States. One moment he was in the family home, and the next he was back in the jungle on patrol. As always, dreams and memories combined into an alternate reality that he went along with without issue.

None of this was enough to wake him until finally some great demon appeared before him. It snapped and snarled, and then began to devour all around it. People, cars, even houses, and then it approached him. It opened its great mouth so wide that it was all he could see. Then it came closer and closer, and the next moment Billy was falling from the heavens and into an unending pit of darkness. He began to scream, and that was the moment his eyes finally opened. At that second, he knew he'd been out cold, and as he felt his parched and uncomfortable throat, he knew he was back in the real world, and not the one of make believe.

What was that?

His eyes might be wide open, but the place was in complete darkness. He blinked a few times and tried to move. He caught his hand on something sharp, and then yelped in pain. But his voice quickly quietened when he realised how alone he was. His gut instinct was to get up and run, but he had no idea where he was or what had happened. Billy rolled to his right and lifted himself up slowly into a crouch. He blinked a few more times, but the only source of light came far off to the right and gave little more than a gentle hue to the shapes around him.

Flashlight.

Billy reached for his MX-991/U Flashlight and gasped in relief as his hands found the device. It was a right-angle-head flashlight developed from the same devices used decades ago and could be used while attached to his jacket or gear. He fumbled with it and cried out as he lost his grip. He had not realised his hands were covered with something wet, probably mud. The torch hit the ground with a thud, but at least it hadn't crashed into rock or metal. He moved his hands over the surface, finding patches of tepid fluid all around him. There were hard objects scattered about, as well as what felt like pieces of fabric.

There it is!

He grasped the torch and pulled it close to his chest. Though tough and reliable, it still did not take much to crack the flashlight or break the bulb, rendering the entire thing useless. His thumb moved to the slider switch, and he readied himself before pushing it. Deep down he was terrified he might be behind North Vietnamese lines, or what if his comrades were all dead, and he was now alone on the battlefield. If they caught him, he could expect no mercy, and that sent his pulse racing.

Do it!

He threw caution to the wind and pushed the switch all the way. For a second nothing happened, and he had to tap the flashlight before it finally sprung to light. The dull orange glow was hardly a searchlight, but it was more than enough to light the area around him.

"Uh…okay. Where the hell am I?" he asked himself quietly.

He was not on the surface, that much was obvious. The walls were made from stone and arched like a sewer tunnel. He reached up and touched the stonework. As expected, it was hard and damp to the feel. Billy then moved the beam around to check himself over. The light shone over his jacket that was torn in places, but he was relieved in seeing his limbs were intact. He'd half expected to find part of his body had been blown apart by bombs or burnt away by napalm. Perhaps even better was that his jacket and bandoliers were still there. He ran his hand over the bandolier and found magazines in place and untouched. If he still carried ammunition, then he had not been captured.

"Thank God," he said almost in a whisper, "Stay calm."

His hand moved down his leg, and he winced as his fingers

touched just below his knee. His pants were torn and there was matted blood all around the area. He pulled at the material and sighed as he looked at the exposed skin of his leg. It was swollen and bruised, but the cuts were all on the surface. Lacerations had drawn blood but had stopped at some point in the night. He scrambled about before dragging out a field dressing as well as his canteen. He took a few gulps, and then poured the rest over the wound. Once relatively clean, he applied the field dressing and tied it down nice and tight, but not too tightly. He grunted a little in discomfort, and then began to look further inside the tunnel.

He used the flashlight to look around his immediate area. There was water running along the base of the chamber, and as he scanned along it, he noticed piles of refuse. Pieces of clothing, packs, even water flasks. But as his torch lingered, he noticed something else. An object stuck up from the heap, and it was glistening white in colour. It was not a colour one might expect to see in such a place, and it left him feeling even more uneasy. He struggled to move closer, his aching legs still hurting from the beating he'd taken. Once close enough, he reached forward to touch the branch, but as his hand touched it, he knew right away what it was.

"Holy Jesus! An arm! I'm looking at an arm!"

He stumbled backwards, knocking over some of the items, and scattering a few boxes into the shallow stream of running water. Tiny pieces of broken metal scattered along the floor, and he bent down to find corroded coins that could easily have been hundreds of years old. He rubbed his fingers over them, but the markings were so severely damaged he couldn't make them out. Something moved in the distance, and he turned to look in the direction of the sound.

What was that?

He could hear was the pounding of his heart, and he felt like he was going to have a heart attack there and then. Billy pressed on, and with each step he could feel the pain and numbing sensation in his leg. The more he moved, the more numb it became. Soon he had to slow and adjust the dressing. By making it looser the pain quickly softened, but the blood began to drip once more.

Dammit.

One thing he definitely knew that with blood loss came unconsciousness. And if that happened, who knew what terrible fate might become him. He pointed the torch at his wound and checked before realising the blood was dripping from a much deeper laceration higher up the leg. As he looked, he could see the flesh pulled open to reveal a deep cut. Billy looked away and retched, but then forced himself to look back. It was like a knife cut, though quite rough as though done with a serrated edge. Fortuitously, it was only two inches long, and with careful use of the dressing he was able to put pressure on it in the right way. He grunted with discomfort as it tightened around his wound, but then he heard something. It was like the rasping breath of a large buffalo, but close. He pulled himself back into the shadow, and at the same time managed to drop the bloodied bandage he had just removed.

Quiet!

He expected to find the wall of the tunnel, but there was an opening and cooler air coming from behind. As the sound became louder, he switched off his flashlight and began to move away from the tunnel and into this next passage. It was drier than the tunnel, and he moved as quickly as he could, doing his best not to make too much noise. The breathing became louder, and then it roared. Billy threw all caution to the wind and broke into a run. He kept one hand out to the right to touch the sidewall and kept on moving. Directly ahead was a faint light, though it was impossible to tell what the source was. The roar came again, and Billy slowed for a second and looked back.

What is it?

He could barely make out the opening into the tunnel that he'd just vacated. But there was a little light. He blinked twice, and then something turned red at the far end. For a short moment it looked like the rising Sun, but then he realised it was something much more sinister. It moved, and Billy pulled himself to the sidewall and held his breath. The thing inhaled deeply, as though it could suck his body back through and into the tunnel. This went on for several deep breaths before finally it moved away, leaving nothing but darkness in the passage. He started to panic and nearly hyperventilated before fighting against it.

Get it together, Billy. You can do this.

His hands moved to his body, checking his clothing and gear for anything he might be able to use. And then his fingers found a shape he had all but forgotten about. The rough finish of the machete scabbard was a welcome relief, and as his hands moved along to the end, he found the handle. In a fraction of a second, he had withdrawn it from its sheath and held it out in front of him. Even in the low light it was able to slightly reflect the gentle glow, and Billy instantly felt safer. It was of course all nonsense. If he ran into a North Vietnamese Army unit in this place, he'd be a dead man. What could he do with a machete against men with rifles? Nonetheless, with the weapon in hand he waited in the dark. The sound of the creature was gone, as was the red light.

I have to see. I can't fumble about in the dark. I could fall into a pit...or worse.

He reached for the flashlight controls and pushed the switch, terrified the sinister shape would be right there with him, but he was inside the new passage, and with not a soul to be seen. Instead, he could make out markings on the walls. He moved closer and rubbed his eyes to look more closely. There were letters or shapes, he wasn't quite sure of the difference. They might be written in some local language, or something from the long distant past. But what really made him gasp were the pictorial engravings that went with them. They were cut into the stonework, and many retained signs of coloured pigment. He lifted a finger to touch one, and the paint began to crumble away.

Incredible. This must be a long-lost temple or something. And I found it.

All thought of the war or even his own wounds were long gone. His childhood curiosity kicked in, and all he could see were the strange shapes cut into the wall. He moved along, smiling as he found animals he was familiar with. There were reptiles and birds, some being of the type he'd already seen since arriving in South East Asia. But then he stopped at reaching something quite different. There were buildings rising up high, people were bowing or lying prostrate on the ground. The stonework was cracked, and he could only make out the shape of a leg, and at the end where the foot was were long, brutal looking talons. Just seeing them sent a spark of pain racing through his leg, and the memories of that savage alien-looking limb locked around his.

Billy shook his head and tried to shake the thoughts from his mind. He turned to move away, and then stopped. There was a ribbed column that was missing a third of the stonework. But it wasn't the damage that caught his eye, but the deep lacerations in the stonework itself. Specifically, deep gouges as though a clawed hand had been dragged along it. He placed a finger into the furrow created in the metalwork and recoiled. Streaks of dark red and black covered the wall, as well as more of the scratches. He shook his head and stepped away. His feet crunched on something fragile, and even as he lowered the flashlight, he knew what it was.

"No," he whispered, "It can't be."

The dulled orange beam flooded the passageway. There were heaps of dirt, sodden fabric, and litter everywhere. All along the floor were pieces of bone and scores, upon scores of skulls. He bent down and lifted one, holding it close to his face. It was completely clear as it if had been left in the Sun for centuries before being brought down here. One part was missing, and the temple bore deep scratches. Billy dropped it and cried out in horror. There were claw marks and bloodstains on the walls, and damage from the talons or claws of some great beast. But as he walked amongst the myriad of bodies, he knew he had walked into something so much worse.

"It's a den or lair of some creature," he said, shaking his head, "Why am I here?"

He stepped away from the skulls, but no matter where he stepped, he seemed to find a fragile piece of bone that cracked and splintered beneath his military boots. His slow walk quickly increased in speed, and soon he broke into a panicked run. Billy crashed over the bones and finally reached a wider space that was slightly higher. Water drained from the sides and ran into the other passages, but more important, this area was partially lit from above.

"Moonlight!"

Billy stepped into the centre of the circular chamber and looked up. A narrow shaft rose vertically up so far, he couldn't see the top, save for a small circle of light. It was pale white, like the face of the Moon, and provided enough illumination that when he switched off his flashlight, he could still make out the shape of the wide chamber. He looked around him, noting new passages running off into other parts of the vast, labyrinthine structure. Seeing nothing of note, he moved to the nearest wall and began climbing. When first built the walls would have been smooth, but the passage of time had left entire sections to break away, leaving exposed stonework to grab onto. Up he went, past several deep cracks it the walls, and further up to the light. It took time because he was being careful. He moved a single limb at a time, making sure that he was attached to the wall at three points at all times.

How much further?

Water dripped down from the surface and ran like a small waterfall down the side of the pit. He blinked again and was sure he could make out a metal grate above him. It was nearly ten feet more to get there, and when he looked back down, he almost lost his grip.

Easy now...be calm.

Billy hung there, doing his best to calm his breathing. He'd never been much for heights, but he knew that if he fell it could leave him with broken limbs or much worse. He lifted one hand to continue upwards as a shape appeared before him. For a second it seemed to be little more than a vine shifting before him, but then the green shape of a snake emerged. He tried to move backwards and nearly fell from his precarious position. The snake slithered out from the hole and began to work its way past him. It moved near his hand, and he tensed for a second, half expecting the thing to embed its fangs in him. But it did nothing of the sort and slithered directly over his fingers and back into the vines.

Phew. Finally, things are looking my way.

He reached forward and took careful hold of the vines. They felt slippery to hold, and he had to check twice to make sure he was not holding onto the green snake. Once certain he was safe, he pulled on it, and continued his slow, perilous climb to the light. One step after another, and as he climbed, he could see that this chamber was getting narrower and narrower the closer he moved to the top. What had started as nine feet wide was now half of that.

"…giup toi."

What…the Hell?

Billy looked back and squinted. The white light from the Moon had dazzled him, making it almost impossible to make out anything below him as anything more than utter darkness. He blinked and listened carefully. He was sure he'd heard something back inside the vast complex. But he waited there, like a spider hanging inside its web.

"Lam on giup toi."

Billy felt his grip loosen, and he scrambled to hold on, but it was to no avail. His foot slipped from the rocks and stonework, and he dropped nearly a foot. He grabbed at the walls, but clumps of dirt and moss pulled out. He slipped again, and then fell back through the shaft. It was a drop of nearly ten feet and would have caused serious injury had he not crashed on top of a grassy mound of dirt and moss in the centre. Even so, the fall was enough to stun him, and he lay there on his back unable to move. He blinked several times and tried to move when he spotted movement. He suddenly stopped moving and held his breath.

There's somebody else here. And they're not American.

CHAPTER TWELVE

An eerie wind seemed to settle around the clearing as the three moved to the mouth of the pit. Each waited there, with their rifles at their shoulders and pointing down into the darkness. Linh Hoa angled her head to concentrate her hearing on the pit, but instead her mind was filled with a thousand other sounds coming from the mountain. There was the wind, the rustling of vegetation, the sounds of birds and other animals, and the constant annoying buzz of insects. No matter how hard she tried, it was impossible to tell if there was anybody else out there. Sergeant Thanh moved closer and past the bodies that remained in their bizarre circle around the entrance. He peered over the edge and down into the pit. It was nothing but darkness, but as he waited, he seemed to hear something.

"The Captain. He's down there."

Corporal Quang Cong moved to his side and looked down into the hole in the ground. It was difficult to make out what was down there, even when he concentrated on the darkest sections.

"You could hear him, Sergeant?"

Sergeant Thanh bared his teeth in a smile and then shrugged.

"Who else would be down there?"

Without waiting for a reply, Sergeant Thanh moved to the first of the steps. He peered into the darkness, and then proceeded down them one at a time, all while keeping his AK47 pointing directly ahead.

"We have a duty to keep the Captain out of danger. Dead or alive, we must find him, and quickly."

Linh Hoa nodded.

"Yes. We must. He would do the same for us."

In just a few seconds he was gone, and the other two quickly followed. It did not take long for the moonlight to have almost completely vanished, and then he stopped for no apparent reason. Linh looked back up in the direction they had entered from, but there were no signs of anybody else there. When she turned back, she found the Sergeant reaching for what appeared to be an old torch fitted to a hole cut into the rock wall. There were several of them, though Linh Hoa had discounted them as being little more than decorative.

"I can smell something down there."

Sergeant Thanh held the torch close to his mouth and smelt it. He then grunted, let his rifle fall to his side on its sling, and reached for his cigarette lighter. It was a tarnished brass device, one he must have found or taken from a dead enemy solider in the past. He flicked it three times before a steady flame appeared, and he held it against the combustible materials wrapped around the carefully crafted stick. After a couple of puffs, it came to life. He took another, lit it from the one burning, and then continued until all three were carrying the torches. Linh Hoa held hers out and looked around at the spiral staircase cut into the rock that wound its way down and down. In the centre was the pit, with no rail to stop them from falling. She placed a hand on the sidewall, pulled a small rock free, and then held out her arm over the pit. Sergeant Thanh gave her the nod, and she released the rock. Down and down it fell, but there was no sound of it hitting the ground. Either the pit was even deeper than they'd expected, or it had hit foliage on the way down to cushion and deaden the sound of its fall.

"That is a long way down," said Linh Hoa.

"This place is a prison, nothing more," said Sergeant Thanh, "Come with me."

He signalled for Linh Hoa and Quang Cong to follow right behind. They were all armed, but with the flaming torches in hand they had to hold their rifles in one hand, supported by the slings, or just leave the weapons hanging. The steps ran lower and lower into the darkness. Soon they were far underground and working their way down a pit that seemed unending.

"What is this place?" Sergeant Thanh asked.

Corporal Quang ran his fingers along the markings on the walls as they travelled further and further.

"I have never seen a place like this before."

They were about thirty yards from the surface, perhaps more, and there were now narrow passages leading away from the shaft, while steps continued downwards. Sergeant Thanh placed his hands on the walls and pulled away vegetation to reveal the remains of iron fittings.

"There were gates on these passages," said Corporal Quang, "The hinges are still there, and look, there's one of the bars."

He bent down and lifted the aged and rusted piece of metal. It was so badly corroded that when he lifted it, an entire section crumbled away.

"Gates do not interest me," said the Sergeant, "I want the Captain found. Then we leave. This place…it is unnatural."

For a second, Linh Hoa could see his face clearly in the flickering flames of the torches. He was one of those men that was unafraid of anything, yet the further they descended, the more unnerved he seemed to become.

"Where do we go now?" She pointed into the passage leading away from the pit, "Should we split up?"

Sergeant Thanh considered that for a second.

"No, we stay together. Something took the Captain. We are stronger together than apart."

It was a classic piece of Communist dogma, but on this occasion, she thought he was probably correct. The life of the individual meant little compared to the collective, and right now they were a collective of just three people, four if they ever found their Captain. They moved on further, taking care not to slip on the vines that seemed to always find their way in the wrong place. As before, Linh Hoa dropped a rock to try and gauge the depth, and it hit something almost immediately. She stopped and leaned over the edge while waving her torch ahead of her. She nodded towards the blackness in the centre of the pit below them.

"I have seen a place like this before. It is like an animal pit. They were used in Imperial menageries to house gifts and captured animals."

"Like a zoo?"

"Yes, Sergeant," said Corporal Quang, "Like the Saigon Zoo. A place used to collect animals from around the world."

"This is not Saigon. Why would anybody keep animals here?"

There was silence as the three continued downwards. It was dangerous, and they kept apart to ensure no one slipped or pushed the other.

"Maybe it was used to keep people, not animals," suggested Linh Hoa.

"That's not an animal pit, then," said Sergeant Thanh, "That's a prison."

The flames from the torches cast strange patterns on the walls but finally they reached the bottom. The staircase angled away from the floor and into a small passage that ran to a metal arch blocked by a rusty iron gate. The three moved closer, and as they looked through, they could see the circular base of the great pit.

"Stay back." The Sergeant handed Linh Hoa his torch.

"What are you going to do?"

Without speaking, he used the butt of his rifle as a hammer. He struck the gate at its hinges just three times before they split apart, and the gate half collapsed. He pushed it, and the remaining sections hit the ground with a thud. The three then waited in case the sound brought the attention of a hidden foe, but after several seconds, nobody appeared to challenge them. One by one they moved past the damage and to the centre of the pit. Sergeant Thanh moved to the middle and bent down. There were massive hoops of iron fitted into the rock, and each was big enough to fit an arm inside.

"These are for…"

"Chains," said Linh Hoa.

She looked about the place, and then nodded towards several broken rings on the ground a short distance from the massive hoops. From a distance they looked like the kind of thing that might be used to chain up a lion, but it was obvious that they were much too large for that.

"Look."

She leant her burning torch against the metal hoops fitted to the ground, and then reached down. It took all her strength to lift the three iron rings from the floor. She could hold them only for a few seconds before dropping them with a heavy thud.

"They are not like the gates," said Sergeant Thanh, "They are not as old."

Linh Hoa ran her hands over the rings.

"They're heavy, and they've been split. It is like something big was being kept down here, and it escaped."

She pointed to one that was partially broken. The inside of the metal was gleaming, as though it had recently been split open with something very heavy.

"Or it was released," said Sergeant Thanh, "Don't forget the bodies."

He looked up at the distant moonlight from the opening far above them.

"Sergeant."

They both turned to look as the Corporal ran his hands

along the walls.

"Look at this."

They moved closer, but Linh already recognised the marks. Sergeant Thanh bent down and lifted one of the pieces of broken chain before moving closer to the Corporal. He ran a finger over the metal, as though by touching it some great secret would be revealed.

"Claw marks," said Corporal Quang, "And these are fresh. If I…" He stopped as a shrill sound echoed through the chambers of the underground structure. They seemed to bounce around this particular chamber far from the surface, "What is that noise?"

Linh Hoa turned back to look at him, and then lifted a hand to her face. Incredibly, she said nothing, though it was clear she wanted to scream.

"The Captain," said Sergeant Thanh with relief, "He's alive. Hurry!"

He dropped the heavy iron chains to the ground, clambered back over the broken gate, and began to climb up to several yards from floor. Linn Hoa hesitated, but Corporal Quang gave her a nod.

"We stay together, or we die alone."

She gave him a short smile, and then followed after him. They made it just a few yards when the scream returned.

"Hurry!"

* * *

The scream filled Billy with dread, and it was coming from a short distance away. He'd heard the sounds of men in pain before, and he'd also heard the sounds of terror when faced with certain death. The sounds he was hearing combined the two into a terrifying cacophony. Billy's chest felt like it would explode as he moved closer and closer towards the sound of breathing. They were short, pained breaths of a wounded man. Billy held his machete in one hand. His gut instinct was to try and climb back out, but with somebody else inside, it was simply too dangerous. While climbing he could do little to protect himself. First, he would have to deal with whoever else was down there with him.

I've got this. Just get in first, and don't stop till they do.

Memories of his training back home flooded in, but they seemed so petty compared to what he was about to face. Running at dummies hanging from ropes was one thing; looking for a hidden enemy underground was quite another. His training had always felt incredibly basic, as if they had never intended for him to do much more than eat, sleep, be carried in choppers, and then walk about in the open. Rifle drill and discipline seemed to be all that mattered, and today neither were going to help him. He gripped his machete even tighter and struggled to slow himself down. He wanted to rush ahead, but what if there was a trap?

Billy audibly gasped at that realisation. With his flashlight off there was no way to tell, and the thought of walking onto a mine or punji stake filled him with dread. He stopped for a few seconds, and in the silence his body seemed to exude sounds, the creaking of his limbs, the heavy breathing, and even the occasional rumble of his belly. No matter how hard he tried, his own body seemed determined to kill him.

Keep moving.

The passage seemed much smaller as he tried to move as quietly as he could. The flashlight was off, the only illumination coming from the vertical shaft that was now at his back.

"Lam on giup toi," said the voice.

This time Billy knew it was Vietnamese, and that put him on edge. He'd heard the stories of the Tunnel Rats, those poor, brutalised men sent into the tunnels after the enemy. They entered with a flashlight, pistol, and a knife, and were expected to hunt and kill any enemy that they found. Unwilling to use either the light source or their guns, the fights often became unarmed battles underground, or perhaps with nothing more than knives. Just thinking about it filled Billy with dread, but that was still not enough to stop him for pushing forward. With his left hand he ran down his clothing, checking for any other gear or weapons he might use. He didn't have a bayonet or sidearm, though he still carried magazines for a rifle he no longer carried.

Damn it. Only a FNG loses his weapons so fast.

Then his hands settled on two cylinders. He knew right away that they were the M18 smoke grenades that they all carried into combat. The simple device was used for everything from as a ground-to-ground or ground-to-air signalling device, as well as target or landing zone marking. There was the third use that he'd seen frequently during training, and that was a screening device for unit manoeuvring. The reality of Vietnam was that battles of manoeuvre were perfect on paper, and little more than confusion in reality. Billy took one of the devices and held it in his left hand.

Only a little further.

It was just a dozen yards or so until the passage widened into what seemed to be a room or storage area. Light came in from a passage to the left and provided pale illumination of the area from one side. Shelves were cut into the walls, though they were covered in lichen and other greenery now. Air blew in gently from the left, and he could make out the shapes of entrances to two more passages on both sides. But then Billy spotted movement directly ahead. It stopped, and then for a second there was a flash of red. Billy gulped nervously and then reached for the ring fitted to the M201A1 fuse on the top of the smoke grenade. It hissed into life with the bright indigo smoke belching from it. As he held it there, he saw the thing turn to face him. It was no great beast, but simply a man, and he could see blood running from its open mouth. The man wore nothing from the waist up and looked the stuff of nightmares. It was still crouched over, and there on the ground was the shape of another, possibly its victim. The thing howled in a low, unnatural tone and then rose up to its full height to face him. Billy screamed as he tossed the grenade towards the creature. It howled in some unnatural and terrifying sound as Billy ran forward with his machete lifted up high.

Everything seemed so slow and calm as the pair moved in to fight, and with the smoke filling the place, Billy had an advantage. Just as they moved into range in the thickening smoke, he started to hack and slash. Left and right came the attacks as though he was cutting his way through the jungle. The thing groaned and howled from the attack, and then with the sixth blow it screeched and ran. Billy stood there with his bloody machete in one hand, and then started to cough.

Idiot. You didn't think of that, did you?

He grabbed at his throat and found the thin black scarf that was always tied around his neck and pulled it up over his mouth and nostrils. He then stepped up to the hissing grenade and kicked it off into the passage to the right. It continued to belch smoke, but thankfully the gentle current of air pushed it away. As visibility slowly returned, he looked for the figure that had been on the floor. But with each passing second it was clear the shape had moved.

Where is…

Something breathed nearby, and he stepped away as a blade narrowly missed his face. Billy swung with his machete, but the smoke and his lack of training or skill meant the machete flew past the target and scraped along the wall. He could see enough now to make out the shape of a man. He was bloodied and wore the torn and damaged uniform of the North Vietnamese Army. Seeing the man sank Billy's spirits in an instant. He'd thought he was hunting down a missing comrade, but instead he'd somehow ended up inside the one place he wanted to avoid.

You idiot. You're in a Vietnamese tunnel complex!

The man shouted something unintelligible and then came right at him. It would have been terrifying enough having to fight him under normal circumstances, but underground, with no friends and doused with indigo smoke was the stuff of nightmares. The man seemed wounded, but that didn't slow him down. He stabbed with skill and precision, and Billy found himself backing off to avoid his attacks.

"Why you here, American?"

He spoke in such a thick accent that it took a second for Billy to even realise it was English. As he tried to answer, the man leapt forward and crashed into him. The pair fell against the wall and shattered some kind of stone shelf, scattering pottery and other objects to the ground. Billy dropped his machete, and as he reached for it, the soldier's knife came for his face. He lifted his left elbow and held off the attack, and then locked the man's arm as he'd been taught. With his right hand he grasped around his foe's throat and squeezed.

"Why are you here?" Billy asked, "This isn't your…"

He stopped as something snarled off to his side. Billy knew right away it wasn't the man, but he was still struggling against the knife. The enemy soldier adjusted his grip, and Billy had to release his throat as he used both hands to keep the tip of the blade from his chest. It was now just a few inches away from penetrating, but then the hiss came again, and Billy could see the Vietnamese soldier looking off into the smoke to Billy's side.

"Yeu quai!" he hissed through his teeth.

Billy had no idea what he meant and turned his head a fraction to get a better look. Just a few feet away were six pairs of red eyes, and they waited in the smoke, staring at the two men as they struggled.

"What the…" Billy said, as the soldier pushed back and released his grip. He then turned and pointed the blade at the red eyes. Billy turned as well and looked into the eyes that he'd seen several times before. A pair on their own didn't seem so intimidating. But having them arrayed before him in a mass of flesh, and with them seemingly unaffected by the smoke was a chilling sight. He looked to the Vietnamese soldier who said something, and then pointed at the things.

"What?"

The man then did something Billy never would have expected. He stepped towards the point where Billy's machete had landed and placed the toe of his foot against the handle. He wore an old pair of army boots, of a type Billy didn't recognise. But then he kicked hard, and the weapon spun across the floor, stopping just a few inches from Billy. He bent down and picked up the weapon.

"We fight?"

The man pointed at the glowing eyes and adopted a fighting stance. Billy did the same and moved the machete out in front of him. Neither really looked like they knew what they were doing, but all their attention was now focused on the creatures as they hissed and snarled. As one they moved closer, and Billy shuddered upon seeing who they were. They were not faceless beasts, but North Vietnamese soldiers, wearing bloodied uniforms much like the man Billy had been fighting. One had a pistol, while the others carried staves and knives. Billy looked to the officer one last time, half convinced the man would leap onto him, but nothing happened. He knew that this threat was an unnatural one, and as they prepared for what might be their last battle, Billy actually felt more confident. He might be alongside an enemy, but at this exact moment he was not alone. He pointed the blade at the first creature.

"Yeah. We fight!"

That was when the pistol fired, and the bullet glanced along his forearm, cutting a furrow in the skin and spraying blood on the Vietnamese soldier nearby. Billy had no time to check on the severity of the wound. Instead, he stepped ahead and began hacking away while screaming at the top of his voice.

CHAPTER THIRTEEN

It was still dark, yet the scene of the brutal mountain battle was as noisy and chaotic as they'd ever been. The noise of aircraft engines could have been heard for miles as it made its way back to Da Nang or wherever else it had flown from. Small crates slung under parachutes fell to the ground all around the battlefield. No sooner had they crashed to the surface, and the men were at them. Hands, picks, and other tools went right to work as they split them open and removed the desperately needed contents. Food and water were important, but nothing was more critical than ammunition. None of them even saw the plane as the sound of its engines vanished into the night.

The sound of chainsaws filled the early hours of the morning as the men went to work cutting a wide clearing for the helicopters to land. They had chosen a spot roughly in the middle of the defensive facility where the ground was reasonably level, though it did contain two bunkers and a trench that were now being systematically pulled down and filled in.

"Well there we go, more bullets for the meat grinder."

Lance Corporal Johnson leant back against the trench wall and sucked on a cigarette. There were a few of the squad around him as they took a short break before getting back into the hard grind of preparing the ground. The rest of the platoon was hard at work, as was what remained of Charlie Company. But while they were all busy, there was also a shift in the mood of the men. They had seen a lot of death and destruction over the last days, and many were still too shaken to even speak. One wiped dirt from his face, and Johnson could see the young soldier's hand shaking.

"Kid…take a drag."

He leant in a little closer, and the Private drew in a deep breath, causing him to cough, much to the nervous laughter of the other three men.

"Don't mean nothing, kid." Johnson took the cigarette back, "This is just another day in 'Nam. Trust me. Give it a few weeks, and we'll be back on another field."

"Don't mean nothing," muttered some of the others.

Johnson leant forward and struck one of them on the back before rising to his feet.

"You've all made it this far. Get out of this valley, and you'll have respect like nothing else in this here army."

He then pulled himself up onto the side of the trench, with his M60 resting like a trusted friend up against it.

"You know last year this all happened before?"

"You're kidding?" asked a surprised, spectacled soldier of

no more than twenty-one."

"I shit you not, Private. Almost a year ago, Command launched...what was it...Oh, yeah..."

He raised out his arms to his sides as though proclaiming something from a church pulpit. One by one the men nearby looked to him. He might only be a Lance Corporal, but something about him and the confidence that exuded from him demanded they listen. The belt of ammunition slung about his body and the marks to his face might have helped. He was clearly more than just a tough soldier. He was an experienced veteran that had survived untold numbers of battles. When he had something important to say, it was wise to listen.

"Operation Delaware. That's what they called it, another crappy name in a long list of names. What else was there last year...we have Operation Leap Frog, Gator, Napoleon for the Marines, and my personal favourite, Operation Cranberry Bog."

One of the privates burst out laughing, but Johnson remained completely serious.

"I shit you not, Private. We had Golden Fleece and War Bonnet as well."

Another of the men whistled in amazement.

"Anyway. You see, last year, back in the glorious '68, we had the shitstorm going down at Khe Sahn. The Marines as always had to claim all the glory for themselves. They were having a tough time of it with their backs to the wall, but we were kicking Charlie hard. Arc Light every day, and the Gooks being smashed in every direction. They were beat, right?"

The soldier with the glasses nodded slowly. He seemed nervous to even respond, perhaps knowing that whatever response he gave would be the wrong one.

"Wrong. While all this was going down, thousands more of those sneaky bastards were pouring through the jungle. Some came from the North, but a shit-ton came in through the border with Laos. That's why we keep screwing up. You see; we're obsessed with body count."

He looked to each of them, making sure they were listening to his story.

"As long as they kill more of them than us, we're winning, right?"

A few nodded and were answered, but a groaning noise came from Johnson. Sergeant Jones smiled, but he was looking away from them, and off into the distant valley. He wasn't looking for anything in particular, just something to take his mind off the brutality he'd just witnessed.

"Wrong again."

"Thousands of them streamed across the border and right down into this here Valley. It happens every year. They built bunkers and trenches just like this place and site heavy guns to knock down our choppers. And so in went the Air Cav."

"Hell, yeah," said a soldier, "Kick ass."

"Kick ass they did. The 1st Cavalry Division…Airmobile went in hard and pushed back three regiments of North Vietnamese regulars. They captured tons of enemy war materiel and killed large numbers of soldiers. You'd think that would be enough, wouldn't you?"

Sergeant Jones, who until now had been silent, nodded to himself.

"Listen to the Corporal. He's been in the thick of it. We went in hard last year, and we lost over a hundred of our men and half again ARVN."

Two of the soldiers chuckled at the loss of the ARVN, as though that was little more than a joke to them.

"Between us and the South Vietnamese deaths in the operation, we took over five hundred wounded as well as about thirty choppers. Hueys, Chinooks, and Sikorsky Skycranes. That's a lot to lose on a victory."

"Yeah, but it was a win. Wasn't it?" asked one Private.

Sergeant Jones looked to Johnson, and the two shared a look. Neither needed to say a word, but it was obvious that they'd learnt some great secret since being here, and neither wanted to mention it out loud. Johnson spoke first, and Sergeant Jones nodded along as he listened.

"Yeah, it was a win, but so what? We killed loads of them, and then we left. You see, you can't control this place, not unless you build bases and deploy a couple of divisions here permanently. And then a year later, here we are!"

He pointed to the men walking past with a stretcher. The wounded man seemed quite animated as he spoke with his comrades. It didn't take long for them to move away, but it was more than enough to make the point that Johnson was making.

"The NVA likely never even left. Sure, we smashed them, but some stayed, and more crept back until we arrived. We're never gonna secure this region this year, not without help. Trust me, give it a few more days, and we'll be sending in thousands of men again."

He pointed off into the darkness. It was not easy to see, with just the light from the flashlights, and a number of open fires that still burned along the hillside. At the same time, groups of soldiers continued to drag bodies from out of the trenches and bunkers, and piled them up in hastily dug pits.

"It will just be the first step in a long, bloody battle."

He shook his head and sighed.

"That's our body count," said Lance Corporal Johnson as he continued shaking his head.

"It's a fact," grumbled Sergeant Jones, "That's what a victory looks like."

A few of the men rose up from the trench to look at the damage. The destruction wrought on the place was substantial, with the ground scorched by fire and bullets. Napalm had removed what little foliage had been left by the NVA, and bombs had left dozens of craters, many of which held the broken remains of the dead. One man appeared from behind the smoke and then walked down the hillside towards Jones. Behind him was Radioman Jeffries, with the heavy radio pack on his back as always. He could always be found trailing the Lieutenant like a loyal dog.

"Lieutenant Weston."

"Sergeant. How are you holding up?"

"Just fine, Sir. Had time for some chow, a hot drink, and ten minutes shut eye. What more could a soldier in the field ask for?"

"Quite."

The two said nothing for more than a minute, and as they waited in the darkness, Jeffries plopped himself down amongst the rest of the men. Lance Corporal Johnson held out his flask, and Jeffries took it, took two swigs, and passed it back.

"Thanks."

Johnson gave him a nod just as Lieutenant Weston began speaking. His attention was on Sergeant Jones, but he spoke loud enough so that all of them could hear what he had to say.

"Captain Harper had three squads out on the tracks looking for signs of Charlie. So far, nothing. We broke a company strength assault here and sent two more packing. The Captain says they have been chased back, along with other remnants of the NVA regiment. It looks like they have withdrawn and broken through our blocking forces."

"You mean the ARVN that were supposed to be watching our flank?" Jones asked.

The Lieutenant smiled, but Johnson said what most of them were already thinking.

"Great, so another Search and Avoid mission, right?"

"No, Corporal," said Lieutenant Weston, "That force took significant losses in combat before being forced to withdrawal. Last we heard, the ARVN were tracking them and reporting their position on the hour, every hour."

He rubbed at his nose and looked back to the battlefield There was an American flag hanging from one of the few vertical spars still remaining from a bunker, but in the moonlight and low wind it hung limp and ignored. Lance Corporal Brandes, a relatively short soldier leant in close to Johnson's ear. Though wearing the same gear as the rest of the platoon, he carried a distinctive weapon at his shoulder, a Springfield M1903A4 bolt-action rifle. It was based on the World War II vintage M1903A3, modified to be a sniper rifle using an M73B1 2.5× Weaver telescopic sight. The rifle was also fitted with an improved stock its iron sights had been removed. He'd quickly picked up a reputation of being the company's crack shot. While the others would pray and spray in combat, he was known for his careful and accurate fire. He'd been given a crash course in advanced marksmanship within weeks of arriving in Vietnam, and now found himself being posted to whichever squad needed his help.

"Search and avoid?"

"Yeah," he replied with a grumble, "You know, it's an All ARVN operation."

It took a second before Lance Corporal Brandes began to laugh, much to the irritation of Sergeant Jones.

"Yeah…Search and avoid. I like it. That's actually…"

He looked to the man and then stopped laughing as quickly as it started.

"Sorry, Sergeant."

Lieutenant Weston ignored what they'd been saying and continued as though nothing had happened. It was Jones' job to maintain the discipline and combat effectiveness of his squad, and he knew he'd do whatever was needed to get them into shape.

"Command is calling this operation a big success. Hell, there's even talk of medal for the Corporal here."

"Medals?" Johnson said in a mocking tone, "I'd take a month's leave over medals."

"Hell, yeah!" Lance Corporal Brandes added to that.

"As best we can tell, we were in pursuit of a small force, and we've broken them and scattered the rest to the mountains."

"A big success. Yeah, I bet they do, Sir," said an embittered Sergeant Jones, "We're fifty percent effective, Sir. The rest need to be pulled off the line, and for what? We ain't keeping this hill, and Charlie is still in this valley. We say we scattered them to the mountains, but that's what they do anyway. Charlie ain't dumb."

There was little respite to wait, and to really give much thought to what had happened. This was their first break so far, and in just a few more minutes they would be right back at it.

"Our job is over for now," said Lieutenant Weston, "Like it or not, we've stopped them moving further South. The 101st is mustering for a major operation in this area. Rumour has it they're bringing in ten battalions to hunt down what's left. We bloodied their nose, and they're coming in to finish the job."

Johnson sighed.

"They'll just dig in again, and they'll be sent to chase 'em back up, just like always."

Lieutenant Weston licked his lips and considered what they were saying for a moment. There was a fine line between staying close enough to his men to ensure camaraderie and loyalty, but a certain degree of distance was also required. He was their commanding officer, not their friend. But as he looked at the two men, he found it hard not to simply become one of them.

"Command screwed up here, big time."

"Don't mean nothing, Lt. This whole war has been one clusterfuck after another since we got here. Westmoreland should have been kicked out a month after he arrived."

"Maybe, maybe not." Sergeant Jones rested a foot atop the broken wooden beams that had been used to construct the small wood bunker. His rifle hung down on its sling while he tipped the contents from his flask down his throat.

"But we're just the grunts on the ground. We go where we're sent, and we do what they ask us to do. All we can change is how many of us get back out of here on their own two feet. Because trust me, there's enough officers out here that will see a battalion killed to the last man in the name of orders. And killing a battalion isn't gonna win a damn here out in the 'Nam."

Even after all these hours the side of the hill looked like the middle of a warzone. Most of them had seen images of the last war, and a few of the first war back in Europe. The imagery of strongholds and trenches didn't seem so far removed from the world they all now lived in. Sergeant Jones sighed as the soldiers filed on past, heading back down the hill. Many were carrying the wounded back on stretchers to where a clearing was being created. He placed his canteen back at his side and reached for his rifle.

"Sergeant," Lieutenant Weston asked, "What about the two privates of yours?"

"Still no sign of them, Sir. Private William Richards and Private Jordan Harrison. Last thing anybody saw was somebody dragging them both to the North. I've had my men scour this site for signs of them. We've gone as far as we dare, and there's just nothing. If there were any signs we could use, the bombs and napalm cleared them up."

"Dammit. So they're gone. And somebody took them? Must be the NVA. There's nothing they like more than more prisoners to barter with."

"Someone took them," muttered one of the men, "More like something. I tell you, that thing wasn't a man. It was a…"

"Secure that shit," Sergeant Jones snapped back, "You'll speak when spoken to. We all know what we saw. Now let it rest."

There was silence for a few seconds, and not one of them dared broach the subject that was on all of their minds. They had all seen something different out there in the battles of the last few days. A mixture of crazed enemy soldiers, as well as the clouds of mist and the red lights. Some had been muttering about strange, supernatural threats, while others had been more circumspect and pointed out that the NVA and their Viet Cong local allies were the real danger. It wasn't a beast that had shot and blown up so many of them, but flesh and blood men that they knew could be killed, just like any other.

"I know this fight has left a bitter taste," said Lieutenant Weston, "But believe me, this was a fight that needed to be done." He nodded off into the distance, "This Valley is part of the Ho Chi Minh trail, a critical part of it. If we leave it in the hands of Charlie, we can expect them to pour through, and who knows, they might mass enough forces for another Tet. For now, we're out of the line, our entire platoon is rendered inoperable."

"Inoperable, Sir?" Johnson said, "It's FUBAR, Sir. In every sense of the word."

Lieutenant Weston was about to speak when Private Hohner approached from a short distance away. He'd been further along the trench and resting due to the heavy concussion he'd sustained. He was missing his helmet and wearing a bandage wrapped around his head. He stopped and pointed up into the distance.

"Get your hand down, Private," said Lieutenant Weston.

"But, Sir, look!"

The small group all looked up at the side of the moonlit mountainside, but all they could see was the dark shadows of the massive trees.

"It's not dawn yet, Private. And you're already…"

He then stopped and rose up tall.

"Smoke."

One by one they looked up. It was impossible to tell the source from back there, but as the first glimpse of light began to fill the valley, if was obvious that the smoke was tinged with green.

"That's indigo, US issue."

Sergeant Jones moved to his side and strained as he looked up at the smoke.

"It's ours, but Charlie could have taken it from us or the Rangers."

"Maybe," said Lieutenant Weston, "Maybe not. What if that's Private Richards or Harrison? They might have popped it to show us their position, and to call for help."

"Sir, that's a stretch. But it's possible."

Just the possibility that some of the men might have survived spread like wildfire amongst the weary men, and one by one they sprung to life.

"Billy's alive?" Private Hohner asked, "I thought he was…"

Sergeant Jones lifted a hand to silence him.

"You didn't think anything. He could be anywhere right now."

The Lieutenant rubbed his chin as he looked at the column of smoke. It was partially scattered, probably due to the tree canopy.

"Choppers are not coming back until daylight, and even then, not until we've got all the surrounded area clear. No way will they risk landing them until then."

"What?" Sergeant Jones spun around and silenced the enlisted man with little more than a look.

"We've got most of the day before we're being evaced. You thinking of a little search and rescue, Sir?"

Lieutenant Weston looked back at him, and there was something about his face that chilled Sergeant Jones. It wasn't fear. All of them had experienced that, and found ways to work past it, even if it left them a wreck inside. No, there was something much darker and stranger about the way he looked back at him. He gave a signal, and Radioman Jeffries moved alongside him.

"I need to speak with the Captain."

Jeffries nodded and called up the officer on the radio set. At the same time, Sergeant Jones looked to the rest of the squad. They were down in numbers by quite a margin, just Hohner, himself, Johnson, and three privates. Nearly half of the squad was out of action now but every one of them looked keen.

"We thought they were long gone." Johnson lifted his M60 up and onto his shoulder, as though carrying a heavy log somewhere, "But we leave nobody behind. If they're out there, we've got to bring 'em back."

Sergeant Jones looked concerned, perhaps even worried, and that was the most unnerving thing so far. He looked to the jungle canopy and then at the men around him. They might have thought he was worried about the dangers present. In reality, he was thinking about the squad. He knew they'd been shattered in combat, but no matter how bad it was, it could always get so much worse. He almost said something when Lieutenant Weston finished speaking and turned back to him.

"Sir?" Sergeant Jones asked.

"The Captain has given me clearance to go, if I want it. It's one thing to lose men in combat, Sergeant. But to leave them behind when you don't even know if they're alive. It's not right."

"You're not wrong, Sir. They might be dead, or more likely prisoners of the NVA. And there's always the chance this is just the NVA setting up an ambush. We could find the smoke, and then they hit us."

"This whole damn war is a game of risk. Either way, we owe it to them. It's the unspoken rule out here, and now we have a target to aim for."

He nodded towards the smoke while he wiped the sweat from his brow and then gave Sergeant Jones a nod.

"I think we have to do it, but we don't go up there half-cocked. The Captain is loaning us an ARVN tracker and as much gear as we can carry."

"Yes, Sir," said Sergeant Jones.

He then turned from the Lieutenant and towards the group of eager young soldiers. It seemed incredible that after all they'd been through that they would see this new plan as being a welcome relief. But deep down he knew it was everyone's worst fear that they'd be left behind on the battlefield. It was a simple contract each had with the other. No matter what happened, and how bad it got, they would never leave the wounded behind for the enemy. They'd rather lose more soldiers.

The man then barked orders that snapped the rest of the squad to attention. One man moved quite slowly and was jerked to his feet by a comrade.

"We've got a man down, and half a day to bring him back."

"Yes!" Private Hohner scrambled about for his helmet. Lance Corporal Brandes tossed it over to him, and almost struck him in the face with the battered helmet. The man next to him, Private Sutherland never seemed to have anything to say other than jokes, and he quickly burst out laughing. He carried an M79 over his shoulder, as well as the grenade bandolier around his body.

"Hey!" Private Hohner struggled to get the thing to fit while keeping the bandages on.

"Private, you're gonna have to sit this one out," said Sergeant Jones.

"No way, Sarge."

"What did you say?"

Jones moved closer, but Private Hohner remained uncharacteristically brave, and stood his ground before the confident-looking Sergeant.

"He's my friend, and I was supposed to be his right-hand man, Sergeant. I need to come with you."

"You're no good to us holding us back, Private. You'll make it an hour, and then what? We'll have to carry you." He shook his head in an almost apologetic fashion, "Wait here for the choppers. In twelve hours, all of this will be just a bad memory."

That seemed to flip something inside the soldier's head. He removed the helmet and grabbed at the bandage that had been so carefully woven around his head. He acted as though it would come off right away, but it took dozens of rotations before finally releasing, and he ducked it into one of the many pouches that festooned his gear. He reached for the helmet, pulled it on, and tucked the strap under his chin.

"I'm good to go, Sergeant. I won't let you down."

"Very well," said Lieutenant Weston, "We're down

enough men as it is."

The relief on the young soldier's face was obvious. He grabbed his rifle and checked that it was clean and serviceable. Lieutenant Weston looked up to the darkness of the mountain, and the light sky that still showed the wisps of green smoke.

"It's one hell of a chance we're taking here. The Captain is giving us twelve hours. If we're not back by then, we're not coming back. He's got a flight of Phantoms on standby to burn this place ten minutes after we leave. So we're on a tight deadline."

He looked to the small group of mentally shattered young men, but there was no doubt in his mind that this was the right thing to do. He'd already conjured up all manner of evils in his mind that could have befallen the two Privates. He was a junior officer, but the platoon was his responsibility. Every single life in the unit was in his hands, and he felt a little part of him die with each man he lost. And he knew that deep down the unit would be stronger for it if they could find their missing men.

"Sergeant. See if Rodriguez can spare what's left of his squad to join us. Combined, we might be able to rustle up a dozen to march into the jungle."

"Yes, Sir, I'll get on it."

And with that, the unit disintegrated as they moved to the supplies and grabbed all they could find. He moved up with them to collect the same ammunition for his own carbine.

"Take as much as you can carry. If we run into trouble, we'll need to cover our withdrawal. And there's nothing better than a torrent of fire for that."

Lance Corporal Johnson had already taken an additional belt for his M60 and was calling for every man there to carry more than they might normally.

"Don't wimp out on me now." He handed two belts to Lance Corporal Brandes, "When the shit hits the fan, you'll be thankful you carried more than normal."

It took a few more minutes, but finally Rodriguez arrived, along with the single group of four men. They were all riflemen, though one carried an M79 on a sling over his shoulder.

"Mock and Sutherland are coming as well."

Lieutenant Weston nodded.

"Good, we need all the men we can get."

One more moved along over the mud, but this one was unlike any of the others in the platoon. He was an ARVN soldier, with a loose-fitting jacket giving him a messy, unkempt look little different to the Americans. Though clearly a military man, his clothing was half civilian. He carried the same M16 as they did, though wore nothing on his head.

"Sir, this is Corporal Trinh. He's our guide."

"He doesn't look like ARVN. He looks more like a Viet Cong trooper to me."

"He's a local man, Sir. From one of the mountain tribes."

"Ah… Montagnards?"

"Yes, Sir."

Lieutenant Weston held out a hand, but instead of taking it the man began to speak. His accent was thick, and the words came out too fast even for the Lieutenant to fully understand.

"He says we need to hurry. The NVA soldiers will not stay in the area for long."

"NVA? He thinks they have him?"

Sergeant Rodriguez nodded.

"He thinks they took them prisoner."

"And the smoke?"

Rodriguez shrugged. "Maybe they escaped."

Lieutenant Weston nodded and looked to the Montagnard. They were a powerful ally in this region, and people with local knowledge he and his men could only dream of.

"And this is all that can be spared?" Sergeant Jones asked.

Lieutenant Weston nodded. He seemed confident, but incredibly weary about their plan.

"The Captain needs everybody else working on the landing ground. So this will have to be enough. Grab every round you can carry. We march in ten."

The men acknowledged him and then moved to join Johnson and the others as they grabbed all that they could. Some took it as an opportunity to chew down on what food they still had on them. Lieutenant Weston looked to his two sergeants, and then beckoned towards the hillside. The place looked as hostile and unfriendly as it ever had, and each of them knew the dangers waiting out there for them. There were a hundred different ways to be injured in the jungle, and that was without being harassed or attacked by the VC or NVA.

"We go in quickly and get to the source of the smoke. If we run into trouble, we have orders to fall back, and fast. We do not stand and fight."

"Sounds good," said Sergeant Jones, "We don't have the time or the numbers for a stand-up fight."

"We got any artillery support?" Sergeant Rodriguez asked, "It's a lot easier to do what we need to with one squad with some shells coming down."

"The 105s back at our lower base are out of range, but the

Colonel assures me we'll have mortars deployed and ready should we need them in the next hour. Four in total."

"Okay, then. That'll work. Let's get this done, and bring our boys home."

The other soldiers were by now forming up around them. It was a small force of around a dozen men, with two sergeants and led by Lieutenant Weston. The reality was that it was little more than a standard combat squad, but as the Lieutenant looked at them; he knew he couldn't ask for a better unit to come with him.

"We bringing our guys back, Sir?" Private Mock asked.

"We don't leave our people behind. The NVA have taken enough prisoners to parade on the TV as it is. We go in fast, and bring back anybody we find. Then we get back here faster than you can throw a grenade. Understood."

"Yes, Sir!"

The Lieutenant looked to his ARVN guide and gave him a nod. Without saying a word, the gaunt-looking man crept away into the jungle. Sergeant Jones gave a nod to the rest of the squad.

"Okay, ladies, let's move out."

CHAPTER FOURTEEN

Sergeant Thanh moved quickly through the passage, his flaming torch casting fearsome shadows along the walls. Linh Hoa and Quang Cong were right behind him as they leapt over the fallen rocks and bones littering the place. The passages went on for hundreds of yards and it did not take long for them to completely lose track of where they were. But while the torches still burned, they continued to move ahead. At one point, the Sergeant stopped and lifted a hand. Linh Hoa and Quang stopped, and lifted their rifles as though they were about to be attacked.

"Can you hear that?"

He looked back at the two of them, and Linh Hoa turned her head a little to hear more clearly.

"I can hear…shouting!"

"Yes," said Sergeant Thanh, "There are people above us. We need to find a way to reach them."

Linh Hoa circled while holding out her flaming torch. The passage was quite narrow, but occasionally another would lead off to the side, with many having completely collapsed. The flickering light from the torch did little to help calm her already shredded nerves. The light altered the shadows, conjuring up a hundred different evils in her mind.

"Find a way up. Hurry!" Sergeant Thanh said.

The trio split up, and Linh Hoa could feel the night terrors creeping into her soul as she lost sight of her comrades. If her torch were extinguished for any reason, she would be trapped in the darkness, perhaps forever. She moved into the next passage and looked inside. There were the remains of shelves on the wall, but whatever the contents had been were now smashed and in ruin on the floor. She moved the torch along the walls, but there was nothing but aged and broken stonework. She was about to turn away when she spotted something glistening on the ground. She bent down and picked up a green-coloured metal weapon. It was nearly two feet long, and when she rubbed her hand along it and removed the dust, she could find pitted metalwork beneath it.

"A sword."

Linh Hoa knew little of old weapons, but this one was clearly very old and unlike anything she'd ever seen, not even during special ceremonies. She took it and began to move away when she noticed something else. As she lifted the object, it at first appeared to be a metal bowl with the same discoloration as the sword. But when she turned it over, there was a sphere at the top that stopped it being placed on a flat surface. There were also small bumps along the surface; each carefully made to fit in a pattern all over the top.

"That's a helmet," said a voice behind her.

She turned and found the spectacled face of Quang Cong. He moved closer and stretched out towards the object. As he touched it, he gasped as though it held magical properties.

"This is old, incredibly old. I've seen drawings of armour like this, from the old Chinese Warring States period, before China was unified by the Qin Dynasty."

"How do you know this, Cong?"

He took the helmet and placed it on his head. Incredibly, is seemed an almost perfect fit. He gasped with excitement, much to Linh's surprise, especially given their current predicament.

"I was studying before being in the army. This was a period…"

The Sergeant appeared at the entrance. "There are steps this way."

He was about to turn away but stopped and looked at the helmet.

"What are you doing?"

"It is an ancient Chinese…"

Sergeant Thanh moved closer, grabbed the helmet, and threw it to the ground. Part of the side smashed apart, causing Quang Cong to gasp.

"We are not tomb raiders and robbers. We are looking for the Captain. Come with me."

"Yes, Sergeant."

He walked away, and the two followed him, but not before Linh Hoa hid the sword inside her clothing, and then stayed close behind Quang. As they left the room, she looked back at the broken helmet on the ground and wondered who its last owner had been. Any more thoughts vanished as the terrifying scream filled the chamber, along with what sounded like metal hitting metal.

"Quickly!"

They ran into the passage and moved through two more severely damaged sections until reaching a partially collapsed set of steps. Due to the narrow passage, they had to follow each other in single file. It was made worse by the cracked stonework and foliage that seemed to be everywhere. Water dripped down the corner, leaving a channel in the stonework, and making the surface treacherous to walk over. Up and up they went until finally reaching a half collapsed arch. The other two were waiting there and listening carefully.

The sound of the screams had stopped, and without the noise, there was no way to track them. Linh Hoa looked to the right with her torch. She could see perhaps ten yards, maybe a little more. There were objects scattered on the ground that glinted in the light, and for just a second she was tempted to run out and investigate them. But when she looked back, she saw the taut face of Sergeant Thanh looking at her. He was all business now, and he'd as likely shoot her if she did anything other than what she was told to do.

"Listen!" he said quietly.

She struggled to calm her breathing, and just as she exhaled, the sound of shouting echoed back to them. It was close, but nowhere as close as she'd expected them to be.

"Run," said the Sergeant, and once more they moved off into the massive underground structure. The passages seemed unending, and they passed even more chambers containing objects. But much worse were the bones scattered about the place. Some were partially dressed, but in fabric and materials she had never seen before. Finally, they ran into a small open space with bodies scattered about the floor. The trio moved to investigate, with the first one making her gasp.

"American!"

Normally, she would not touch the body, but she knew that this was an extraordinary moment. She bent down to touch him and was surprised to feel warmth from his flesh. The uniform was dull green, and he wore a bandolier and other equipment. There was no helmet, though a rifle lay discarded on the ground next to him.

"Sergeant, I think this…"

The body moved, and then to her horror it sat up and stared right back at her. Its eyes were a malignant red, more like something she'd expect to find on a recent corpse. But then the redness intensified and created something close to a glow. She took a step back as it rose from the ground.

"Sergeant!"

"Get back!" He lifted his rifle to point at the walking body. It looked to each of them in turn, and then hissed before lurching towards Linh Hoa. She lifted the muzzle of her Kalashnikov, but it was too late. Sergeant Thanh opened fire with a short burst of gunfire.

Underground in this secretive cavern the sound was deafening, and it was all but impossible to miss. The bullets punched through the thing's body with ease and still it came on. Linh Hoa aimed high and pulled the trigger. The bullets ran from the thing's belly to its neck before striking it in the face. As the round hit the forehead, it collapsed face down to the ground just a few inches before her feet.

"Are you hurt?" Quang asked.

She tried to answer, but her pulse was so fast, and the adrenaline surge so great, she could barely breathe, let alone speak. The words came out one at a time, and she nearly collapsed as her body took control from her. He rushed to her side and stopped her from collapsing.

"Linh Hoa?"

"I…I am fine," she said weakly.

Sergeant Thanh moved among the other bodies and checked them for anything they might be able to use. From one he found a flashlight and another a pistol. Then he stopped and shook his head.

"What is it?" Quang asked.

"One of our soldiers. He was brought here, too."

He bent down and touched the man's tunic. Almost immediately his red eyes blinked, but this time the Sergeant knew what to do. Before it could even consider rising to its feet, he put a single bullet into its forehead. Others in the heap began to rise from the ground, and now they could see it was a mixture of soldiers with all of them sharing the dreaded red eyes. Some were armed with bayonets in their hands, and a handful even carried firearms.

"Kill them!" Sergeant Thanh shouted.

Assault rifles flashed as they blasted left and right, cutting down the strange things before they could strike. As the last one fell to the ground, the echoes from their weapons continued to rattle off into the far distance. But the sound was supplanted by shouting and screams.

"Hurry! Follow 'em!"

The three ran from the scene of the massacre, leaving the dead behind. But as they turned the next corner, Linh Hoa made the mistake of looking back. She expected to see nothing but darkness, but instead she could see the red eyes, and not just a few. There were scores of them, and they were moving from rooms and compartments throughout the underground structure. She turned back and used all her energy to run as quickly as she could.

* * *

Billy leant against the wall and struggled to take in more air. He panted violently while blood dripped from the soaked machete. The battle in the tunnels had quickly turned from bad to worse, and the two men had fought off several of the creatures, but the site had been impossible to defend. So now they kept on moving towards the sound of the trees and the animals outside. There was no obvious way out, save for a light far in the distance, and above their current position. It could have been little more than a crack in the surface letting in light, but as they moved closer, Billy was certain he could make out roughly hewn steps rising to the light. It looked like a ventilation shaft or similar, and right now he did not care. He just wanted to get out of this hellhole.

"Not much further," he said, stepping over more bones.

Billy moved as quickly as he could, but when he looked back, he could see the officer was struggling to keep up. The man was bloodied enough as it was, but there were also deep wounds to his body that he'd sustained before he'd arrived on the scene. Billy had no idea if the man would live, but he also knew he had a much better chance of escaping this place with his own life if he was not alone. After all, he was just one man with a machete.

"For God's sake," he muttered, "You can rest when you're dead. Run!"

The officer looked at him, but in the darkness, he was little more than a shadow. Billy flicked on his flashlight, and already the light level was beginning to dim. He moved back to help and looked at the man who until recently had been fighting him for his life. The Vietnamese regular officer was battered and bloody, yet able to lean against the inside wall.

"Come on."

He turned and pointed to the light.

"Look, we're nearly out of this place."

He looked back at the man as he struggled to speak. Billy knew basic phrases in Vietnamese, and he had absolutely no idea what the man was saying. He could ask for a beer, greet people, and swear at them. But he had no chance holding a conversation with a native of the country, and until now, and had not really thought it would be necessary. So, he leant in closer, and the flashlight lip up both of their faces.

"Say what?"

But then the officer's eyes widened in terror, and Billy knew he was in trouble. He spun around, and there was one more of the foul creatures. A tall man, this time in American military fatigues and carrying a bayoneted rifle, he could just as easily have been a friend had it not been for the glowing eyes. Billy lifted his machete and stepped in front of the gravely injured officer.

"Back off, pal. Now I'm really pissed."

It was little more than bravado, but Billy had finally reached his breaking point. The unliving soldiers seemed to have no strategy or plan other than to simply kill all that they found, for the sake of nothing more than killing. The soldier came running at him, and for a second Billy nearly panicked that it might be a friend. But as it came closer, he could see the eyes, like something from Hell itself, and the man was coming for him. The bayonet came right for his chest, and he cut away at it with his machete. The blade hit the plastic fittings, leaving a gouge in the material.

Billy moved back, but the soldier pulled back and stabbed again. This was no undead monster from the movies, but a man like him, and intent on killing him. The soldier opened his mouth, but the only sound that came out was an unnatural hiss that surprised Billy. He stumbled back while hacking left and right.

"Help me!"

The officer did what he could, but the fighting of the last few minutes must have exhausted his already weakened body. He tried to help, but ended up getting in the way. The bayonet came forward again, and Billy cut at it, but this time his attacker did something he hadn't expected. The tip dropped below his blade and then stabbed up. It went right past his arm and then struck in the upper arm. He screamed in pain and dropped his weapon. The two stumbled backwards, crashing into the officer and sending them all falling to the ground in a heap.

"Christ, help me!"

Billy punched with both arms, but the thing would not stay back. He was now flat on his back, and the foul soldier began to push the bayonet down to his neck. Billy used both hands to hold it back, but his attacker seemed to have almost superhuman strength. His arms began to weaken, especially the one already wounded in the attack. Blood ran from the wound, and he knew any moment now the bayonet was going to impale him and end his life, slowly and cruelly.

Something screamed to his side, and he saw a shape moving towards the soldier. The rifle fell to the ground, and then he spotted the officer pushing the soldier back. He carried Billy's machete in his hand and went to work as though butchering a carcass. Billy had never seen such an act of outright savagery as this, and he remained on the ground, mesmerised by what was happening. The officer must have hit the soldier twenty times before he stopped. He could barely breathe as the torn apart carcass dropped to the ground with a satisfying thud.

"Outstanding," he muttered under his breath, "I owe you for that."

He struggled up to his feet and then felt his wounded arm. There was blood, but his muscles seemed fine.

"We've got bigger problems right now," he said, looking back into the passage. There were glowing red shapes in the distance, and he knew it was time to leave.

"We've got to get the hell out of this place. Hold onto me."

The two staggered up the slippery steps, with Billy occasionally losing his footing on the broken masonry. No matter how exhausted he felt, he knew he had to keep moving, one step after another as they headed towards the surface. The light was brighter now, and he almost cried out as he spotted the greenery. But any relief he felt was spoilt by the sound of those chasing from behind. He glanced back and spotted five or six of them coming, and all carried blades and other weapons.

"Run!"

They moved up another ten steps and then pushed upwards. Billy moved through the foliage first, expecting to find jungle. But he came across a wide-open space, with curved walls and a hole nearly ten yards above his head. Darkened passages led away in three different directions.

"No," he said bitterly as he waited there, shaking his head, "I thought we'd made it this time."

The sounds of the footsteps were getting louder, and he pulled the officer back to the wall to protect him. The man could barely stand and handed the machete back to Billy. He held it out in front; ready to fight to the last against their attackers.

"Screw this, come on!"

He pulled the officer away from the wall, but they made it just a few feet when shapes raced out from the shadows directly ahead.

"Dung lai!"

Billy didn't know much Vietnamese, but he could tell from the anger buried behind the words that he needed to stop. A Vietnamese woman stepped out from the shadows with her AK47 pointing right at him. Her face was hard, almost cruel as she looked into his eyes. But then as she looked across to the man on his shoulder, she cried out, and the expression softened before Billy's eyes.

"Captain Nguyen!"

Then the creatures burst out from the passage they'd just left. There were lots of them, and they came out with a ferocity and intensity even greater than before. They opened fire, and the rattle of automatic fire cut down one after another. Some remained down, but others groaned and then rose back to their feet. Three staggered through the storm of bullets and threw themselves at the officer. At that moment he passed out, either from sheer exhaustion, or more likely lack of blood from his injuries.

"Captain Nguyen!" called out the woman once more, but it was too late. The unliving soldiers were on him, and he would have been cut apart were it not for Billy. He held out his left hand to hold them back, and then went to work with the machete as though whittling down a piece of timber. This wasn't fencing, combat, or even a form of swordplay. It was machinelike, and he went to work hacking them apart. As the first fell apart before him, the next two waded in. A dozen more went for the Vietnamese, and though were shot apart, soon they were reloading, and the things were upon them.

"Keep hitting them!" Billy shouted, "Fight!"

It was a strange thing to hear from him, and even he was a little stunned at what he was telling them, but he knew it was the truth. These things were not superhuman. They were men, just like him. And they could be injured, maimed, and even killed. Another fell, but now Billy had transformed. There was no reason or concern for their lives or even his. He was attacking with wild abandon and ran through their ranks to attack those fighting the struggling Vietnamese. In seconds, the melee turned into some cruel mixture of barfight and slaughterhouse. One of the North Vietnamese soldiers fell screaming as the creatures dived down onto his wounded form.

"Quang Cong!" cried out the woman.

Two of the unliving soldiers stabbed the man with their bayoneted weapons, and then turned away from the dying man.

Billy looked at them for a moment, and he could tell they were not who they had once been. They might wear the uniforms of soldiers, but their faces were pale, and when they opened their mouths, the black pits hissed something as though coming from Hell itself. It was both mesmerising and terrifying. The two broke away and headed towards the fallen officer. It was as though they could sense his injuries and his weakness.

"Kill them!" Billy screamed as he crashed into them.

Gunfire erupted again, and finally Billy was alone in a mass of bodies, and with his arm around the delirious officer who was now on his feet, though supported by Billy. The female soldier came forward, and had Billy been armed with a rifle, he might have even fired. But the woman seemed little interested in him, and she pulled the wounded man from his shoulder and lowered him to the ground. She spoke to him in a rapid series of words, all while the other soldier moved out, and waited with a rifle pointing at Billy's head. He wore the markings of a Sergeant.

"What you doing here, GI?"

"The creature, it attacked me and brought me here. Like your Captain?"

Billy pointed to the man being cradled by the woman.

"You help him…why?"

Billy leant against the nearest tree and looked at the carnage around him. A day ago, he would have been terrified to be anywhere near these people. But today was a very different day. Instead of being a soldier in the US Army, he was now just a man trying to survive in the jungle, against a foe that made no sense whatsoever.

"That thing. It hunts my people and it hunts yours."

"Thing?" asked the woman.

"Yes, the beast with the red eyes, and claws and the tail. It killed a lot of my buddies."

She moved closer, and then looked around him as if hunting for something specific. Once she'd finished, she stopped and looked at his face.

"You are a GI. What you know of the creature?"

"It's big, like a bear crossed with a dragon."

"A dragon?"

The woman looked to her comrades, and then to the bloodied body of Quang Cong. He'd been stabbed multiple times, and the blood around him looked as though he'd been partially butchered on the spot. Her eyes moved back to the American, and try as she might, she couldn't hide her disdain for him.

"Yeah, a dragon. You know, like in the kid's book, the Hobbit."

Linh Hoa shook her head and shrugged.

"It is not a…dragon. It is a creature of the ancients. It is a benevolent creature, the Ky Lan. They are divine and peaceful creatures and do not harm or consume flesh."

Billy's eyes opened wide in both interest and surprise. He'd caught only glimpses of the thing, and even now he was not completely sure what it was he had seen.

"It is said that the Ky Lan only appears in areas ruled by a wise leader."

"I hate to break it to you, but this Ky Lan, or whatever you call it. It's been hunting my people since we found it in the mist. It's no friend of nature."

The Vietnamese Sergeant barked something, and Linh Hoa lowered her gaze for a moment. But then something came over her, and she turned to face the man. An animated argument went on for almost a minute before the disgruntled soldier moved away to check on the Captain, leaving Linh Hoa with Billy.

"What was that?"

Linh Hoa gave a weak smile.

"He doesn't trust an American soldier."

"Good. I don't trust an NVA sergeant."

"We are not NVA. We are the People's Army of Vietnam."

"Potato, potahto." said Billy.

"What you say?"

Billy shrugged.

"Go on…you were telling me about this pure and noble creature, the Ky Lan. If it is so peaceful, why does it hunt us?"

Before she could answer, a low growl echoed through the trees. It was mixture of a lion's roar and the thunder of a coming storm. The Sergeant lifted the exhausted officer and poured water down his throat. His eyes flickered, but he was struggling to remain conscious. Billy, meanwhile, stepped aside and looked at the bodies. There were American, Vietnamese, and even civilians mixed among them. One carried an M16, and he pulled it from the cold fingers.

"The Ky Lan can become fierce and dangerous if the…How you say? Good, untainted?"

"Pure?" Billy suggested.

"Yes, if a pure person is threatened by a malicious one, the Ky Lan will rise, and it will bring death with it."

Billy took a bandolier from one of the bodies and slung it over his shoulder. He reached inside and sighed with relief at finding several intact and unused magazines. He pulled one out and was about to push it into the rifle when the Sergeant shouted at him.

"He says to drop rifle," said Linh Hoa.

Billy looked at her, and then just a short distance behind her he saw the shape. He said nothing, but Linh Hoa turned and cried out as it emerged from the shadows. This time it was closer than it had ever been before, a great monstrous beast, with its forms distorted by the trees and the foliage. Its mouth opened and revealed a gaping maw that glowed brightly. It roared, and the trees rustled with the power.

"Run!" Billy shouted, "Run for your lives!"

CHAPTER FIFTEEN

Billy had no idea where they were anymore as he ran for his life. The jungle was a confusing maze at the best of times, but now he couldn't even tell which direction they had run from. The Sun was well above the horizon, yet it did little to help them as the trio struggled through the jungle while helping to carry the exhausted Captain with them. Every time they slowed down, they could hear the thunder of feet and the grunt and snarl of the dreaded beast. It was as though the mountain itself had come to life to end theirs.

I can hear it. It's close, really close.

It was one thing facing the unliving soldiers. Though they were numerous, they could be defeated with bullets and with force. But the illusive creature never seemed near them long enough for him to do a thing about it. One second the teeth or tail were nearby, and then it was gone, with only the stench of death marking its presence. A flash of lightning overhead lit up the trees, and in that moment, Billy slipped in the mud. He scrambled about, but he couldn't find purchase in the sloppy filth. He struggled again and tried to grab a nearby tree only to pull out a clump of greenery. He finally lost his balance completely and went down hard, nearly taking the officer down with him. The gruff Sergeant held his man up as Billy flailed about in the mud.

"Help me up!"

The rain was now an almost continuous deluge that soaked them to the skin, as well as reducing visibility to little than they'd managed at night. The heat and the water created a haze, like a smoke generator that gave a mystical, ethereal look to the place. The Sergeant muttered something and then reached out a hand to help him. They locked hands, and for a second it seemed as though they might come to blows. But then the man pulled harder on Billy, and he was back on his feet. The two carried the weight of the officer between them, while Linh Hoa ran a short distance ahead to scout the path. At the same time the noises increased behind them.

"Keep running!" Billy yelled, "Faster!"

They moved to the next ridge as shapes jumped out from the right. They were the unliving soldiers, and without thinking, Billy opened fire immediately. It was difficult to aim as he held onto the officer, and the first few rounds went wild. The Sergeant joined in, and the female soldier took aim with a French submachine gun and opened fire. Between the three of them they put down a withering hail of fire. Billy watched the glowing eyes as he fired and tracked from left to right, hammering them with bullets. All three continued to fire, and then reloaded to keep shooting. The shapes moved about, but it seemed the shooting was holding them back. Finally, Billy was empty, and as he started to reload, he noticed the shapes were gone. The other two fired a few more bullets before also reloading.

"Where are they?" Billy whispered.

As they reloaded, the crackling echo of the shooting bounced around them, muffling almost every other sound save for the unending rain. Billy was ready in just a few seconds and lifted his M16, but there were no cries of pain or screams. But the shapes stopped moving and then became very still.

Linh Hoa said something quietly in Vietnamese and then looked across to Billy.

"What is happening, GI?"

"I'm Private William S. Richards," he said in an irritated tone, "My friends call me Billy. And I have no idea…no idea at all what's happening!"

"Look!" Linh Hoa nodded towards the trees. Billy strained his eyes, but the constant rain and poor light meant his mind was beginning to play tricks on him. Every branch and every shadow were an enemy out to kill him. But as he watched them, they amounted to nothing.

"What?"

But then Billy heard something behind him. It was slow and cautious, like a man moving slowly and carefully along a trail. He checked his weapon, and then ever so slowly turned. His rifle rose to his shoulder as it tracked from right to left. All it would take was a gentle squeeze to unleash a stream of automatic fire. But as he turned, he spotted the thing crashing through the jungle behind them. It was little more than a shadow, but he knew it was the creature that Linh Hoa had called the Ky Lan. Foliage tore apart as he came for them, and in front of it was a scattered line of people, like a unit in skirmish formation.

"Not good," he said as he prepared to fire, "Not good at all."

He opened fire as before, and the other two joined in. This time the weary and injured officer also opened fire. He used a pistol of a type Billy was unfamiliar with and blasted off into the distance. Single shots, that seemed so petty and insignificant based on their terrible circumstances. Several of the soldiers fell to the ground, but more took their place, with the terrifying glowing eyes and brandishing weaponry. They were getting close, and as Billy tried to reload, he dropped the magazine. He reached down for it in the mud and spotted his shaking hands. He'd been frightened since first arriving in Vietnam, and every time he'd left the base, he felt a sick feeling deep inside his belly. But this was different. Now he was suffering a gripping, stifling mortal fear of the unknown. Whatever was out there was bigger and deadlier than any living thing he'd seen in his life.

"Kill it!"

More shapes came out, but then he saw the front half of the beast, and it sent a chill down his spine. His teeth rattled with terror as it came charging towards them. The head was massive, and the maw glowed like the inside of a volcano. Much of it looked like a dragon, and yet its skin looked like the rock that the canyon was built upon. It seemed unnatural and terrifying at the same time. Two of the unliving soldiers were trampled as it came. Billy fired his weapon until empty, and though many of the shots landed on target, still it came. The Sergeant tossed a grenade, and it exploded in front of the monster. The flash halted its attack, and it rose up on its hind legs like a bucking horse rising up tall into the trees. Billy fumbled for another magazine, and then shook his head.

"Hell, no."

He glanced at the others, and then broke from his position, physically dragging the arm of the wounded officer.

"Run!" he screamed louder than he'd ever screamed before, "Run!"

The beast roared, and the trees shook as it howled with rage. Billy didn't wait to see what was happening, and he ran and slid over the mud, pulling the Vietnamese Captain so roughly that he dislocated his arm. They reached yet another ridge, and as they moved to the other side, they came across a steep drop, almost like a cliff edge. Billy struggled to hold on, but he was moving too fast. The entire group vanished over the edge, tumbling and rolling down the hillside.

* * *

The rain came down heavier by the second as Lieutenant Weston and his understrength platoon worked their way through the jungle, moving along the narrow tracks created by the wildlife that filled the valley. They were forced to use their flashlights due not just to the low light, but because of the heavy cloud cover and rain. Their ponchos were soaked through and every step an effort. The men had been fired up and eager when they'd left, but each passing minute sapped their reserves of energy, and their willingness to move so much further away from their comrades on the side of the valley wall. The trails used by animals were sometimes easy to spot, but there were entire sections where there was nothing but foliage, and they either had to work around the thicker sections or revert to the use of the machete. Either option slowed their advance further.

"Lt!" Sergeant Jones called out.

He pointed ahead to a pair of shattered trees. Lieutenant Weston waited for several seconds for his eyes to adjust. At first, he had difficulty in making out quite what he was looking at. The men moved closer, but not too close. But even as Weston moved to the trees, he looked confused.

"What am I looking at, Sergeant? Looks like a couple of blasted apart trees."

"The trees, they've been cut down."

"Probably a stray bomb from our top cover. At least they blew up a tree this time, and not us. Take it from me, if this was intended for us, we'd be scattered all over this hillside."

The Sergeant moved closer and ran his fingers along the destruction. He shook his head as he looked more closely with his flashlight.

"Yeah, as I thought. It's been hacked down by something serrated, and recently."

He turned to look to Weston with a look of concern at his face.

"Sir, it's got to be those shell-shocked soldiers or something."

"The what?"

Sergeant Jones moved closer and lowered his voice.

"The soldiers that attacked us in the night. You know, the ones the Private said were like the zombies in that movie he saw."

Lieutenant Weston shook his head.

"Children's stories and fantasies," he said as he tried to convince them both, "All kinds of chemicals have been dumped in this valley over the last decade. I promise you, Sergeant. What we encountered were crazed junkies, not some creature from a horror movie."

Sergeant Jones placed a hand on the shredded trees.

"There were more than just those men, Sir. There was the shadow, that shape we saw in the smoke. It was big, and fast. And there's no reason to cut down two trees out in the middle of nowhere. There's no…"

A shape moved up ahead, and a single soldier rose from the undergrowth. He was only twenty yards or so away, by Lance Corporal Brandes had an uncanny skill for being able to melt into the background.

"Sergeant! We've got bodies on the trail."

The young soldier pointed to the greenery a few feet from his position. Sergeant Jones moved his way from the felled trees, and then lifted a hand to his face. There were two bodies on the ground, both cut in half by a powerful blow. Their bodies had been severed at the belly, leaving the area looking like a slaughterhouse. There were bullet casings all around them.

"They had it bad," said Lance Corporal Brandes, "Really bad. They were cut in half by something with a lot of power. A man with a sword couldn't have managed this."

He lifted his hand to wipe the rain from his face. There was a look to his eyes that made Lieutenant Weston's hair raise on the back of his neck.

"That's not gunfire, and it's not explosives that did this," said Sergeant Jones, "They were slashed apart, like a scythe attached to a tractor."

The two men looked to each other, but neither dared to say more. Each knew what the other was thinking, but even mentioning the terrors that they'd seen in the jungle might make them all the more real. The broken remains on the ground were clearly North Vietnamese soldiers. Their uniforms were bloodied, and their pith helmets lay on the ground alongside them. Their weapons were bloodied, and yet for all the gore, they seemed undamaged elsewhere.

"This isn't looking good," said Lieutenant Weston, "We've almost run out of time, and all we've found so far are two bodies and a lot of mud."

He leant against a tree and pulled out his map case. The rain poured down, dripping from his helmet and onto the plastic covered paper. He lifted his flashlight and couched it next to his left hand to hide the glow of the light. Not that it really mattered; the weather was so bad it would be barely visible more than ten feet away.

"Another thirty minutes top, and we need to turn back. They must have taken them by now."

"You might be right," said Sergeant Jones, "Corporal Trinh is having trouble even finding a trail now."

"Sir," said Lance Corporal Brandes, "Let me move on ahead with Trinh. I can cover twice the ground in half the time. If we run into trouble, we'll fire a warning shot and get the hell back here."

Lieutenant Weston considered that for a moment. He wanted his missing men found, but he also wanted to keep what few men he had left in one piece. If something happened to Brandes, he could not leave him behind as well. His unit was in one place at the moment, and with the weather the way it was, it needed to stay like that.

"I think it might…"

He stopped speaking as Sergeant Jones lifted his arm with a clenched fist. The entire squad dropped to their knees and prepared for combat. Each was an experienced soldier by now, and only those who knew how to react in the jungle could have made it this far, even over just the last few days. Every one of them sank into the greenery, becoming one with the jungle.

"What is it, Jones?"

The man remained utterly still as he watched off into the distance, listening to the gunfire. It wasn't the sporadic crackle of a long-range firefight, but something very different and rather unsettling. Lance Corporal Johnson crept forward and waited alongside the Sergeant. The M60 was down at his waist, ready to be fired the moment they encountered the enemy.

"What the hell was that?"

"Firefight," said Sergeant Jones, "And a close one. Looks like somebody ran into a little trouble."

The men checked all around them as they waited for the enemy to attack. A green unit might have opened fire immediately, but not them. So far, no shots had come near them. And hopefully that meant they hadn't been spotted. Sergeant Jones lifted a finger to his ear.

"Listen."

A shape moved slowly ahead, but they already knew it was the phantom like Corporal Trinh. The man was a true ghost as he slipped through the jungle, silently and effortlessly. At first glance any man might think the Corporal cared nothing for discipline based on how he looked. But he inched his way back like a snake and stopped next to the Sergeant. He was filthy, but his rifle was gleaming, with nothing but the water from the never-ending rain running down its plastic furniture.

"Battle ahead, Sergeant. At bottom of hillside."

"How many?"

The Corporal held out his hand and counted on his fingers.

"Small fight, four of five firearms."

"That's a lot of shooting for just five people."

He nodded off into the distance. Although it was not obvious there was a hillside, only the blackness of the jungle and the unending rain. As they waited, the gunfire started again. Sergeant Jones listened to the weapons, and his face seemed to light up. Lance Corporal Brandes lifted his rifle and aimed through the scope, but he could see nothing more than they could.

"We need to get closer." He moved off ahead of the squad. He held the rifle out in front of him, cradled in both arms as though an infant being carried by an overprotective parent. Sergeant Jones listened to the firefight as two long bursts rattled away. They were much longer than normal practice, perhaps even a single burst to empty the magazine. He counted the shots to perfection, nodding along as they stopped to reload.

"At least two AKs…" he said as he nodded to himself, "And they're fighting up close and in a panic. This isn't a battle between two units in the jungle. It's a brawl."

Again the guns fired, and this time he sighed.

"And that's definitely an M16…being fired on full auto, and in short bursts."

His eyes met the Lieutenant's.

"Somebody is in a lot of trouble."

"Private Richards?"

Sergeant Jones nodded.

"Could be. If I had to guess, I'd say we've got one of our guys being pursued. No idea why they're firing so many shots at him, though."

He looked ahead where the Vietnamese scout and Lance Corporal Brandes pushed ahead of the rest of them. Right then the distant thump of mortars going off made him look back.

"That's ours."

There were more and more, but the rain made it difficult to fully make out the exact direction of the sounds, let alone the type.

"Okay…Brandes, go with the Corporal and deploy a hundred yards ahead of us. I don't want to run headfirst into an NVA battalion."

Lance Corporal Brandes nodded, and then turned away with the Corporal.

"And, Corporal, if you find them, wait for us. Don't start a fight until we've moved up."

They both left with little noise as the rest of the squad prepared to follow them. Lieutenant Weston put the map case away and looked to an agitated Radioman Jeffries. He was a few yards away and in the middle of a conversation over the radio.

"Sir, the Colonel reports they're engaged in combat with two attack from the North and the North East. Estimated strength one hundred plus."

"Dammit. We're running out of time. You know our status, Jeffries. Give him our current position and status. We're about to make contact."

"Yes, Sir."

Only then did he look to Sergeant Jones.

"Move them on, Sergeant. We've got work to go. I reckon the Colonel is going to need help, and very soon."

"Sir. What if we run into the same enemy? We're barely a full-strength squad out here."

"We'll deal with what we find."

"Yes, Sir."

Corporal Trinh was ahead, and the rest of the soldiers followed slowly behind, working their way through the jungle. As promised, they soon hit a steep gradient that took them to a darker part of the valley wall. Trees and mud blocked their path, and most of them slipped as they struggled to remain upright. At the same time, the crackle of gunfire increased their desire to get into action. Every one of them knew that they could arrive just a few seconds too late, and all of this would have been for naught.

"Contact!" Lance Corporal Brandes shouted back to them.

* * *

Billy struggled to load in another magazine as more of the unliving soldiers moved closer and closer. The rain was unrelenting and running down his body and all over his weapon. He scrambled back over the mud and branches, desperately struggling to get away from them. He opened fire, and this time there was little chance of aimed fire. He was shooting like a madman, with some bullets hitting the enemy, and others slamming into the trees. He stopped as he crashed into Linh Hoa. The woman took aim with the French submachine gun, but for some reason the attacking soldiers slowed, and then halted.

"Screw this," said Billy, "Kill em!"

Maybe it was simply bravado, or more likely sheer terror. But for some reason his breathing calmed, and he began to fire single shots to the head and torso as he'd been taught. He watched with satisfaction as one after another fell to the ground. Four were knocked down, and as he aimed at the fifth, they turned and melted away into the jungle.

"Uh…what happened? Did we win?"

He looked to Linh Hoa, and she shrugged.

"I do not think so."

He looked into her eyes and could see a mixture of young passion, but also rage. There was something about her that was utterly different to him. He'd been uncertain about taking part in the war right off the bat. And even once he'd arrived, he had no driving passion to see victory, only to survive, and to come back home. This woman on the other hand, she was here to win, that much was obvious.

"Listen." She placed a hand over her mouth, "Americans, they are coming."

Billy could hardly believe what she was saying. He'd been separated from his platoon for so long he'd considered himself truly lost. All he wanted was to live long enough for some kind of payback against the thing killing them. As he looked around the place where they'd landed, the Sun was rising ever higher, and it cast yellow and white streaks through the treetops and down around him. The creatures were gone, but there was the sound of movement from three directions.

"Get back!" Billy said.

He slipped as he tried to move away from the scene of the battle, but then all hell broke loose. Bullets hammered into the foliage, and he ducked down to avoid being hit. The shots were wild and sporadic, with streams of fire coming over their heads.

"Take cover!"

The tiny group hid behind the stumps, felled trees, and the vast tree trunks that rose up to the sky, aiming their weapons at the shadows. Billy checked his bandolier and gulped at finding every single pouch empty. He removed the magazine in his rifle and checked. It was close to full, but he could tell that it didn't contain a complete twenty rounds. He pushed it back in and checked a round remained in the chamber. The branches parted, and then more fire hit around them.

The Vietnamese Sergeant opened fire and was quickly hit in the shoulder by a single shot. He staggered backwards and dropped to the floor. Linh Hoa screamed something loudly, and then five of the unliving warriors came charging towards them. Linh Hoa was about to fire, but Billy pushed her weapon down and dragged her to the floor.

"No!"

But then a massed volley of fire hammered over their heads. The creatures were torn apart, and behind them came a thin skirmish line of soldiers. Billy instantly called out into the jungle.

"US Army. Hold your fire!"

He stepped in front of the three Vietnamese soldiers, using his body as a shield to protect them from the advancing soldiers. More moved out from cover, and one gasped in excitement.

"Billy!"

"Jayden?" he asked in surprise.

More of the soldiers swept in, and they kept their weapons trained on the three Vietnamese. Even now, completely outnumbered, the two men and one woman refused to lower their firearms.

"What's going on here, Private?"

The confident shape of Sergeant Jones stepped out, flanked but two more men, as well as Lance Corporal Johnson who swung his M60 back and forth, looking for targets.

"Holy shit, Sarge," said Billy, "Are you a sight for sore…"

"Answer the question. Who are these…"

A roar shook the branches, followed by unnatural howls. The rest of the Americans were now there, and they began checking the trees around them for signs of the danger.

"The creature, it's out there, Sergeant."

"Creature?"

"Ky Lan!" Linh Hoa said.

Sergeant Jones moved towards her, with his carbine pointing at her chest.

"What did you say?"

"She said it is the Ky Lan. A monster."

Sergeant Jones sniggered, and that was the second the thing emerged from the jungle. There was no hiding or pretence this time. It came right for them like a freight train hurtling down a pair of tracks. Linh Hoa lifted her submachine gun higher, and Sergeant Jones began to pull the trigger.

"Not today," he muttered.

Then the creature was amongst them, and for the first time every one of them could see the sheer size and power of the thing. It swung around and leapt towards the soldiers. One rifleman was too slow, and its tail slashed horizontally, splitting the man in half, and showering blood over the trees. The rest continued to back away, with Sergeant Jones and Billy standing alongside the Vietnamese as they opened fire. A mixture of Soviet, French, and American weapons rattled away as they struck the monster's flank. It roared and hissed and turned to face them.

"What in the name of shit is that thing?" Lance Corporal Brandes yelled.

He'd already shouldered his rifle and turned to his automatic. The pistol fired four times, and each shot hit its mark. Johnson didn't need to use a bipod or a prone position. He just aimed in the beast's rough direction and unleashed hell. The legs were as big as a bear, and it lashed out with them, slashing down trees and men with equal ease. Another solder went down, and it caught the dead man with the barbs of its tail and dragged him away. Before the man vanished from sight, Billy was sure he could see a red glow around his face.

"Jesus!" he said under his breath, "It turns the dead."

The creature slowed and turned back to snarl as though it had heard him. Its front legs rose, and it extended those terrifying talons in his direction. It looked as though it was about to charge when Linh Hoa appeared at Billy's side, holding up a dulled bronze relic. That seemed to catch the beast's attention, if only for a moment. As it watched, Private Sutherland called out as he took aim with his M79.

"Fire in the hole!"

He yelled as the weapon thudded back. The 40mm high explosive grenade struck the creature in the head and detonated with a bright flash. At the same time, the soldiers used every weapon at their disposal to blast it. Trees tore down, and hundreds of bullets churned up the hillside until nothing remained but the echoes of gunfire and the smoke of the guns.

"Yes, you bastard!" Lance Corporal Johnson shouted, "You want some more of that?"

He stepped forward, but Sergeant Rodriguez grabbed his shoulder and shook his head.

"We need to chase it down, end it once and for all."

"Cease fire!" Lieutenant Weston crept forward. It took several more seconds for the smoke to begin to clear, but it was clear the beast was well and truly gone.

"Sir. We need to pursue it. We hurt it!"

"Lieutenant," Sergeant Rodriguez said, "Look!"

They looked off in the direction they'd come from as a flare detonated in the sky, and then began to fall back.

"Distress flare," said Sergeant Jones, "And it's from the NVA camp we captured."

He turned and moved towards the Vietnamese soldiers. At the same time, Lieutenant Weston signalled to Jeffries.

"Get in touch with…"

Another boom shook the ground, but they all knew it was something much more significant that artillery. It was the booming shake of bombs exploding. Second later, screaming jet engines confirmed that fighter-bombers were in the area.

"Sir. The Colonel is in a bad way. He says shadows came from the trees and attacked. Hundreds of them."

"What?"

"They've been overwhelmed. The last fifteen men have entrenched in their command post. They're calling in a…"

"Give me that."

The Lieutenant reached for the telephone style handset.

"Colonel. What is your status? Colonel!"

He listened carefully to the sound of the Colonel's voice.

"Say again. Our position is being overrun. Estimated numbers, three hundred plus! Continuous fire until all rounds expended. Cannot observe, over."

"Dammit," said Lieutenant Weston, "They're calling in artillery on their own position."

He spoke into the handset and then jerked back as if he'd just heard a loud sound. He was silent for several seconds before he looked back to his men.

"His last words were they're not firing. Red eyes. Stabbing. Those things made it inside the CP. They're dead," he said, dropping the handset, "Every one of them."

All attention turned to Linh Hoa and the others.

"Somebody needs to tell me what in the fuck is going on out here."

He pointed to her.

"You seem to know something. Talk."

"Sir. I've seen its lair. I know where it comes from."

The Sergeant looked at her, before turning to Billy.

"Lair?" Sergeant Jones asked, "What exactly are you saying, Private?"

"It took me there after the fight. The place is full of bones. It must hide down there."

"The Ky Lan waits in the mountains until it is summoned," said Linh Hoa, "We cannot defeat it."

"Bullshit. Those were my men it killed. It's more like…"

"It's true," said Billy, "I woke up and I was alone in some ancient catacombs. There are markings all around it."

"Wait…you said lair?"

"Yes, Sergeant."

Lieutenant Weston approached. Blood covered the side of his face though he moved and acted as though uninjured.

"Sir, you're hurt?"

"No. It's not my blood. Look, I've contacted Command. They're saying the entire company has been wiped out. Our orders are to get out of here and get to the designated open ground. We've got an evac order in effect."

He held out his map case.

"If we move fast, we can be there within three hours."

"What about the Colonel?"

"T Plus Ten and the Air Force will initiate an Arclight strike throughout this area. They're gonna destroy whatever the NVA have left out here."

Linh Hoa looked mortified at the news, but when she looked back to her people, there was nothing but hardness in their faces. Sergeant Thanh clutched his newly wrapped wound, while Captain Nguyen spoke for the first time in what seemed an eternity.

"These are not our soldiers," he said in his thickly accented English, "You say they are attacking you. Our orders are to defend this valley. We do not throw our soldiers away needlessly."

He coughed, and then spat blood on the floor.

"Whatever you say," said Lance Corporal Johnson.

He swung his M60 around to face them, while snarling.

"Let me grease 'em, 'Sarge. They've just gonna slow us down."

His finger started to depress the trigger, but something

about what they were saying intrigued Lieutenant Weston.

"So who are they?"

The officer muttered and turned away, but the female soldier spoke for him.

"That all of our people are dead."

"Who are you?"

"Private Linh Hoa, People's Army of Vietnam, and these soldiers that attacked your men. They attack us also."

Lieutenant Weston seemed to have an idea of what was going on, but he persisted in questioning.

"They?"

She seemed confused, so Billy interceded.

"The soldiers with the red eyes."

The rest of the unit placed the remains of the men into body bags to take back with them, while the rest checked their ammunition. The rain was starting to ease off a little, though the saturated trees continued to create the effect of heavy rain for the time being.

"We need to get out of here, and fast," said Lieutenant Weston, "This entire place is…"

Then something happened that terrified every single one of the men there. One of the body bags began to move. Johnson moved back and pointed his M60 down at the moving bag. Even Linh Hoa seemed stunned by what was happening and tried to move away, only to be grabbed by her Captain. He said a few words, but she stopped in her tracks.

"What the fuck," said Sergeant Rodriguez as he arrived from checking on the state of the unit's ammunition, "Get back."

The bag moved again, and then the man inside began

clawing at the material. The fingers could be seen on the rain-covered material of the bag.

"Get him out of there!" Lance Corporal Brandes, "He's still alive."

One of the privates moved close and swung his rifle over his shoulder before bending down. The hands were still clutching to get out. He unzipped the bag, and immediately the hands reached out to grab him. Both hands were around his neck as the dismembered body pulled itself from the bag. The legs were still inside, and the broken remains of the man clung to the rifleman.

"Get him off me!"

Sergeant Jones stepped in, along with two others as they grabbed the broken man and tried to pull him away. They succeed but were left with the biting, snapping shape.

"Drop him and get back!" Jones said.

Each let go and did as ordered, letting the body of their comrade fall to the mud. But once there he used his arms to pull himself along the ground towards them. His flesh was already becoming pallid, his eyes a dull red, and becoming brighter by the second. It then reached to its side and drew out his machete from its long sheath.

"Hey, now," said Sergeant Jones as he pointed the muzzle of his carbine at the head of the dismembered soldier, "Back off. It's us."

The man looked up, and it was obvious to every one of them that the thing they were looking at was no longer the man they knew. The life that had inhabited his body had long gone, and in its place the strange unliving shell of a man, more a husk than anything living. The blade of the machete extended out, and it began to move even closer. One of the soldiers panicked and turned to run, only to crash into Lance Corporal Johnson, sending both of them crashing to the ground. Perhaps sensing opportunity, the thing went for them. A shot crashed out, hitting the man in the forehead, and he dropped to the mud, finally devoid of movement or life.

"Who did that?" Sergeant Jones demanded as he turned to check on the others. Standing in the open, and with a smoking gun, was Linh Hoa.

"You killed him!" Jones accused her, "One of our own, and you cut him down in cold blood."

His carbine was back up and pointing at her face when Johnson called out.

"The body. He's as cold as ice. He was dead when he attacked us."

"That makes no sense."

"No," said the Lieutenant, "That creature, you saw it grabbed him with its tail. It glowed as it touched him, like it was giving life to the dead or something."

"What?" Sergeant Rodriguez shouted, "You can't be serious?"

"Yeah," said Johnson, "You're seriously saying this is some black magic bullshit?"

A few of the others started to argue, and it didn't take long before all sense of order had broken down amongst the carnage and the blood. They had lost three men now, and it seemed as though the entire company had been wiped out, save for the few of them remaining. Lance Corporal Brandes stepped away and moved back towards the trees, checking where the enemy had come from. It didn't take long before he called back to them.

"More bodies over here. They've been dead for some time. Looks like we shot corpses." He bent down and then gasped, "You're not gonna believe this."

He stepped away and moved a few feet back towards the stunned looking men.

"What?" Lieutenant Weston asked.

"It's the ARVN Rangers."

"They followed us here?"

Lance Corporal Brandes looked back at the bodies.

"They're carrying blades like the others. They must have been killed, and then brought here by the…"

He hesitated, as though even mentioning the thing they'd all encountered would cause him trouble.

"The Ky Lan," said Linh Hoa.

"I said it before, and I'll say it again. We hurt that thing and it ran off. If we're gonna kill it, this is the best time."

Sergeant Jones seemed to agree.

"Johnson is right. This thing keeps picking us off. By the time we get to the choppers it could come back. If we hurt it before, then we can finish it off." He wiped his cheek with the back of his hand, "I reckon I can chase after it with a single fireteam. We'll have its head within an hour."

"No," said Lieutenant Weston, "We've got our orders. And those things have already gone. Whatever threat it was, it has dissipated, for now. That's our chance to bug out."

Lance Corporal Brandes then looked furtively to his left, stepping back slowly and carefully, as if he was trying to avoid making too much noise.

"What is it?" Sergeant Jones asked.

The other soldiers picked up their weapons.

"Uh, Sir, look."

Billy pointed to the North, and to a clump of trees. Around the base were dozens upon dozens of red eyes. And as they watched them, more appeared.

"More of them over here, Sir," said Sergeant Jones.

As they looked around their position, it was clear there were scores of the unliving things. They formed a line of unliving flesh directly in the path the monstrous creature had taken just moments earlier.

"Why are they back?" Johnson asked.

Billy readied his rifle while shaking his head.

"They're keeping us from the creature, it must be."

"What? How do you know that?"

"Screw this," said the Lieutenant, "I've had just about enough of all this. Screw all of them."

He pulled back the charging handle on his M16.

"If they come any closer, we open fire. Understood?"

"Yes, Sir!" replied every man in the unit.

Had he looked behind him he might have changed his mind, but Billy could see what was happening. The three Vietnamese were all armed, and perhaps for the first time in decades they were not pointing the weapons at each other, and instead they joined the Americans as they aimed at the shadows. The shapes began to move, and then the trees rustled as they moved towards the small band of soldiers. This time they were being much more cautious, with many of them staying low, or hiding behind the foliage to avoid being spotted.

"Why don't they attack?" Private Mock asked, "We're right here."

"Because it's not an attack," said Billy, "They're slowing

us down."

Lieutenant Weston looked right back at him and nodded.

"Private…I think you might actually be right on this one."

He then looked back at the shapes.

"We're not waiting for them, not this time."

He reached to his side and lifted a grenade. He primed it and began counting in his head. Then he tossed it far away and into the mass of half hidden enemy warriors.

"Right. Drop 'em!"

The grenade detonated a fraction of a section after the first rifle fired.

CHAPTER SIXTEEN

The rain had stopped, and a gentle trickle of water dropped down through the branches onto the men below. And with the rain now gone, it should have been quieter. But that was little more than a dream for Billy. The running battle against their dead, soulless enemy continued unabated, and it became more horrific with each passing second. He could no longer hear as the combined force of US and Vietnamese soldiers destroyed anything that came close to them. The sound of gunfire was so great that the echoing sound in his eardrums was continuous. Vegetation, trees, soldiers, and even the earth at their feet was blown apart in the maelstrom of violence. Scores of bodies lay around them, with many more coming out of the jungle without a care for their lives.

"Stand your ground!" Lieutenant Weston called out as he reloaded, "Don't let them touch you!"

Even as the bodies fell, more slithered out from beneath them. One made it close enough to grab Billy's left foot and was about to stab him when Sergeant Jones dragged him back. He then lifted his carbine and fired just two bullets. Several more grenades exploded, and then the fight was over as quickly as it had begun. A few had sustained light injuries and were tended to, while Billy and Mock moved out with Sergeant Jones to check the perimeter. He said nothing but communicated with hand signals. Billy held onto his rifle with a death grip, ever fearful he might be disarmed again.

The rain had stopped, but the ground was as treacherous as ever. He had to hold onto the nearest foliage to stop him from slipping over. Once he was almost twenty yards from the others, and when he looked back, he gasped at finding they were almost hidden from sight.

"See anything?" Private Mock whispered.

Billy looked off into the jungle and shook his head.

"Nothing out here. Nothing but…wait…that's weird."

Private Mock began to lift his rifle.

"Weird good? Weird Bad?"

Billy stepped away a little further, and then ran his hands over the trees on each side. There was a roughly beaten path through the jungle, but it was the deep, fresh lacerations in the trees that told a very specific story.

"It came this way. And it was moving fast."

He moved even closer and placed his fingers on the cuts in the material. At first nothing happened, but then he noticed a slimy material covered the damage, as though the creature had left it. No sooner had he touched the material than a flash of light and pain struck his head. A white light blinded him for a second, though he was sure he could see shapes moving about in the light. It felt like the worst headache he'd ever had and left a throbbing in his temples.

"Billy! You okay, man? You hit?"

Billy looked across to Private Mock. The soldier was one of those men close to the end of his tour of duty. He had been in country long enough to know the ropes, and to not take unnecessary risks. He suspected he was asking more to find out if he was going to be a liability, rather than an asset to the unit.

"Yeah…it's just a headache, came on fast."

He shook his head a few more times, and the pain vanished as quickly as it had arrived. Billy had felt similar pains before, but never had they come and gone so quickly. He touched his head but felt nothing of the numbness of before.

"I…I…uh. This is weird."

He reached forward and touched the damaged tree. Nothing happened, but then as his fingers moved to the lacerations in the surface, the pain returned, but far less violently than before. But more shocking was the imagery in his mind. The white light had subsided, and in its place were trees and greenery, and they were moving. He removed his hand and looked back to the others. The imagery vanished, and try as he might, he could no longer even remember what he'd seen exactly. It was like the fleeting moment upon waking from a deep sleep where the dream fades in seconds.

"Sergeant!"

The man moved quickly, and with his carbine at the ready, just as if he expected the enemy to leap out and attack once more.

"What is it, Private?"

"The creature, it caused this damage when it fled."

Sergeant Jones looked at the tree and at the trail through the jungle. The light was increasing, and they could all see much further, even with the faint mist that seemed ever present first thing in the morning.

"Yeah, I thought as much."

He whistled, and Lance Corporal Brandes worked his way back through the foliage to join them.

"Scout ahead that ridgeline. Stay in sight, and watch for signs of those little bastards."

"Yes, Sarge."

The marksman slinked off into the jungle, leaving Mock, Billy, and Sergeant Jones together.

"Sarge, there's more."

"What is it?"

"The damage. When I touched it, I felt something."

The Sergeant pulled his head back as though he'd just said something offensive.

"What are you talking about, kid? You felt what, the moving spirit of our Lord and Saviour? Because trust me, right now we could do with a little of his help."

He then looked up at the sky and placed his clenched fist at his sternum, where a small metal cross was hanging low from his neck.

"The creature. I think I saw what it was seeing."

Sergeant Jones laughed, but Billy remained stone-faced. He knew what he had seen, no matter what the others might think or say.

"Try it," said Billy, daring the man to do what he had just done. Sergeant Jones wasn't the kind of man to take suggestions from a private in such a manner and shook his head. He hadn't risen through the ranks to be played with by rookies thinking they knew how reverse psychology worked.

"Private, I ain't poking my fingers into no damn tree."

He laughed as he looked away. It was a dismissive gesture, but as he turned, it gave Billy a chance, one he knew he would be unlikely to get again.

"Now, get back to…"

To the Sergeant's astonishment, Billy grabbed his left arm and forced the hand against the damaged tree. Billy was not particularly strong, but he had caught the Sergeant by surprise.

"What the!"

He yelled in anger, but then as he made contact, the sound stopped. It was as though he had just been electrocuted as he was pinned there, held by Billy who seemed equally stunned. He remained in contact with the tree for three seconds before releasing and falling backwards. Private Mock caught him before he could fall down, while Billy staggered away and somehow managed to remain upright.

"Sarge! You okay? What did he do to you?"

The man shuddered, shook his head, and then pushed them away.

"Holy shit."

He looked back and forth, and for a brief moment the men thought his eyesight might have been affected.

"What did I just see?"

Lieutenant Weston was now there and trying to see what all the commotion was about.

"Everything all right in there? We need to get moving, and fast."

Sergeant Jones looked to the Lieutenant with glazed and confused eyes.

"Sergeant, are you okay?"

"That's the lot," Lance Corporal Brandes called out from his position far away from the others, "There's more bodies, but no sign of any more coming this way."

The Lieutenant nodded and turned back to Sergeant Jones. Rodriguez was also there and grabbed onto the forearm of his comrade.

"Sergeant!"

"I just saw some kind of underground structure. Like a stone fortress with chambers, rooms, and…it was a little weird."

His eyes met Billy's, and right away Billy knew he now understood. Lieutenant Weston, on the other hand, had no idea what was happening.

"That's great. We don't have time for cultural sightseeing right now. We have to leave, and fast."

"Sir, you don't understand. The Private here spotted the damage caused by that creature. I believe it can see anything that its followers can see."

Lieutenant Weston might have laughed, but the look on the Sergeant's face allowed him to dismiss that idea out of hand.

"Touch it," said Billy.

Lieutenant Weston was hesitant, but when he placed his hand on the tree, his reaction was much less surprising. Finally, he released and gasped while looking at the transparent fluid he'd caught on his fingers. It evaporated almost immediately.

"I saw something moving through the ruins of the defences we captured, the destroyed CP of the Colonel's. I…"

He dropped to one knee and vomited. Billy and Sergeant

Jones moved to his side and helped him back up.

"What is it, Sir?" Jones asked.

"I saw the Colonel. He was gathering up soldiers."

"He survived," said Sergeant Jones with relief, but the Lieutenant shook his head.

"No. That's just it. His eyes, they were like the ones that attacked us. Red, and glowing."

Billy wiped his brow while shaking his head.

"So they've fallen under that thing's control as well. Were they dead?"

Lieutenant Weston shrugged.

"I couldn't tell, but they're definitely under that thing's control."

They moved their way back to the rest of the depleted squad and tried to avoid looking at the mutilated remains now in the body bags.

"Lieutenant," said Radioman Jeffries, "Contact from Command. 101st are being prepped for an all out offensive in this area in the next week. They'll take the hills and recover any bodies."

"101st," said the Lieutenant angrily, "We do the work, and they'll come in and claim the victory."

"Victory, Sir?" Sergeant Jones asked, surprised, "There ain't no victory here, not this time. All we can do is bug out and salvage what we have left."

"No!" called out a woman's voice. Each of them turned to face the trio of Vietnamese soldiers. They'd almost been forgotten in the thrill and terror of the battle. But now they were there, under the carefully watch of two soldiers.

"What did you day?" Lance Corporal Johnson demanded

as he moved closer and swung the M60 around to face them. To the amusement of the others, Linh Hoa batted the weapon aside.

"Stop pointing that at us, you child."

She then focussed on Lieutenant Weston.

"The Ky Lan. It has been summoned to this valley. It will kill my people when it finds them."

"And? We're having this valley, one way or another."

"Yeah," said Johnson, though this time he kept the barrel of his weapon lowered, "Try and stop us, and we'll keep coming back."

"It will not matter. Ky Lan will kill your people. No Vietnamese, no American. All will die until Ky Lan is dead."

A silence befell the group. Sergeant Rodriguez approached and looked even grimmer than before.

"We're ready to go. What are your orders, Lieutenant?"

Lieutenant Weston grunted, looked to Linh Hoa, and then to Billy.

"What do you know about this group? Can they be trusted?"

Billy's eyebrow's rose in surprise.

"Trust? No idea, Sir. But we fought together against that creature and its…"

"Slaves," said Linh Hoa, "You have seen its work. It controls the dead and uses them for its bidding. For all of us…we must kill it."

"You're serious?" Weston asked, "You want to go and kill it? No way am I letting you out of here."

The Vietnamese Captain moved to her side and spoke in short bursts. It was impossible even for those with some knowledge of his language to understand him. Linh Hoa nodded along and then said just a few words before returning to English.

"My Captain proposes a truce."

"And?"

"A truce until the beast is killed."

"No way," said Johnson, "No way do we trust these Gooks. Waste 'em now before they try and waste us."

Linh Hoa seemed to become angry and had to be physically held back by her commander. They exchanged words before she spoke to Weston once more.

"You will never leave this valley. Neither will we."

"You threatening us, Missy?" Johnson demanded, much to the annoyance of Sergeant Jones.

"Johnson, secure that shit. This ain't the time or the place."

Weston moved closer to his enemies, and the tension quickly rose in the small group. The American Squad had been cut down to size, leaving a quarter of its number now brutally slain. It would take only one or two minor incidents to leave them vulnerable to the three Vietnamese regulars, people who probably knew the land a lot better than they did.

"Go on," he said, lowering his weapon.

"The Ky Lan has been summoned. It will kill your people, and it will kill mine. We have truce and fight it. Kill it."

She made a gesture with one hand and repeated herself.

"Kill it!"

Billy watched all of this with interest. Unlike the others, he'd been up close with the creature and its enslaved soldiers. But he'd also seen its lair and had an idea of where it had come from. He knew there was much more to this thing than it being some wild beast or ethereal spirit wandering the valley.

"Sir, I think she might be right," said Billy, "It has killed her people and ours, and it attacks when we're at our weakest."

"Then we should leave this place, and fast. Let the B52s do what we cannot."

"Sir. I don't think we'll ever make it to the choppers."

"Why not?"

"It has killed hundreds, and now the Colonel and his men have joined it. What they see, it sees. What they smell, it smells. And what the dead hear, the creature hears. We're outnumbered twenty to one. There's only one way out now."

"We kill it?" Sergeant Jones asked.

Linh Hoa and the Captain both nodded, and then replied in English.

"Yes."

"Yeah," said Johnson, "The Gooks…"

"Zip it, Johnson," snapped back Sergeant Jones. There was anger in his voice that transcended mere discipline in the unit. Even Billy was surprised to hear the outburst, and when he looked to the man, he could tell he was hurting. Billy had forgotten that the Sergeant had already lost a number of men in his unit, with the possibility of losing many more. Each of them was his personal responsibility. He expected them to perform to the best of their ability, and in exchange he would do his utmost to keep them alive. It was the unwritten covenant between them.

"Do you know where it lives? Is there somewhere that it hides?"

"I've been there," said Billy, "It dragged me there."

One by one the soldiers moved in closer.

"We getting some payback, Sir?" asked one.

Private Mock nodded along eagerly.

"We can't let this one slide, Sir. That thing chewed up our entire company and spat out the bones to come back at us again."

"How will killing the creature help us get past the hundreds of dead blocking our route to the LZ?"

Linh Hoa considered his question for a moment. Everybody was now looking at her, including her two comrades. But for some reason she did not answer.

"Well?"

"Lieutenant," said Billy, "How can we know? My guess is without the creature there would be nothing controlling those it had killed. But who knows?"

"Your soldier is correct," said Linh Hoa, "But we will only truly know once we have tracked it back to its lair and killed it."

"Yeah!" Private Mock said, "Let's kill that bastard!"

"Very well," said Lieutenant Weston, "We'll track this thing down, kill it, and then withdraw to the LZ. The B52s can finish whatever we've left behind for them. Any questions?"

"Just one," said Sergeant Rodriquez, "What about our dead? We can't leave them behind for those things. And there's not enough of us to carry them and be able to hunt."

Lieutenant Weston considered that, but he already knew what he was going to say. It was a painful decision, but his duty was to the living more than to the dead. They had all fought hard against the creatures, but for those that had fallen there was little else he could offer them.

"There's no time for burial. The choppers are already waiting for us. If we don't hurry, we'll be barbecued by the B52s."

His eyes met with Sergeant Jones, and it was as though

they were able to communicate without speaking. Finally, the Lieutenant said something none of them expected. He sounded calm, yet assertive, something especially surprising considering the circumstances.

"Burn the bodies."

There was silence in the group, but the two Sergeants quickly nodded in agreement.

"If we can't bring them back, then by hell we're not leaving them for this creature, or for the enemy."

He cast a quick glance towards the North Vietnamese soldiers.

"Make sure you take their personal effects, dog tags, and any weapons and ammo they have left. I don't want a thing left but their burnt bones if anybody finds them before the 101st."

"Yes, Sir!" replied the pair of NCOs.

They then turned to leave, barking orders to the men as they prepared to create a small pyre for the bodies. There was no time for something individual, and they worked quickly. Each knew the evac chopper would come as soon as they were near the LZ, and if they delayed even by a few minutes, they'd miss their chance to get back to base.

"You heard the Lieutenant. Take care of the bodies. We've got some hunting to do."

The remains of the squad got to work, all while the Lieutenant remained with the Vietnamese soldiers. Billy stayed back as well as he looked at each of them. Linh Hoa looked shattered, but she did her utmost to hide it from the men around her. It was obvious she trusted none of them. Lieutenant Weston moved to the side of the wounded Captain and looked at his wounds.

"You were attacked by the creature?"

Linh Hoa translated, and then quickly responded.

"He was attacked by the beast. He fought it with his knife before it took him. He says he was woken twice in the jungle and once more underground. It bit him once."

"Bit him?"

Linh Hoa nodded.

"Yes."

"Was he able to hurt it?"

The Captain began to chuckle, and though he answered, his voice was too shallow and fast to understand. At the same time, he pulled up his shirt to show deep slashes to his body. At first glance they appeared mortal wounds, but most of the blood was around the edges of the wound. Even so, it looked like a bear had gone to work on him.

"He says he does not know. He was screaming as it slashed at his body."

Lieutenant Weston pulled the light scarf from his neck and wiped away the sweat. The Sun was rising quickly, and already the heat and humidity of the early day in the valley was getting to him.

"Can your wounded still walk?"

Linh Hoa spoke with the Captain and Sergeant Thanh. Luckily, the bullet was little more than a flesh wound for the Sergeant, and though his arm was bloody, he seemed more than capable of walking. He watched the Americans with suspicion and scorn.

"Yes, we can walk."

"Good. Then you can go at the front. Lead us to this creature's lair."

"And then we kill it."

The Lieutenant be pulled back the charging handle of his M16 and nodded.

"We kill it."

CHAPTER SEVENTEEN

Billy could still smell the smoke from the burning bodies as he inched his way through the jungle. The column wound its way along the animal trails. Any sign of the beast was gone, as the trees and greenery seemed to move back to cover its tracks. Luckily, they had the combined efforts of Lance Corporal Brandes, Linh Hoa, and Corporal Trinh, their local guide. Billy carried his M16 across his body, ready for action in case attacked. The men had by now all seen the creature and faced off against its unrelenting hordes. The last encounter had sobered them, but it had done something else. There was a mood amongst them, one of anger, but also a need for revenge.

"How much further?" Lieutenant Weston called out.

A face turned back from the front of the unit. It was Linh Hoa, and she looked frustrated at how slowly they were moving through the jungle.

"Less than a mile."

She then gestured with one hand, causing Sergeant Jones to chuckle.

"She wants us to be quieter," he said.

Even Lieutenant Weston seemed amused by that.

"Cute."

The two wounded NVA soldiers hobbled along, and somehow managed to maintain the pace of the Americans. It may have been a determination to save face in front of the Americans, or just as likely they'd been encouraged to move by Lance Corporal Johnson following behind with his M60 pointed directly at them.

"Keep moving, Dinks."

His voice was quiet enough that Sergeant Jones didn't hear him, or perhaps he merely pretended so. Billy felt a little safer being further back, and with Mock and Sutherland around him. The Lieutenant was right in front of them, along with Jeffries. Sergeant Rodriquez brought up the rear and moved nearly twenty feet further back to cover their rear. He was able to match their speed, while also constantly travelling off to their flanks to check the trail.

"What happened to you with them?" Sutherland nodded towards the Vietnamese soldiers, "Did they find you, and take you there?"

Billy shook his head.

"The creature took me. I'm sure of it."

"Holy shit," said Private Mock, "For real?"

"It left me in a pile of bones. When I woke, I was in some underground temple. It was full of those walking corpses. I was trying to escape when I found the Captain. They were biting him when I arrived."

"How did you get away?" Mock asked.

"We fought our way out to the light. And all the time those things…they came for us."

He placed his left hand on his chest and could still feel the bruises. Images and thoughts of those tunnels came back to him as though he were living them once more. But it was the drooling dead soldiers that sent shivers through his body. The way they moved right at him, brandishing blades, and other weapons as they sought to kill him.

"How many?"

"Too many. We had no firearms, so it was all blade work."

Private Sutherland raised his eyebrows and threw a quick glance across to Mock. Any sense of doubt over his story was well and truly gone. They'd seen the creatures, and they knew the truth of the danger they faced.

"But what about those other two? The Sergeant, and the woman?"

Billy lifted his canteen and poured several mouthfuls of water down his throat. He was a little too eager, and almost choked as half of the fluid ran down his front, instead of into his body.

"Hey, buddy. Easy there."

"It's okay." Billy coughed twice, "Just thinking about that place turns my throat dry. I can't believe we're going back."

They reached a long tree that had fallen some time ago. It had completely blocked the trail from left to right. Branches were torn apart much higher up, but there was just enough space for each of them to crawl underneath and to the other side. By the time it was Billy's turn several minutes had passed, and the noises of the jungle had quietened down, as though even the trees knew something would soon happen, something bloody, and destructive. Hands pulled him up on the other side, and once upright he could see the shapes of rocks two hundred feet away in a clearing. He blinked several times and then knew it was more than just rocks.

"What is it?" Private Sutherland asked as Private Mock helped his comrade from under the tree.

"That's the place."

"What place?"

"Where it took me."

He turned and looked at the pair of soldiers. They looked deadly, and yet also vulnerable in their military fatigues, their loose jackets now soaked and muddy. Their helmets appeared as though they had been on patrol for months, not days, and their faces were pale and damp.

"That's not far from creature's lair."

That was the moment Sergeant Jones clenched his fist and then lifted up an arm calling them all to halt. The squad was bunched up around the tree, with only Sergeant Rodriguez left on the other side. As the men sank to their knees, the Sergeant pulled himself up over the tree, and then waited there in a raised position.

"What's happening?" Mock whispered.

Billy placed a finger on his lips, and they waited as quietly as they could. Billy could see nothing immediately that was a problem, but then as they waited, he noticed one of their men was gone. At the same time, Sergeant Jones looked back and mouthed words quietly to the nearby Lieutenant.

"Corporal Trinh has gone."

"What?"

"He was first under this tree. Now he's gone."

"Tracking?"

Sergeant Jones considered that, and then shook his head.

"That bastard has left us."

"He is from the hill tribes," said Linh Hoa as she rose to her full height. One by one the others did the same and continued checking the trees for signs of danger, and for the missing man.

"Brandes. You're on point."

They continued forward at a slower pace, while Brandes inched his way ahead. He looked not just for signs of the enemy, but also for the telltale signs of an ambush, hidden traps, and other potential dangers.

"Your tracker is no fool, Lieutenant," said Ling Hoa, "His loyalty is not to you, or to me."

"What do you mean?"

"Your man, he of the mountain people of Thua Thien-Hue Province and of Quang Tri Province."

"What of it?"

"The mountain people have no interest in king, presidents, nobility, and leaders. They want Vietnam kept as it is. They do not want you here, American."

"Well, you could have fooled me. Because they fight hard for us."

"No. They do not fight for you. They fight because they see Communism as the greater danger."

He nodded ahead towards Brandes who was now crawling through the undergrowth as he reached the rocks.

"Perhaps he believes the Ky Lan knows what is best for

us all."

A branch snapped up ahead, and Brandes looked back at them.

"Sorry."

Then came a roar, and the trees shifted apart as the monstrous creature revealed itself. It swung around, slamming its tail against Lance Corporal Brandes as he struggled to escape. The impact lifted him from the ground and hurled him fifteen feet through the air. He crashed through branches until ending up impaled on one of the split branches. The thick wooden spike punched through his body and burst out through his chest. Blood sprayed from the wound as he flailed for several seconds. Before the others could get close to him, he was dead, hanging from the tree like a parachute caught up its branches.

"What the fuck!" Private Sutherland cried out. His voice was so high-pitched it almost broke out into a scream. He turned to the others, and then tried to fire his M79, but in his haste or confusion he'd forgotten to reload it.

"You idiot," he snarled as he removed a grenade from the grenade bandolier and snapped open the weapon. He slid in the 40mm high explosive shell and snapped it shut with a reassuring clunk.

"Yeah, baby."

"Light it up!" Sergeant Jones shouted.

The creature turned towards them and roared, its fiery throat shaking and glowing as hot as a furnace. What remained of the squad opened fire with every weapon they had. More than a hundred rounds hit the beast as the men showered it with gunfire. The 5.56mm bullets were more than capable of punching into the hide of the creature, sending spurts of blood into the air. Private Sutherland was still screaming as he took an aim at the beast and fired. The M79 sounded feeble as it clunked and then hurled the M406 40mm high explosive grenade at a muzzle velocity of just seventy-five metres per second. This was more like a man throwing a grenade when compared to over nine hundred metres per second from the M16s. For all its lack of speed, the effect of the grenade hitting the side of the beast was a sight to behold. It staggered backwards, groaning in pain.

"Advance, and don't let up," said Lieutenant Weston, "We don't leave until we've put that thing down! For the Platoon!"

The men shouted as they blasted away with abandon. Billy was right next to Lance Corporal Johnson and could hear him shouting as he opened fire. The M60 was a brutal weapon, and in the muscular hands of Johnson he was able to wield it like an assault rifle. It shook violently with each burst, but this close it did not seem to matter.

"Yeah! Not so tough now!"

Johnson stopped shooting as he reloaded, with Private Mock helping him load on the next belt. They worked quickly, but as the creature roared again, Billy found himself unable to pay attention to anything else but the creature. He aimed at the centre, fired three short bursts, then released the empty magazine, and loaded in the next.

"It won't go down!"

One of the soldiers ran through the smoke with his rifle blazing. Billy had no idea who it was, and he vanished as a grenade exploded nearby. Another landed next to the creature, but as it twisted about, it knocked the weapon aside, and it detonated impotently several yards away. Billy took aim once more as Private Mock ran out into the open. He was muttering words deliriously to himself, as he lowered his rifle and swung the heavy tube he had been carrying on his back since they arrived. It was an M72 LAW, a disposable Light Anti-Tank Weapon that gave an infantryman the ability to destroy armour, bunkers, and reinforced emplacements. He took aim and shouted so the others knew that he was about to firing.

"Firing!"

"Oh, shit!" Johnson stepped away from the weapon. Some of the others ducked down, but most continued fighting as the flash from the weapon marked the launch of the high explosive warhead. Billy had heard stories of the LAW rocket launchers failing spectacularly in battle, with some exploding before hitting their targets, causing injuries and even deaths. He knew he should duck, but he wanted to see the creature killed. It appeared to know what was happening and turned head on as the rocket struck its flank and detonated. The explosion shook the ground and was followed by a grenade from the M79.

"We've got him!" Jones said, "Keep moving. I think we really have got him!"

Billy felt the adrenaline pumping through his body as he moved up towards the position of the creature. The area was still flooded with smoke, and a fire burned where one of the warheads had managed to ignite a small part of the jungle. The leaves moved as they approached, and as he reached the top, he could see the thing was still there. It was on its side, with its belly facing away from them. The creature was bigger than any animal Billy had seen in his entire life. From a distance it looked similar in overall mass to an elephant, but now he could see the torso was at least the size of an elephant, with legs as big as a bear. The head was just as large, while the tail extended out like an

Anaconda, with three quarters of it being quite narrow, and cloaked up along the ground. The edges of the razor-sharp tail glowed red in the early morning light.

"We killed the bastard!" Lance Corporal Johnson said as he put another six rounds into its skin. He looked to his right where Linh Hoa waited with her weapon raised. The barrel was smoking much like his. He gave her a grudging nod.

"It ain't getting back up, not now."

The others moved closer, but Billy refused to get too close. He'd spent enough time around death over the last days to avoid taking any unnecessary risks.

"Stay back," he said nervously, "It's not stupid."

Few of them listened and circled around the massive beast. Johnson pushed the muzzle of his M60 against the thick hide of the creature and laughed.

"Holy shit, that skin is thick."

"Look at it," said Private Mock, "It looks just like Smaug, the dragon!"

Billy turned and looked at him, and almost laughed at the mention of the dragon from the children's book. Of all the absurd things they might talk of, a fantasy dragon was not the first he would have expected during his tour of duty. But his laughter stopped as spotted he bloody corpse of Lance Corporal Brandes still hanging from the tree. His rifle hung from its sling where it had dropped, and now held onto his foot, like a climber holding onto the edge of a cliff side. It swayed gently in the morning breeze and then slipped off his boot, vanishing into the undergrowth.

"No…not Brandes."

He took a step towards the fallen soldier but then lifted a

hand to cover his mouth as he found another body, near to the tree where the marksman was now impaled.

"What do we do now, Lt?" Sergeant Jones asked.

The Lieutenant was close now and placed a boot on the beast's back. He tried to push it, but the mass of the creature meant there was no chance of that.

"We blow it to Kingdom come."

"Hallelujah!" said one of the men in a mocking tone. Sergeant Jones nodded to himself and moved towards the front of the creature.

"I want every grenade and Claymore you can get your hands on. We'll rig this mother."

Billy reached for a grenade, but he soon stopped and leant in closer towards the creature. He thought he heard something, but as he waited there, he could hear nothing but the noises of the jungle, and of the soldiers now surrounding the fallen monster.

"This is one weird animal." Johnson kicked it again.

"It is not an animal." Linh Hoa moved closer to the front of the creature, "It is the Ky Lan, a creature of ancient myth. It was said that they appeared in times of great prosperity, during the rule of only the wisest men."

"I hate to break it to you, sweetheart," said Johnson, to the chuckles of the others, "But there's no wise men in Vietnam. Not in Hanoi, and not in Saigon."

That drew immediate shouts from the NVA Captain. But then Billy heard something, a noise that chilled his very soul. His lifted a hand and looked directly at the Captain.

"Quiet."

He then leant down towards the monster, even as another

Claymore was positioned at its side. The noise vanished as quickly as it had arrived, but he was sure it was the rumble of heavy breathing.

"It's dying, or dead," said Sergeant Jones, "Creatures make all kinds of sounds in their last seconds."

The man turned away and continued giving orders to the others. They were relatively lightly equipped, but they still carried enough Claymores and grenades to leave a crater in the hillside.

"Sarge."

The man ignored him as he continued barking orders, forcing Billy to shout much louder than he would have liked.

"Sarge. I think it's playing possum!"

Jones glanced across to him, and then at the creature. He took a few careful steps backwards, signalling for the others to do the same. Every one of them lowered their weapons at it, ready to fire. Billy was sure he could see the body of the thing starting to move. It was little, but enough to show it was breathing.

"Oh…shit, it's alive!"

In that moment it sprang into action. The dormant mass spun on the ground, with flailing limbs lashing out. The tail moved like a whip and slashed through the neck of Captain Nguyen. Somehow the head remained atop the body as he slumped to his knees. The red line ran through the stump, and blood gushed from the sides. Linh Hoa screamed and began moving forward. Billy ran away from the beast and leapt on her as the Claymores detonated. A massive thump shook the ground as the explosives and steel balls shredded the woodland. The creature howled in pain, but still it fought on. It pounced on

Private Mock, biting off a leg, and leaving the man screaming as his life drained away before their eyes. Next it faced off against Sergeant Rodriguez and Private Hohner who were caught out in the open.

"Shit!" The Sergeant he did all he could think of and opened fire. Hohner turned to run as the thing's head came in for the kill. The teeth were like swords, and it seemed to ignore the bullets as it came for them, biting the Sergeant clean in half. Private Hohner made it to within six feet of Billy's outstretched arm when the Ky Lan's front leg slashed at him. Hohner spun around like a ballet dancer, and as he turned, they could all see he'd been disembowelled, with his internal organs dropping from the gaping wound. He crashed to the ground in a pool of blood.

"Put it down!" Sergeant Jones shouted, "Kill it!

The soldiers opened fire once more, but they were scattered about, and as the beast moved among them, they were unable to hit it without striking their comrades. Sergeant Thanh ran out of ammunition and ran at it screaming in his own tongue with a hand grenade in one hand.

"Take cover!" Sergeant Jones shouted.

Those that could hear dropped to the ground, but others remained upright and blasted away, including Lance Corporal Johnson. His M60 thundered away while Linh Hoa shouted for Sergeant Thanh to stay back as the bullets flew. Two rounds hit his shoulder, and he half fell onto the monster and then exploded. Shattered flesh scattered around them, and the beast stumbled away from them. Johnson put another twenty rounds into it, and this time the beast began to give ground. It snapped and snarled, and then turned away.

"Chase it down!" Lieutenant Weston ordered, "Do not let it escape, not this time!"

The Americans broke from cover and charged the short distance to the peak. There was blood and gore everywhere, both from the slaughtered men, as well as damage caused to the creature. Right in front of them were stone ruins, like that of a tiny castle or temple complex. It was so old that trees were growing up and through the remains, making the place appear truly ancient. And there in the middle was the monster. It rose up onto its hind legs and roared so loudly that the trees shook.

"Fire at will!"

The final volley hammered into the beast with such unrelenting force it was unable to come closer. It lashed out with its tail, but the soldiers stayed far enough back. It howled in pain and staggered backwards.

"Forward!"

The soldiers moved one step at a time over the slippery mud, with each step making the ground even more difficult to traverse. Billy slipped, but waiting hands pushed him forward and stopped him the humiliation of falling backwards down the gentle slope. The soldiers continued reloading and firing until the barrels of their weapons hissed under the strain. The monster lurched forward and snapped at Billy, but he leapt aide as the tail narrowly avoided him, and slashed a tree in half. Two grenades sailed through the air, and the creature turned to flee as they detonated. The broken beast staggered and then collapsed to the ground. It hit the surface hard, causing the floor to buckle and then fall away. The creature howled and crawled at the sky as it was pulled down underground.

"Holy shit!" Johnson rushed to the edge. With the heavy

M60 pulling him to one side, he almost fell over and joined the creature in its death spiral down into the depths of the Earth.

"Yeah…enjoy the ride!" he laughed.

Sergeant Jones was next up, and with Linh Hoa and Billy at his side. The unit had been torn apart, leaving just them plus Lieutenant Weston, Lance Corporal Johnson, and Private Sutherland.

"Is this it?" Johnson looked at the small group. There were just five remaining plus himself of the entire company that had stormed into the valley. His look of victory and self-satisfaction vanished as he realised that the others were now all gone. Their victory that had seemed such an achievement quickly paled.

"What happened to Jeffries?" Sergeant Jones asked, "He was alive a minute ago. He was standing right next to me."

Private Sutherland placed his M79 grenade launcher on the ground and bent down to check the body of the radioman. He ran his hands over his clothing and pulled open the man's jacket. Fresh blood oozed out from a multitude of deep wounds. He lifted a hand to his face, and through incredible self-control managed to avoid vomiting. He then turned back and shook his head.

"It looks like he was hit by debris from one of the blasts. Something cut into his chest and neck, serrated and very sharp. There're splinters of metal here. I just don't know…"

He dropped down next to the man and placed his hand on the man's face. He'd been dead for a matter of seconds, and already his face was pale. He reached for the man's eyes and gently moved the eyelids back down. He then slumped down next to the soldier.

"It's the Dinks' fault," he muttered angrily.

"Bullshit," said Billy as attention shifted to Linh Hoa, "You mean the soldiers that are dead as well. Two of them died in this fight. It's just her left. Screw the war."

Sutherland pulled off his helmet and tossed it to the ground in a fit of helpless rage. The helmet bounced once and then sunk partially into the mud. He'd transformed from a man keen and eager to fight, to one mentally and physically broken by the carnage he'd witnessed. The fighting against the NVA seemed to pale next to the brutality of this creature and its summoned hordes. He looked up, and his eyes looked sunken and red from sheer exhaustion.

"It ain't right," said Private Sutherland as he looked away, "It ain't right at all. We shouldn't be here."

The others knew that Jeffries and Sutherland were hardly the closest of friends. They'd said few words to each other, but they had fought together, and this last death seemed to be the last straw for him. The cumulative effect of seeing his platoon killed one by one must have been too much for him. He looked around at the bodies and the blood and began to sob. The others spread out around the pit that the creature had vanished into, each staring carefully down into the abyss.

"Private, get back on the line."

Billy could see the man was going through a complete and utter breakdown. The same had happened to him when he'd been underground. And in his experience, there were only two outcomes, one was madness and despair, and the second, perhaps the most dangerous, was an uncontrollable rage.

"Lieutenant," said Linh Hoa.

Weston turned to her, and perhaps for the first time there was no reservation about her loyalty. She was just a woman and a soldier now. She'd seen as much death as he had, and both were splattered in mud and blood from the fighting.

"I heard something in the pit."

"What?" Sergeant Jones moved up beside his Lieutenant, "You've got to be kidding me."

He leant over the ledge and then waved to Johnson.

"Flare…now!"

Johnson muttered as he rummaged for the flares. It took a moment until he found one and handed it across. Sergeant Jones activated it and held it over the top of the pit.

"Be ready."

Lieutenant Weston pulled his rifle to his shoulder and nodded. Sergeant Jones released the flare, and it fell down into the pit, lighting up the sides as it went. It made it five or six yards where it hit something and stopped. Each of them leaned over the edge and looked down at the fizzling flames.

"I thought it would be deeper," said Sergeant Jones.

"Wait," said Linh Hoa.

The flare then began to move and then rolled to the side. A second later, a red glow become brighter and brighter until it turned to yellow and then almost pure white.

"No…fucking way," said Lance Corporal Johnson, "It's still alive."

The burning maw roared and howled, and the pit began to shake. Johnson tried to aim at the thing far below, but the edges of the pit began to crumble and collapse inwards. He leapt away, dropping his weapon down into the blackness. As he landed, Linh Hoa wobbled and then fell. She vanished from sight, but Billy threw himself to the floor and caught her arm as she disappeared. For a second, he lay there holding her, but then he began to slide in the mud. Billy kicked out wildly, but no matter how hard he tried, he continued to move to the edge.

"Let me go!" Linh Hoa shouted.

Billy shook his head and called out for help.

"Over here! Help!"

The others were so busy looking at the glowing light in the pit they had barely noticed what was happening. Johnson was reaching for a grenade when he saw what was happening.

"Private!"

Lieutenant Weston was the closest and turned to the right as he watched Billy about to go over the ledge and fall to his potential death. He swore to himself while dropped to his knees. At the same time, part of the mud gave way to reveal steps off to the side of the pit that circled their way down into the darkness.

"Screw the beast, grab him! Now!"

All thoughts of combat vanished as Lieutenant Weston and Sergeant Jones rushed to their falling comrade. Willing hands grabbed onto his mud splattered boots and pants, but still he slipped away. Only when Johnson joined in, were they able to stop the movement, and then slowly but surely, they dragged him back from the ledge. They were stunned to find a terrified Linh Hoa holding onto his hands. With Billy safe, Johnson reached down to take her hand. She hesitated, and then released one hand from Billy and grasped Johnson's forearm. They locked grip, and he pulled her up so fast she landed on her knees.

"I've got ya," he said helpfully.

But once she was safe, he released his grip and turned to the mud-soaked Billy.

"You crazy fuck. You nearly got yourself killed, and for

what?"

All of them were there, with the exception of Private Sutherland who still seemed to be inconsolable. He was sitting on the ground next to the numerous bodies. There was no need to answer as the creature roared and howled. The ground shook as before, and this time Lieutenant Weston seemed to be losing his patience.

"Any grenades left?"

Johnson and Sergeant Jones both withdraw a single weapon each.

"That's it?"

"Yes, Sir," said Johnson.

"Give them to me."

He took the grenades and held them over the ledge.

"Any last words?"

"Nuke the bastard!" Johnson said.

"Yeah," agreed Sergeant Jones.

Private Sutherland moved up alongside them. His face was sweaty, and he was breathing so heavily it sounded as though he might hyperventilate at any moment. He held out his M79 and snapped it open to load in a grenade.

"You okay, Sutherland?" Sergeant Jones asked.

"I just want to send that thing right to Hell!"

He snapped the weapon closed and pointed it down into the pit.

"Amen to that." The Lieutenant primed the two grenades and stepped back. Sutherland remained there, silent and still for a full two seconds before he shook his head and then pulled the trigger. The weapon clunked, and he moved back as it hit the monster. An almighty boom shook the ground as the combined weapons detonated in the close confines of the pit. A plume of smoke burst upwards, and the soldiers waited and watched. They began to cheer as blood rained down on them.

"Finally," said Sergeant Jones, "We got him."

One by one they moved back to the edge of the pit and looked down. The sides were partially burning, but they could see much further down now. The flames lit up the sides, giving it the impression of some ancient passageway into Hell itself.

"About time," said Lieutenant Weston.

He noticed the spiral steps cut into the rocks as they wound their way down. Roughly a third was missing from large section of gaps, and presumably settled at the bottom of the pit.

"I've never seen anything like this."

"We have." Linh Hoa looked across to Billy.

"She's right. I was held in a place just like this."

"It looks old," said Sergeant Jones, "The stonework must be two or three hundred-years-old."

Linh Hoa laughed and then sighed.

"Americans. You have no history. This pit is many hundreds of years old. Perhaps even a thousand."

"Bullshit," said Johnson, "Now…all we…"

A distant rumble seemed to come from far away, and Sergeant Jones looked away to try and see where it was coming from. The rustling of trees followed it.

"I heard that," said Lieutenant Weston.

They all turned from the pit, all except for Billy who looked down at the quickly receding fires. He was sure he'd seen some movement down there, the flicker of light, or the movement of a shadow far below.

"I heard it, too," said Private Sutherland while loading in

another grenade into the M79 grenade launcher, "In the trees."

Lieutenant Weston, Sergeant Jones, and Lance Corporal Johnson lifted their weapons and aimed off into the jungle. It was a pitiful firing line compared to the numbers they'd taken to search for Billy and the others, and a fraction less than those that had first entered the jungle days earlier. Billy remained looking down into the pit, while Linh Hoa moved closer to his side as he pulled back the charging handle of his rifle.

"What now, Sir?" Lance Corporal Johnson asked.

Lieutenant Weston wiped his forehead with the back of his hand and then took careful aim.

"I think we've got more of those things coming back for us."

The foliage shook, and then more shapes joined them. They were close, but not close enough to be fully seen in the early morning light.

"Watch your ammo," said Sergeant Jones, "Once you're empty, you're dead."

The Sergeant glanced back to Linh Hoa.

"I thought you reckoned this would be over when that beast of yours was dead?"

She opened her mouth to speak, but instead of her voice, the grumbling snarl of the terrifying creature filled their ears.

"No way!" Private Sutherland turned back and looked down into the pit. He took aim, but the red glow deep in the pit vanished, leaving nothing but darkness.

"It lives?"

Billy nodded slowly. "I think so."

The shapes were moving quickly now, and a matter of seconds away from breach in the tree line. The soldiers inched backwards until they were almost upon the pit. Billy moved to the steps at the side, and then began the slow descent into the pit.

"Private, what are you doing?" Jones asked.

"We can't hold off those things forever. We need to get away from them."

"And into its lair, are you shitting me?"

The first wave came out of the trees on the other side of the pit; men and women brandishing all manner of edged and pointed weapons. Some carried rifles tipped with bayonets, while others brandished knives or sharped stakes. But for the first time ever, those towards the front opened fire. Shots crashed around the Americans as they fell back, abandoning the pit where Billy and Linh Hoa remained.

"Drop 'em!" Sergeant Jones yelled.

They opened fire with fully automatic bursts of fire, cutting down the first wave with relative ease.

"They're using guns now?" Johnson grumbled.

"The creature is learning," said Linh Hoa, more in surprise than as an actual statement. She stepped down next to Billy to avoid the fire from both sides, "It has been awakened."

"Wait," said Billy even as the battle continued to rage, "You're saying the more that thing watches us, the greater the threat?"

Linh Hoa looked at Johnson and back to Billy.

"I am not an expert, Private."

"Yes, you can say that again.

Billy threw Johnson a hard stare, but Linh Hoa spoke before he could begin yet another argument with the machine gunner.

"When we first encountered it, the Ky Lan was wild, out of control, and lacked planning or discipline. Now…it takes the living and creates legions of soldiers. It can plan, ambush, feint, and attack." She shook her head and looked up to the sky, "And now it is using its soldiers to use guns. What next, helicopters and jet planes? You can learn what it is to be hunted from the sky."

"You're kidding, right?" Johnson asked, "An animal ain't arming and sending soldiers out to fight us in helicopters. Not today, not ever."

The roar from below the surface came again, and Billy leant out and down into the shadows. He could not see the monster, but he could hear it. He then carefully inched his way to the top so that he could see his comrades.

"Sir, it's still alive. They're trying to protect it."

Another volley crashed overhead, and Sergeant Jones appeared with the others coming right behind him.

"Keep moving. We're hunting that thing down if it's the last thing we ever do!"

"Hell, yeah," said Johnson, "About damned time. Let's put this…Ky Lan down, for good this time."

CHAPTER EIGHTEEN

The descent into the pit was one of the most terrifying experiences of Billy's life. Unlike other parts of the underground structure that he'd already seen, this one seemed as though it had been abandoned to nature longer than the rest. Plants grew out of the walls and across the wide shaft, many completely blocking progress. Entire sections broke away as they moved further down, with complete steps vanishing beneath their feet. He had to physically pull them aside, or even chop at them with his machete. This was difficult work as it was, but made so much worse by the fact that the others were coming down behind him, while engaged in a firefight with their pursuers.

"Hurry!" Lieutenant Weston said, "They're too many of them."

Billy stepped forward to find his feet were not pushing greenery. He flailed about and then fell down six feet, crashing onto wet plant matter. He tried to grab onto them, but Linh Hoa came down behind him as part of the steps began to give way. Billy slipped and rolled, slamming down onto the hard surface of a dark passageway cut into the rock. One by one the others came crashing down until they were all inside, panting from exhaustion and confusion. One by one their flashlights flickered on, and Billy looked into the bloodshot eyes of the Lieutenant.

"Sir, are you hurt?"

"Nothing serious. Now…where is that thing?"

Billy used his flashlight to look around, but already it was obvious where the thing had gone. They were all standing atop a heap of shattered stone and masonry where the ceiling and part of the inner walls had collapsed. He was about to touch the damaged walls when Linh Hoa placed her hands over his arm.

"Do not touch…remember?"

Billy was confused, and then remembered the slowly evaporating fluid that had been on the trees. He looked to the inner walls and was struck by the damage they'd sustained, both over time, and also in the last few minutes. The passage was substantial, and vastly different in style to those he had seen before. They were atop the rubble, but the passage itself was flooded, and wide enough to take a small boat through. It was full of weeds, dirt, and filthy water, with them being saved only by virtue of the collapsed part of the tunnel.

"What is this place?" Johnson asked, "I've never seen anything like it."

"Looks like a sewer to me," said Sergeant Jones, "Or some kind of underground waterway."

Shapes appeared behind them as the unliving warriors crashed down into the end of the passage. They were not far away, and in seconds would be on top of them.

"Sutherland. Sort that out. Bring down the ceiling on top of them. Everybody else, get back."

The Private nodded and took aim with his M79. On the surface it was a deadly weapon, but in the confines of the underground lair the weapon was monstrous. The group moved as far away as they could atop the platform of rubble, but not so far as to fall into the filthy water. As the grenade exploded, it felt like the complex would collapse around them. Any of the creatures that had made it down to them were blasted apart, with the rest crushed by the falling masonry as part of the ceiling came down, blocking the Americans into the tunnel.

"Looks like we're here to stay now," said Sergeant Jones.

"Better in here than torn apart by those…things," said Lieutenant Weston.

The others continued talking while Billy looked at the wall, and in the flickering light he spotted the lacerations in the stone, the same markings he had seen on the surface. The ones left by the creature as it raced away into the jungle to avoid their gunfire.

"It came this way, and it's badly hurt. I mean really badly."

"You reckon?" Lance Corporal Johnson laughed as he moved ahead. He stopped and pointed at pools of fluid and blood on the ground, "I'd say it's half dead."

A groan reverberated through the tunnel, as if to emphasise the point.

"Wait," said Lieutenant Weston, "What have we got left?"

He looked around at his small group huddled in the dark passage.

"It's just us left, Sir," said Sergeant Jones, "We've got our rifles, a few grenades, and that's it."

"Don't forget the Old Lady." Johnson lifted his M60, as though he was presenting a prized pig at an agricultural fair.

"More of them will come," said the Lieutenant, "So, we chase that beast down. Agreed?"

"Yes, Sir!" said each of them. Even Linh Hoa nodded and spoke up in agreement.

"Yes…we find it, and we stop it."

"Then move out, people. This is it!"

With a cry of bravado, they leapt from the rubble and into the water. It didn't look particularly deep, but soon each of them was up to their ribs in the filthy fluid that quickly slowed their movement. Only Billy remained as he looked at the markings.

"Private, over here," said Sergeant Jones.

All of his attention was on the markings and the fluid that still coated the walls. He knew he should follow the others, but something deep inside told him he needed to know more. He looked at the others as they waded through the water, with only Linh Hoa looking back at him. She called after him in her own tongue, but Billy had to know. He closed his eyes and thrust his hand into the shattered wall. A flash of pain surged through his body, as the light and the images flooded into his mind. He could see so much, the jungle, collapsing rocks, and death. But then he could see the water, and a wide structure full of ancient statues, relics, and water pouring down the walls. He yanked away his arm and shouted.

"It's in here with us."

"What?" Private Sutherland shouted.

Billy stumbled back and collapsed over the rubble and into the water. He vanished under the surface as his vision blacked out. He could hear what was happening for a while, but then even that vanished as his senses became numbed. He had no sense of time now, with only the images to keep him company. He could see the walls, the red eyes, and the monstrous beast waiting for them, like a King sitting upon his throne. He opened his mouth to speak, but all he could do was utter unintelligible sounds. Faces looked back at him, and then he blacked out again. By the time he was conscious again Linh Hoa and Private Sutherland were dragging him through the water.

"What the hell happened to you?" Sutherland asked, "We thought you'd passed out for good this time."

Billy shook his head, and then cried out from the pain. It was like the worst headache he'd ever suffered from in his entire life, even more painful than the one he had before. As he inhaled air into his lungs, the pain returned, and he had to force himself to calm his breathing before speaking.

"Billy, you've been out for twenty minutes. Don't do that again, Okay?" Sutherland said with a strange reverberating sound to his voice. Billy continued trying to calm his breathing, and then opened his eyes fully. It was dark, though light did make its way into the tunnel through distant pinholes high above them. Something squeaked, and half a dozen rats swam on past them. They vanished into the blackness.

"What happened?" Linh Hoa asked, "What did you see?"

Billy started to speak, but the words were gibberish. He slowed down and tried again, one word at a time.

"I saw what the creature saw."

"The creature? It is alive?"

Billy nodded as Sergeant Jones stopped and spoke to them both.

"Of course, it's still alive. Why else were those things chasing us?"

"Sergeant. The creature…it is in this chamber with us. It's waiting."

"What?" Private Sutherland asked.

"It's a trap. It lured us down here to finish us off."

Billy struggled to get his balance and looked around their position. The tunnel had widened out into a large water-filled chamber. Vines hung down from the ceiling to block of parts of the area.

"Good. It's killing time."

"No." Billy grabbed Johnson's arm, "It's right here, with us."

"Everybody stop," said Sergeant Jones.

He then looked back towards Billy.

"You're sure? What did you see?"

"Everybody stop!" Lieutenant Weston repeated the order.

They all stopped, with each of them now in so much water that it almost reached Linh Hoa's armpits. The flashlights moved back and forth as they picked out arches holding up the ceilings, as well as holes in the walls where water continually poured inside.

Private Sutherland muttered to himself, pointing ahead with his M79.

"This place…what the hell is…"

They saw it then, out in the middle, and mostly hidden beneath the dirty water. From a distance it looked like a partially buried platform, but as Billy's eyes adjusted to the darkness, he could make out the top of the head as it lay half under the water. The rest of its form was hidden behind three tall pillars that were damaged, but somehow still attached to the ceiling above.

"There it is," said Johnson, "Let me grease that bastard."

He lifted his M60 to his shoulder and took aim. That was no mean feat, based on the weight of the gun. It wasn't nicknamed The Pig for nothing.

"No," said Billy, "The pillars, hit them and you could bring all of this down on our heads."

"He's right," said Lieutenant Weston, "We need..." He stopped as nine heads rose up out of the water just twenty feet away from them.

"Oh...shit," said Lance Corporal Johnson, "What have we got here?"

They were men, each clearly Vietnamese, but wearing clothing more akin to the local tribesmen than to a military unit. Even stranger, they wore ancient and decaying helmets and breastplates.

"No," said Billy, "I've seen this before."

Linh Hoa reached behind her and drew the bronze blade she'd found. The nine figures stopped, seemingly transfixed by the ancient relic that waited before them.

"They are the mountain men. They sacrificed themselves to the Ky Lan to bring it to life."

"The who?" Sutherland asked.

"Montagnards," Sergeant Jones said in hushed tones, "They brought this thing to the valley."

"Assholes," Private Sutherland laughed nervously, "What do we do with them?"

Lieutenant Weston took aim with his rifle and spat the words as he fired, "We kill them!"

His M16 kicked back into his shoulder as he fired. The

others joined in as they blasted the half-hidden shapes. Two were hit in the head, but the others dropped back under the water.

"Shit," said Lieutenant Weston, "Where are they?"

A burst of water erupted in front of the officer as two of the sword-wielding warriors appeared from the water. One cut to the right, slashing into the rifle and casting it aside. The second then stabbed directly forward and pushed the bronzed blade. His rifle vanished beneath the water, but even with the blade pushed through his chest he was still alive. He reached forward with both hands around the neck of the nearest assailant.

"Help him!" Sergeant Jones took aim and fired individual shots from his carbine. Two hit one of the enemy warriors, but they seemed only to punch holes in its flesh. He waded closer towards them, but the Lieutenant and one of his attackers vanished beneath the water. More shapes rose from the water as the bronze sword-wielding warriors circled around them. A mighty splash sent a wave of water crashing towards them, hitting them hard, and knocking them over. Billy struggled back up, half choking on the filthy water as the line of warriors moved ever closer. But then they stopped, and the writhing shape of the Ky Lan rose out of the water. Its mouth was wide and gleaming red-hot. The warriors' eyes were the same colour, and they seemed to be responding to the creature without even looking at it.

"Oh…Jesus," Private Sutherland cried, "We're fucked!"

The small group was now that much smaller. Billy was in the middle, with Lance Corporal Johnson on his left, and Sergeant Jones on his right, their weapons pointing at the warriors. Private Sutherland was a little further back and next to Linh Hoa. Billy looked back to check on them and could see the man was shaking so much he could barely hold onto his weapon.

"What do we do, Sarge?" Johnson asked.

Before he could answer, the warriors swarmed ahead, while the creature came with them. Its tail lashed overhead, cracking in the air like the largest whip ever created. It narrowly missed Billy and slashed into Sergeant Jones's shoulder, tearing off his arm, and sending blood spraying all over Billy's face. He could see nothing but red now as he stumbled and then fell back into the water. Screams and gunfire filled the air as he struggled to remain upright. Incredibly, he still held his rifle and opened fire while the gun was under the water, hitting two of the creatures. The Ky Lan was close now, and he knew they were seconds from the end. He surfaced a few feet in front of Private Sutherland, who was waiting there, utterly frozen in terror and pointing his M79 down at the water. Linh Hoa was there as well, blasting away with her small French submachine gun, her face as hard as nails, and her expression filled with rage.

"Sutherland, the pillars! Shoot them!"

The terrified Private looked to him, and then at the monster as it snapped and snarled. It came for them, sending water flying around them. The sword-wielding warriors were among them now, hacking away and forcing the few remaining soldiers to use their firearms to parry the attack. One came for Billy, but the one-armed Sergeant blocked its path and cut down with his machete into its neck. A second came for him and stabbed him in the stomach. He grunted and then hacked away again.

"Get on with it, Private," he said as he fought it with his

last dying breaths.

"The what?"

Billy leapt forward and yanked the weapon from Sutherland's arms. He spun around, and everything around him seemed to slow down. The M79 would carry a single warhead, but it was more than capable of blasting whatever it hit apart at this range. He pointed it at the charging Ky Lan. It must have recognised the weapon, as it veered away as he was about to fire.

"Die, you bastards!"

Billy pulled the trigger, and the weapon slammed back into his shoulder. The warhead missed the creature by just a few yards and detonated at the base of the thick pillar. It exploded, blasting out the entire lower section, and sending the rest of the tall pillar crashing down into the water. The second pillar was split down the centre, and began to collapse, and as it did so, parts of the ceiling began to fall. The third then split at the top and tipped over while remaining intact, slamming into the distant wall. As it struck the ancient masonry, huge cracks appeared, with water spraying out at high pressure behind them.

"Billy…what have you done? You should have shot the beast."

Billy tossed the weapon back to the man and then took aim with his own rifle. The entire chamber was falling apart all around them, and the water level had risen up to their necks. Then a massive section burst apart, and water rushed in like a tidal wave. He pulled his rifle to his shoulder and gripped the sling, knowing full well there was nothing a rifle could do against the torrent of water.

"Not good!"

Even he wondered if he'd made the right choice as the

wall of water hit them, washing the soldiers, unliving warriors, and even the Ky Lan with them down into the deepest, darkest parts of the underground structure.

"No!" Sutherland screamed as he vanished beneath the water.

Broken tunnels, heaps of masonry, and the stumps of trees rushed past, but soon the morning light became brighter and brighter, as the outer passages broke apart to reveal the mountainside. The creature was nearby and lashed out at him Twice Billy managed to hold onto branches, only for them to be torn up as he raced on past.

"Hold on!" he shouted to himself.

The torrent of water pushed him onwards. He didn't even realise he was on the surface as he was thrown towards what looked like a cliff. He scrambled to hold onto something as he was pushed along with the water, bodies, and flotsam that had been contained deep underground, and then managed to tangle one arm up just as he reached the precipice. As he hung there, the water roared on past and vanished over the edge. The water was gone in a matter of seconds, leaving a slow running stream, as well as a trail of destruction leading back into the mountain. Billy pulled himself up and looked into the darkness inside the mountain. The water had blasted its way out, revealing the entrance to a vast and complex facility that had now been torn asunder by nothing more than the pressure and speed off the pent-up waters.

"Billy!"

He turned to the right and gasped at seeing friendly faces. There in the middle of the stream of dirty water running towards the cliff edge were three people. Lance Corporal Johnson was there, and somehow, he still carried the battered M60. Sutherland was there, and even more surprising, the bloodied but conscious form of Linh Hoa. She was sitting up and coughing as she forced the water from her lungs.

"We made it," Billy yelled, dropping down beside the others.

Private Sutherland kept shaking his head, and his hands were trembling. Billy placed his hands on the man's shoulders, trying to reassure him that it was over.

"I thought we'd all gone to Hell."

"We did," said Lance Corporal Johnson, "Trust me, that was no picnic."

He grunted in pain as he nodded towards Billy.

"Quick thinking on the M79. I would have just shot the beast. This way you killed two birds with one stone."

Linh Hoa staggered towards them and dropped down beside Billy. She looked almost like the unliving creatures that had attacked them, and yet somehow, she still carried the bronze blade, though part of the edge had chipped away either during the fighting or during their wild escape.

"I can't believe we made it out of there." Billy laughed, but he stopped at seeing Johnson's broken leg. Billy hadn't noticed from where he'd been standing, but now he could see the leg was shattered in at least two places, and part of the bone was pushing out from below the knee.

"What happened?"

"What do you think? I hit rocks on the way out. How did you not?"

Then came the sound none of them had expected, and the sound that filled each of their hearts with dread. It was a low roar that echoed through the jungle and the mountainside of the valley.

"What?" Johnson struggled to lift his M60 from the ground. Now Billy could see how he'd managed to keep it with him, the weapon was fitted to a makeshift sling that attached it to Johnson's torso. He twisted around and looked off into the darkness of the shattered passages leading into the mountains, "Shit, that thing…it's still alive."

Billy stared at the mountain and couldn't say a word. After all that had happened, he was convinced this was all finally over. They'd fought the creature and its minions multiple times, and each fight had left them diminished.

"I know where we are," said Linh Hoa, "We are not as far as you think. The tunnels, they move through the mountains."

Billy looked back and found the female North Vietnamese soldier standing at the cliff's edge, looking off into the valley below. The drop was substantial and would kill any of them foolish enough to fall. She pointed into the distance with the bronze sword in her right hand.

"That is where your officer said the helicopters are coming. Will they be bringing help?"

"No," said Billy, "They're here to evac only."

He looked back to the fallen Lance Corporal.

"What do we do?" Billy asked him.

"You get out of here, and you get to the LZ. Let them know what happened and cook this valley."

"No way. We're not leaving you behind. Me and Sutherland, we can carry you between us."

The roar came again, and each of them knew they were living on borrowed time.

"Bullshit, you are. I'm in command now. Sutherland, you and the Private here, get going."

The Private hesitated and looked to Billy for guidance.

"Don't look at him, look at me. My leg is wasted, and I can't walk. If you help me, we all die. You go on without me, and you have a chance. Just leave me your belts and go. Go!"

Billy reached forward and pulled the last belt of ammunition from around Sutherland's body. Normally, they all carried additional ammunition for the M60, and this was the last full belt. He placed it next to Johnson who now adjusted his position so that he was facing off against the mountain.

"Got any grenades?"

Billy checked his gear and found nothing. But when he looked to Sutherland, he could see one hanging from the man's gear. He reached forward and took it.

"That's the last one."

Johnson grunted as he took it, and then placed it next to him on the ground. Billy hesitated, but Johnson grabbed his arm and gripped it firmly.

"You did well out here, Private. Somebody has to report what happened. Let them know what we did here."

The roar came again, and now a red glow filled the darkness inside the mountain. Black shadows were moving in front of the red, and all of them knew what was coming.

"We can all stay and fight," said Linh Hoa.

Johnson laughed. "With what?"

He settled into a firing position as he rested the M60 on top of the debris that littered the ground. It allowed him to remain in a half-sitting position rather than prone. He checked the ammunition feed was free of junk. At the same time, the first shapes emerged from the half-collapsed complex and came for them. None of them seemed to be carrying weapons.

"Look, their weapons must have been swept away," said Billy, "We can hold them."

A bright flash of light lit up the tunnel, and then a growing silhouette of arms and a massive head showed that the creature was coming. Johnson pulled back the charging handle before looking back at the three.

"Now go. Burn the bastards for me!"

The gun started to clatter as he fired short bursts.

"Yeah…" he said happily, "I've got plenty more!"

Billy placed a hand on the man's shoulder.

"Good luck, Johnson."

"Yeah." He said with a nod, "You, too…Billy."

He reached out and handed a smoke grenade to him. Billy took it, and Johnson wrapped his blood-soaked hand around Billy's.

"You might need this."

The mere mention of his own name nearly made him choke. The two had never been anything close to friends, but right now there was a bond, one so much greater than the bond of friendship or family. It was the bond of brotherhood that only soldiers in combat could ever understand.

"We'll burn every last one of them."

Johnson nodded, then let go and turned away. Linh Hoa was already working her way along the edge of the mountain, a wickedly narrow trail. He wouldn't even have seen it had she not found it first. Billy began the descent, but not before looking back one last time at the Lance Corporal. The man was hunkered down and preparing for his last fight. Billy wished he could have recorded the moment so that he could show others what he had witnessed.

"Soldier. Hurry," said Linh Hoa.

CHAPTER NINETEEN

Billy followed right behind Linh Hoa as they reached the lower parts of the steep mountainside. In all his time in Vietnam he had never walked along such a treacherous trail. There was nothing to stop them falling to their deaths, and on no less than three occasions one of them had slipped, only to be grabbed by the others.

"Where are we going?" Sutherland asked.

"This way," said Linh Hoa, "We are not far from the clearing."

They moved away from the steep trail, and to a narrow path that led to the shallower gradient in the distance. At first the going was exceedingly difficult, with large rocks forcing them to climb over them. Eventually, they reached a shallow stream, and once past it, the route was clear to a flatter area of grassland, pockmarked with tall rocks.

"Is this it?" Billy asked.

The crackle of machinegun fire came from far above them, and all three looked back as though they expected to find Johnson with them and engaged in battle. Sutherland reached for his grenade launcher, but Billy placed a hand on his arm.

"He's still fighting," said Private Sutherland, "We should go back."

"No," said Linh Hoa, "We must leave."

"She's right. Johnson is buying us time with his life. Let's not waste it."

Sutherland muttered something, but then he spotted movement ahead.

"Look."

Billy lifted his M16 and aimed off into the distance. There was a man in NVA uniform and pointing a pistol right at them. He fired once and missed, and then two more soldiers appeared, both ragged and armed.

"It's trying to stop us escaping," said Sutherland, "We're never leaving."

"Screw that." Billy opened fire. Six shots were all it took, and the trio were down, each with a bullet to the head and torso.

"Very good shooting," said Linh Hoa, "Very good."

Sutherland now realised his M789 was unloaded and scrambled for a grenade. At the same time, two more shapes appeared to the right. Linh Hoa lifted her MAT-49 and fired. It was less accurate, especially at this range, and she was forced to fire two short bursts before hitting the enemy. One fired back, with its bullets coming perilously close.

"Run!" Billy shouted, "Run!"

* * *

The entire area in front of him was now littered with bodies. The machine gun hissed from the heat of unleashing so many bullets into the attacking warriors. Lance Corporal Johnson was going to die, he knew that, and accepting it gave him a sense of relief. He looked down at the weapon and shook his head. He should have been in the middle of changing the barrel, but there was no time for that, and even if he'd wanted to, he had no spares with him anymore.

"I never would have guessed I'd go out this way. On a mountain against a wall of the living dead."

He laughed as the shape of the creature moved behind the rocks that partially blocked up the broken entrance to the underground structure. Johnson knew it was there, but it seemed to know he was still a threat, or maybe it was simply watching for its own amusement. He pushed open the top plate and fed the last belt of bullets into the machine gun, gently pushed down the top plate, and pulled back the charging handle. With the weapon loaded he felt strong again, but then a pang of pain from his leg ran up his spine. It sent a shiver through his body, like a jolt of electricity. His jaw clenched tightly, and for a second it seemed as though he would shatter his own jaw until finally his body relaxed.

"Jesus," he muttered, "What's next?"

Any sign of the night was well and truly gone, and now he noticed that both the creature and its minions seemed to do their utmost to remain in the shadows of the mountain or the trees. He chuckled to himself as he took aim. One or two of the raised dead moved into the open, and then lifted their arms to shield their faces. At first Johnson assumed it was to shield them from bullets, but then he noticed the direction of the Sun.

Damn it, if we'd only known that a little earlier!

He squeezed thc trigger, firing three bullets at a time in very short, controlled bursts. One of the warriors fell down and then tried to get back up. So he fired again and cut it down. With that, there was relative calm, and as he took in a few lungfuls of air, he could feel the pain returning. Only the surge of adrenalin could keep it away, and for that he needed combat. He took aim and checked the shadows. More and more shapes moved about, but they refused to come out.

Maybe I should have gone with them.

As he prepared for his final fight, he began to doubt his last decision. Perhaps bluster and bravado would now prove to be his downfall. The Sun was high enough to light the entire area with its warm glow, and it began to warm his battered and damaged body.

At least I won't go out in the dark.

The shapes increased in number, and as they spotted him, they broke into a run. And this time the creature was with them. It snapped and snarled, but made sure its minions took the fire, instead of itself.

Well, shit. Here we go!

Johnson could see thirty or forty of the half-dead men coming at him as they scrambled from cover. They lifted their hands to cover their eyes, and one collapsed before he could even fire on them. The rest clambered over the body as if it was nothing but rags and came directly towards the clearing where he waited. There was no other direction they could go in, and they left the relative safety of the broken tunnels. He took aim and began to fire. The gun worked beautifully, even after being submerged in the filthy water. Shot after shot struck them, with some pushing through the gaps and hitting the beast. Yet still it held back. Forty rounds were gone, then fifty, but still they came.

"Come on!" he shouted.

Two more bursts slowed their attack, and as they fell, some of those he had already shot began to stagger back to their feet. They struggled to move where he had hit them before. The bullets clearly damaged them, but they showed no signs of discomfort or pain, only the difficulty in movement.

"Stay down!"

He raised his aim a little higher. The next shots hit their upper bodies and heads, and then they stayed down for good. Something glinted to the right, and as he turned his head, he spotted two NVA soldiers and an American, all with the glowing eyes, and carrying rifles. They opened fire, and bullets hammered into his lower body and legs. He screamed as he struggled to swing the M60 around and opened fire, cutting them apart. He lay there, panting in exhaustion and pain. Blood pooled around him as they continued to come right at his position.

"I'm not done for yet, you piece of shit."

Johnson moved the M60 back, and this time he ignored the drooling warriors. He knew that more of them would come, and he recalled what either Billy or Linh Hoa had said about the creature. The idea that by stopping or killing it would end the thing's ability to control those it had manipulated to do its bidding.

Maybe if I kill you, I'll have a chance.

He looked down and checked that he still had one smoke grenade left, something that could mark his position when the extraction unit arrived. It was a faint hope, but it gave him enough to keep up the fight. This time he blasted the monster itself, firing a single long burst that caused the barrel to hiss as it overheated.

"Yeah!" he yelled at the top of his voice, "Mess with The Pig, and this is what you get!"

But as the belt ran through the machine gun, the look of rage and glee began to fade. Seventy bullets were gone, then eighty, and still he fired.

"Bastard!"

He used every last ounce of strength and willpower to stagger up onto one knee. The pain was near unbearable, but adrenalin and rage gave him the strength for one last push. He aimed the M60 and fired again until the weapon finally ran dry. The creature must have known, because it howled and then came right at him. The feet crashed to the ground, shaking the rocks so much that Johnson almost fell. He coughed as blood ran from the corner of his mouth, and then began to laugh. It was a short distance away now, and its tail lashed to strike him. He ducked down, narrowly avoiding the impact, and then spotted the grenade. He snatched it up, and without thinking pulled the pin. It was so close now he could smell it, but instead of turning away or closing his eyes, he pulled the grenade close and called out as it leapt upon him, its maw wide open and ready to tear him apart.

"Asshole!"

* * *

Billy and his comrades knew immediately what had happened as the sound of the explosion echoed across the valley. Birds flew from the safety of the trees as the sound continued for several seconds. Billy nearly lost his footing as he looked back. The machine gun had stopped, and that could mean only one thing.

"How much further?" Billy asked.

"Past those trees. See."

She pointed ahead, but Billy could only see the narrow line of trees, like a fortified wall between them and their salvation. They were not particularly dense, but they were an obstruction they would have to pass through before they could escape.

"Good. Now, all we need…"

He stopped speaking as shapes moved around the base of the trees. Sutherland saw his expression and stopped.

"What is it?"

"Look. Soldiers."

Sutherland lifted his weapon, but lowered it as six men emerged. They were US soldiers, fully equipped and brandishing rifles. One carried a shovel, though it was not apparent to Billy as to why.

"They came for us!" said Sutherland, "They must have been dropped to clear the LZ!"

Without looking to the others, he broke into a run towards them, blocking their view of the approaching soldiers as they broke out from the tree line.

"Are they your men?" Linh Hoa asked.

Billy didn't want to raise his rifle for fear of starting a shooting match, especially as his uniform and gear was wrecked and covered in mud and water. God only knew what he looked like right now.

"Get down!" Billy shouted.

He chased after him, but Linh Hoa pulled him back. She lifted her weapon and opened fire on the Americans. One went down fast, and Private Sutherland slowed upon realising his mistake. Billy tried to blast them with his rifle, but Sutherland blocked his view. He blinked, and then fired two shots. One soldier was hit, but then the Colonel pointed a rifle directly at the Private and fired. Sutherland dropped to his knees and collapsed face down to the ground in front of them.

"No!" Billy screamed.

With his friend on the ground, the soldiers were exposed, and Billy ran towards them, his rifle blasting away. All but one was cut down by the time the magazine was empty. Linh Hoa fired, but after two shots she was out of bullets. Only the Colonel remained, and Billy went for him with all the power and rage he could muster. He thrust the muzzle of his rifle into his chest as the soldier fired back. A bullet snapped through Billy's left upper arm, spinning him around. He crashed into the Colonel, and the two collapsed to the ground. The Colonel hissed and snarled, struggling to fire his rifle at him. They rolled on the ground, but somehow the man managed to push Billy onto his back, and then struggled to aim his rifle at Billy's torso. Billy dropped his weapon and held onto the rifle pointing at him. He was able to push it just enough so that the bullet missed him by two inches.

"You bastard!"

He struggled to hold the man back, but his new wound weakened his arm enough that it was almost impossible to stop him. Billy kicked the man in the shin, and his posture shifted just as the Colonel's finger moved on the trigger again. Shots hit the ground, but they were coming closer.

"Help me!" Billy shouted as he felt his muscles beginning to fail him. Fatigue, injury, and the relentless strength of his foe drained what little energy he had left. And yet he refused to quit. Even as the barrel came close, he pushed against it and screamed with all his rage and bitterness exploding from deep inside. Then Linh Hoa was right next to him, unarmed and screaming as she also grabbed the man, but she was unable to pull him away.

"Gun! Get his gun!"

Linh Hoa reached for the rifle and grabbed it, but even together they weren't able to pull it away.

"The other one!"

She stepped back, looked down, and reached to the man's side. In one smooth motion she withdrew his Colt Automatic and pointed it at the Colonel's temple.

"Du ma!"

The gun fired once, and the dead officer collapsed in a heap onto the ground. Billy struggled out from underneath him, helped by Linh Hoa. But instead of leaving the man, Billy removed three magazines he had been carrying. He fitted one into his rifle, grabbed the M16 on the ground and passed it to Linh Hoa, as well as a magazine.

"Take it."

"What happen now?"

"We get to the LZ, and fast."

"And me?"

He looked into her eyes and could see the doubt there. He hadn't even given her any thought when it came to the extraction, but now he realised that what was an escape for him, was something akin to sheer panic for her. Linh Hoa was a North Vietnamese soldier. She might have worked with him, perhaps even befriended him, but there was no chance she would have a normal life if she escaped with him. The likely result would be that she was thrown into prison and interrogated for an eternity.

"I'm sorry," he said, but to his surprise, she merely smiled back at him.

"Your arm."

Billy shook his head as he looked at the bleeding.

"No time for that. I'll live. Come on."

The pair broke into a run as they crashed into the trees. Neither bothered checking for booby traps, trip wires, or even signs of the unliving enemy. They just ran for all they were worth. They burst out through the other side, and to a large open area devoid of much greenery. There were burn marks on the ground where it had been attacked from the air.

"This is the place?"

"It is where your commander said the helicopters would come. The LZ he said."

"All right, then."

Billy ignited the grenade and tossed it into the middle of the clearing, where it hissed away, sending a tall plume of indigo smoke up into the sky. There was relatively little wind, and it rose up above them and towards the clouds.

"If they didn't know we're here, they will now."

"Look!" Linh Hoa moved to his side.

There were red eyes in all directions now as the foul unliving soldiers encircled the pair. Even worse was that distant roar from the beast as it came closer and closer down the canyon. Neither could see it, but the terrifying sound was unmistakable. Billy knew their time was up, but when he looked into the eyes of Linh Hoa, he knew they couldn't give up. They'd both lost everything in this fight, and now it was down to the two of them, the last survivors of the entire force from both sides that had come to fight over the mountains. Now they were all dead, and the mountain once more belonged to the Ky Lan and its slaves. Billy struggled to stay upright as Linh Hoa grabbed his shoulder. Blood loss was finally beginning to affect him, made worse by other minor injuries and the onset of fatigue. She helped support his weight as he lifted his blood-splattered M16.

"We were promised an evacuation, and look. They must have been waiting in the area."

He nodded off to the East, where a dull yellow glow was increasing in intensity second by second. More shapes moved off to the sides, setting in amongst the foliage and even drifting to the tree line where the enemy remained. Billy looked from left to right as the red eyes moved back into the yellow mist from the smoke grenade, but soon it was replaced by scores of smaller, duller pits of red. They spread out in a wide circle so that the pair was completely surrounded. The mist remained around them, blocking off any access to the jungle or the mountainside. But as Billy waited with his rifle raised and ready, he noticed black dots in the sky. They were close, but it would be a few minutes before they arrived.

"Kill them!" he said angrily, "Kill them all!"

He opened fire in a wide arc, while Linh Hoa used the pistol she'd taken from the Colonel. Bullets struck the advancing shapes; all while the menacing beast inched closer. It was now inside the thick wall of trees and hissing at them.

"Nearly here!" Billy said, "Not much longer."

Though out in the open, there was still cover provided by the rough tufts and stumps that littered the ground. The pair ducked down as bullets started to hit around them. More soldiers advanced on them, a mixture of rifle armed Americans and Vietnamese, as well as many more unrecognisable forms brandishing hand weapons.

"Private." Linh Hoa looked back at him.

"Billy. My name is Billy."

"Billy, if you escape, tell your people to stay away from this valley. It will bring only death."

He lifted himself up and blasted the nearest soldiers. Three more came from the right, and he twisted around and fired again. They were coming from all directions, and off in the trees came the beast. It moved quickly, literally tearing down the smaller trees as it came for them.

"Dammit," said Billy, "I thought we'd done enough."

The weapon clicked, and he ejected the magazine, reloading without even looking. The gun fired again and again, while Linh Hoa could do nothing more than grab Billy's machete and hold it out in front of her.

"Don't let them take me," she said as she slashed at the air, "I will not join the dead!"

Billy could only look at her for a moment, but he could see a real fear in her eyes. He knew the Vietnamese treated death hugely different to him and his fellow Americans. Access to the body, and its correct preparation and handling were critical, and she seemed petrified of what would happen if she was forced to join the ranks of shambling soldiers that now fought for the Ky

Lan. As he looked at her, he spotted the dots coming closer. But it was not the shapes that put a smile to his lips. It was the thumping sound that could be one type of helicopter, and they were coming fast.

"Get down! We've got slicks coming in."

The first pair of Bell UH-1 Iroquois helicopters came in from the South, but there was something quite different about them. Both were engulfed in smoke, and for a fraction of a second Billy thought they'd been hit by ground fire.

"No!"

But then dozens of blasts shook the ground. Rockets streaked downwards, followed by a fusillade of fire. They came in and showered the surface with gunfire. As they moved past, he caught a glimpse of their profiles, and right away he knew they were more than regular Hueys.

"Those aren't slicks!" he said with relief, "They sent in Cobras!"

The nickname was one the infantry had used for some time, with slicks referring to the troop transport Hueys, while Cobras or Guns were used for those with weapons. They were UH-1C variants, special version of the Huey designed to carry heavy weapons to support ground troops as well as transport helicopters. While looking the same as a regular Huey, they were fitted with more powerful engines, a new rotor system, longer tail boom, and additional redundancy to protect against damage. But all that Billy really cared about were the weapons. The first helicopter carried rocket launchers on each side, and a pod fitted below the nose that blasted away. The second one carried the same weapons, as well as miniguns pointing out to the sides that it used to shower the ground with gunfire.

"Billy!"

He turned back. A last wave of the creatures was coming at him, and right behind them the Ky Lan. It roared and howled, and Billy could do little more than open fire. Bullets from his M16 crashed into them, and then a trio of rockets struck directly ahead. He saw two rockets strike the beast, exploding, and throwing it onto its side. The flesh was burning, and it appeared dead. More rockets hit around it, finishing the job once and for all.

"Yes! Burn, you bastard!"

The next volley of rockets came a little too close, and the blast blew him onto his back. Linh Hoa pulled him up while the indigo smoke began to circle around them like a tony tornado as more Hueys swept in. A handful of the enemy still came at him, but the creature seemed to have gone. Billy kept his rifle raised and scanned all around him, expecting teeth or hands to come at him. But as the smoke started to clear, he could see only bodies, including many he'd not shot.

"You were right," he said more to himself than to Linh Hoa, "Killing the Ky Lan broke its control of the dead."

"Billy!" Linh Hoa placed a hand on his arm. He was too busy to look at her as he kept scanning for hostiles, "Good luck, American."

She then slipped away and fled towards the trees. Billy didn't even notice until he reloaded and found she had already gone before he could try and speak to her. The smoke from the grenade mixed with the small fires from the rockets, quickly obscuring her from view. His vision was starting to fail, and as he rose to walk away, he stumbled and dropped down to one knee. Shapes were coming for him, and he lifted his now empty rifle. The trigger clicked impotently, and seconds later, strong hands grabbed him and pulled him away.

"No! Let go of me!"

One leant in closer, and he could see the face, and the normal eyes. He should have passed out, but adrenaline kept him going as he was bundled into a transport helicopter. One of the men stripped back his jacket to examine his arm and began cleaning the wound. Another leant directly in front of him. It was a black officer, wearing a green beret.

"Anybody else out there, soldier?"

Billy knew Linh Hoa was out there somewhere. She'd run towards the trees and might easily be dead by now. Johnson had died on the mountainside, and the rest were scattered all over the valley. The creature had been showered with rockets, and he had seen it finally perish in the inferno. He shook his head.

"The whole company has gone, Sir. It's just me."

"Shit," said the man, who then turned and spoke to the man next to him for a few seconds.

"What's happening?" Billy asked.

The officer continued speaking before finally turning back to Billy.

"Phantoms are coming in to burn the LZ to the ground. B52s are coming after them to soften up this valley. By the time we go back, they'll be too afraid to come out of their bunkers."

He placed a hand on Billy's shoulder.

"Don't worry. We'll mop up what's left of them trying to dig in out here. The hills are ours."

Billy nodded and leant back against the seat as he watched the ground move away from them. Other helicopters circled around them, with some still firing down into the smoke. He watched the woodland and the mountainside, but apart from the smoke, there was nothing else of concern. His vision was blurring, and he knew fatigue was about to take him. He tried to focus on the heavily wooded area and then gasped. He was sure he'd seen something, shadows or something else. Using all the strength that remained in his body, he peered forward and almost tumbled from the Huey before grabbing onto the door gun. He swung the M60 around and opened fire on the woodland.

"Hey, buddy, easy now," said the soldier opposite him. His uniform was gleaming, like he'd just arrived fresh from the US, "We're here."

Another helped pull Billy back and moved him onto the stretcher.

"Stay still, you fool. You're losing blood by the gallon! Don't worry about it. There's nothing out there."

Another of the soldiers looked off into the distance.

"Weird," he said, shaking his head.

"I think I saw some guys down there, at the tree line."

"You think it's friendlies?" asked another of the crew.

The Sergeant shrugged.

"They're not firing, so they might be. Maybe we've got more guys down there."

The Sergeant leaned in close and shouted to the two pilots.

"Take us around for another pass. We've got more people on the ground."

They nodded, and the single helicopter swung back around to the left and circled around the landing ground. Smoke from the grenade continued to waft up into the sky, marking the landing ground, as well as the place where so many of the creature's minions had fought and died.

"No," said Billy, "Leave this place."

He tried to get up, but one of the soldiers held him back.

"Stay there, Private. We won't be long now."

The helicopter came in low over the smoke, and then descended until it was little more than ten feet from the ground.

"Where are the bodies?" asked the officer, "We cut down at least ten of them when we arrived."

"VC," suggested the Sergeant, "They take their dead with them."

The helicopter settled onto the ground, and four men climbed out, their rifles raised and scanning around the craft. Billy watched, but he was so weak he could barely move. He blinked, and then saw the shapes staggering out from the smoke. They leapt on the nearest two soldiers and dragged them to the floor.

"Holy shit!" The Sergeant moved to the side and reached for his carbine. He brought it up quickly to his shoulder and took aim.

"Open fire!"

The door gunner grabbed the stock of the M60 that Billy had been using and swung it around. The helicopter vibrated as the gunner opened fire with burst after burst of gunfire into the smoke. At the same, the officer with the green beret was shouting into the headset he was wearing. Two of the men stumbled back towards the Huey as they dragged a wounded man with them. As soon as they were onboard the engines roared, and the Huey rose slowly from the ground.

"Get the Phantoms here, and fast. We need this place cooked. This place is hostile."

Billy's vision was almost gone, and as he looked into the smoke, the helicopter began to rise, and there, looking right back at him was a single pair of red eyes, and the glowing maw that he'd faced so many times before. He opened his mouth and screamed.

THE NIGHT HUNTER WILL RETURN

NEWSLETTER

I have written more than fifty novels with a mixture of science fiction, military, and even horror. If you'd like to receive my latest news, special offers, and free books then please sign up for my **newsletter**. It's a great way of keeping up to date with my latest projects, as well as getting samples and free books throughout the year. Click on the **link** and join up today. You can also visit my official website and Facebook page, links below:

My official website: **www.starcrusader.com**

My Facebook Page:
https://www.facebook.com/starcrusader

Made in the USA
Coppell, TX
04 August 2021

59954842R00163